A SCI-FI THRILLER
BY MICHAEL LIMESKI

FUTUREVIEW

STARTUP

BOOK 1 OF THE FUTUREVIEW SERIES

TABLE OF CONTENTS

This is a history, a timeline of events that have happened—but which now may never occur. You might think that statement strange, but all of our futures are just as fleeting. As chief technician for the development of the FutureView time machine, I have been in the unique position to assemble this history from my personal experience and discussions with others on the FutureView team. It is also essential that I include descriptions of events that occurred in timelines that no longer exist. That is the nature of the time machine—it can provide the power to change the future for the better, or it can become our peril.

–T.A.E.

CHAPTER 1

Texas Hold'em

January 19, 2019, 5:45 a.m.

I HAD NO INCENTIVE TO GET out of bed this early since being laid off from my technician job at Boston Scientific, and it was also bitterly cold. I'd learned about an unusual seminar to be presented today at the Massachusetts Institute of Technology and was determined to attend. I had the clothes, facial hair, and physical condition to pass for a student, though my formal education had never gone beyond Cambridge Latin High, and the electronic student ID card I'd created would get me in the buildings. I slung my laptop case over my shoulder and headed out into the stiff wind, then went underground to the Red Line to Kendall Square.

The buildings on the MIT campus had been built over three different centuries, making for a jumble of layouts and styles. Navigating the campus was a challenge. Outside, the campus "skyscraper," the Green Building, provided an easy visual reference. Walking indoors through hallways and interconnecting tunnels, however, required tracking each turn to maintain your intended vector.

I was fortunate to have found a mention of this seminar in a blog on the internet, but I found no other information about MIT and time travel. The Institute had a history of secret developments in radar, inertial navigation, and magnetics. Could Professor Johnson be part of a secret project on time travel? Is time travel a real possibility, or is it just a creation of science fiction?

I made it to the student center at the other end of the campus and found the conference room on the third floor, clearly marked with a sign at the entrance:

The Rules of Time Travel
Prof Samuel Johnson, PhD
7:00 a.m., Sat, Jan 19th

I didn't realize there were rules. *No one has yet invented a time machine, and already there are rules?* I thought. One rule for sure should be not to have a seminar at seven on a Saturday morning!

I was shocked to find people already there, and they seemed too old to be students. It was soon obvious these were not students early to the seminar but the remains of an all-night poker game among alumni. Six men were still in the game at this hour. One of them was Mr. Harold Hawkins, a man who would have a profound impact on my future. "Hal" was dressed in a black sweatshirt, well-worn cargo pants, and Adidas. He had long, unorganized hair and a goatee, along with stubble befitting the hour. He wore rimless glasses and slouched in his chair, looking like a disheveled Steve Jobs, though not nearly as successful—maybe an early Steve Jobs.

Also in the group was Mr. Kevin Brayton. He also had a profound impact on my future. He had trim, groomed hair and was clean-shaven. Even at this hour, he was still wearing his gray pin-striped suit coat and a red power-tie. His shoes were polished Italian brown leather that fit so perfectly they needed no laces. His socks were pin-striped and gray to match his suit. He sat with a commanding posture and kept his cards deeply buried in his hand.

The game was Texas Hold'em, a vicious version of poker, in which one who knows the future can become extremely rich and one who only thinks he knows the future can become extremely poor. These weren't students playing penny-ante poker. No, there were no chips— just real money—paper money, and lots of it. These were *former* MIT students in a fun game that I doubt I would ever be a part of.

Texas Hold'em is a game in which the winner of the betting pot is the player who produces the highest-value hand of five cards from the two he is dealt and any three of the cards laid faceup on the table by the dealer. It is ironic that, in a game called Texas Hold'em, you only get to hold two cards! It would seem to be a simple game, but the strategies can be complex. A round of betting occurs each time the dealer lays down cards. What makes it interesting is that you can win without ever getting good cards by bluffing the others, hoping to intimidate them into dropping out early and leaving money behind.

I witnessed only the last hand being played. While certainly no player was going to show his cards to a strange visitor, I, like all writers, can see the future! When the game ended, I took a photograph of the cards laid out on the table, allowing me to recreate the last play. Hal was dealt only a six and a seven of spades. A professional player would have immediately folded—so, clearly, he was going for the bluff! As the game progressed, three of the players acquired potentially winning hands. The betting must have been ferocious! Hal should have seen then that a bluff would never work, but he remained in the game anyway.

Hal was always one to take risks. They never fazed him in the least. But he often cashed in his gains early, which seemed inconsistent with his risk-taking but consistent with his lack of a girlfriend. He'd grown a tech business while an electrical engineering student at MIT, dropped out to run the business, then sold out. Some say he sold out too soon. That money was now gone, and he had abandoned his college degree. He did, however, start another tech business, FutureView, that he was now pursuing. It sounded mysterious. I believe he envied Kevin's wealth and success.

Kevin was dealt the king and queen of spades—an excellent hand! His hand got better with each round—first a straight, then a straight flush in spades. Kevin didn't have to hold back on the betting. Hal and the other remaining players did his work by repeatedly raising the stakes.

Kevin played conservatively, as that was his game. He'd made his money by investing in the future—long-range projects in commercial real estate, following in his father's footsteps, and his father's money. Kevin was not a big risk-taker. He was patient with his investments. Perhaps it was because of his MIT degree in economics, the paleontology of the business world. Despite his wealth, the slow pace of the business bored him. Secretly, it gave him a rush to win at poker, where he could make a killing in an instant. I believe he envied Hal's ability to take dashing risks.

Kevin won the game and an extremely large pot. He said nothing, despite the emotions of the minute. He didn't taunt Hal. He didn't gloat. He just gathered up his winnings, sorted the bills by denomination, straightened the stacks, and wrapped each bundle with a red rubber band. He then stuffed the stacks into his various coat pockets. The guy who least needed the money had taken it all. Despite outward appearances, emotions ran high for everyone.

Hal lost more than the cash he had brought to the game. What I learned later was that Hal was expecting winnings from this game to cover next week's payroll. He had bet the company—and lost.

When the poker players left, I straightened up the chairs a bit to ready the room for the seminar. Hal pulled together a few chairs in the back of the room, lay down, and went to sleep.

CHAPTER 2

The Rules of Time Travel
January 19, 2019, 6:55 a.m.

LOOKED UP AT THE CLOCK, remembering the wall clock in this conference room was famous. It showed the time, I have been told, to an accuracy of a billionth of a second. While the clock looked like any round, black-on-white wall clock one would find in any classroom in America, this clock contained a Global Positioning System signal receiver to synchronize its hand movements with the atomic clocks aboard the GPS satellites in orbit. To be that accurate, it even had to compensate for the velocity of the satellites because, as Einstein had predicted, time itself runs slower on these satellites than on earth. The clock looked extremely ordinary, so I was only the more impressed. The time displayed was exactly 06:55 and 20 seconds, as exact as a sweep second hand can be.

By the time the seminar started, twenty had arrived, not counting myself or the guy sleeping in the back of the room. Attendance was open to MIT students and anyone who pretended to be one, as no one was checking IDs. The attendees were of two distinct persuasions. Members of the first group were mostly male, dressed haphazardly, often unshaven with long hair, and of questionable physical fitness. These were those who thought they had once seen aliens and believed in conspiracies and various forms of the afterlife. They based their belief in time travel on little scientific education and a lot of science fiction. These were the type who would walk for hours in the desert sun, looking for unusual pebbles outside Area 51. Any scientific presentation that even mentioned time travel would be sufficient proof of the existence of time travel to this group.

Members of the other group were mostly male, dressed haphazardly, often unshaven with long hair, and of questionable physical fitness. These were those who thought they saw flaws in Einstein's General Theory and spent hours staring at particle traces. They had too much education, especially in science, and little experience working in the real world. They were attracted by the possibility of discovering a new branch of physics and felt that experimental evidence alone sufficed to prove anything.

I was of the former type, as much as I wanted to be of the latter.

Professor Johnson was familiar to the faculty and many students. A joke around campus was that he had been around electrical engineering when you had to wait for the circuits to warm up before taking measurements. His teaching style was more old-school than fashionable and not so much what the younger staff respected. His students wrote it off to his idiosyncrasies, like his penchant for starting classes precisely on time. That explained why those who knew him stopped diddling their iPhones when the digital/analog clock in the room ticked to the hour. True to his style, the lecture started promptly with a sudden darkening of the room and a louder-than-necessary projected video sure to stop any conversation midsentence.

The screen lit up with that famous scene in *Back to the Future* in which a time-traveling DeLorean is off-loaded from a trailer truck full of dry ice. The music faded, and the video froze.

The professor said, "I have invented a time machine. Check the clock time! It is now 7:00 a.m." He dimmed the lights and continued the video.

In the parking lot scene from the limovie, Doc Brown sends his dog, Einstein, one minute into the future. He waits a minute, then stands out of the way as the time machine suddenly reappears. Doc compares the clock time shown on the watch around Einstein's neck against his own watch, showing a one-minute difference.

The lights came on and the prof continued, "What just happened?"

Someone in the audience piped up, "Doc sent Einstein one minute into the future!"

Professor Johnson was strict in the rigor of his logic and demanding of his students. He was nothing like the excitable Doc Brown in the movie, though he pointed his finger at the audience, mocking the pretend physicist, and said, "Look at the clock! It is now 7:05. I just sent this entire seminar five minutes *into the future*!"

That same student replied cynically, "But the trick is to do it faster."

"Actually, Einstein, the person, predicted that we could travel into the future in his derivation of special relativity. We even have experimental evidence today that, if you just travel fast, your clock will run slower than a stationary clock. Or, from your perspective, you end up traveling into the future faster, as fast as Einstein, the dog, did. If you fly in a commercial jet to Los Angeles, you will travel one millionth of a second into the future. You can subtract that from your six-hour travel time. If you could travel closer to the speed of light, even respecting that speed limit, you could travel hours into the future. If you could travel *at* the speed of light, you could travel into the future in no time at all!

"What, then, is 'travel to the future'? Is it just arriving in the future in less time than you perceive passing? I will demonstrate just that right now! Look at the gentleman in the back row. Someone please wake him up."

A student near the back gave Hal a nudge. He sat up in his chair and tried to look nonchalant.

"Welcome to the future, my son! Tell me, what was the last time you saw on this clock?" He pointed to the clock in the front of the room, which now read 7:10.

Hal came to his senses and realized he had been caught sleeping, so he might as well play along with the prof. "Last time I saw on that clock was 6:35 a.m."

"There, everyone. I have transported this gentleman 35 minutes into the future instantly! So, time travel into the future is no big thing. Let's not bother with that any more for now. The real interesting development is a time machine that can travel to the past. The first thing we are going to do is to determine *how* a time machine would work, if a time machine were possible at all. We need to develop a theory of time travel. Let's first assume that a time machine can carry a person back in time. Is everyone OK with that?"

Professor Johnson spoke enthusiastically about time travel. From comments I'd overheard, he was thought to be quite the proponent of rigorous logic and mathematical proof and didn't cater to emotional outbursts and sloppy thinking. He must have been secretly thinking a lot about the science of time travel, a lot more than just watching *Back to the Future*. Even for the hour and the day of the week, his audience was very attentive.

The professor continued, "Now, before we start, I have to say that I subscribe to Occam's Razor. Does anyone know what Occam's Razor is?"

No answer. Perhaps those who knew the answer were reluctant to present a less-than-perfect response. That was certainly my excuse!

"I'll have to assume that your lack of response is owing to the early hour. Occam's Razor is a philosophical dictum attributed to William of Ockham, England, who died in 1347. It basically means that if a simple explanation can satisfy a theory, you shouldn't rationalize a complex answer."

The professor put up a slide on the screen:

Occam's Razor

- If a simple explanation is sufficient, stop!
- If a theory requires changing a Law of Physics, your theory must include revising that law
- Laws of physics are universal and must apply everywhere and at all times

"On the other hand, if you come up with a complex theory of time travel that requires violation of fundamental laws of physics, then you also have to resolve the problems you created, or you don't have a valid theory. That may take you a while. So, let's develop a theory of time travel that avoids, as much as possible, any violation of the current laws of physics.

"First, can a time traveler make changes that result in a change to his future?"

"What if I said 'No'?" a bearded student in a red hoodie asked. He must have been a law student to have presented an answer without taking responsibility for it.

The professor ignored the tone and continued, "There were some early accusers of H. G. Wells who said, with full confidence in their logic, 'The past has already occurred. Therefore, it is fixed and cannot be changed!' Therefore, a time traveler cannot change history. And since if a time traveler so much as says 'hello' to a resident of the past, he has changed history, that rules out *any* time travel!"

The professor changed the projected slide:

Time Traveler's Dilemma

- Can a time traveler change the future?
- Is he not just as capable as any other person of changing his future?
- If he can change his own future, can he prevent himself from traveling to the past?
  - The theory of time travel has to resolve this paradox

"But I have to ask them: If a time traveler travels to the past, is there some weakness in this time traveler that he cannot do what anyone else can? Can he not carve his initials in the oak tree? Can he not write a note to posterity? The answer we see in some early science fiction stories is that the time traveler's arms are forced to move, his written words change in front of his eyes, and his attempts to do anything different from historical records always fail. The result is that history always reverts to the way records say it happened. When he leaves the past and returns to the present, he finds nothing has changed! All of his efforts were for naught!

"I call this 'The Hand of God' theory. Somehow, God is now moving the time traveler's hands, suddenly transporting him to different places, making objects appear or disappear, words change on paper. This violates so many laws of physics that I refuse to even attempt to untangle it! If you have to violate every law of physics and logic to make your theory work, then you may as well call your theory *Magic*."

A student raised his hand. The professor nodded, and the student asked, "What about the multiverse theory? I understand it has support among top scientists."

Ah! Invoking the community defense!

The professor responded, "These scientists postulate that every time a time traveler changes the future, a new universe is created that follows that alternate history. This universe exists in addition to the universe that the time traveler left, where that change did *not* occur, resulting in a 'multiverse' of universes. Of course, there are many people making many other decisions every day that affect the future, so would a new universe be created every time a human makes a decision? What about dogs? Does another universe get created every time a dog makes a decision? This may not happen much in my 8:00 a.m. physics class, but that's a lot of universes.

"It's not that the multiverse assumption does not resolve the problem of a time traveler changing the past. It does. But it can also be the answer to *any* problem. If a fifth-grade student were asked why putting a magnet up against a compass causes the needle to swing, could she answer, 'A new universe is created, an alternate universe where compasses no longer point north?'

"Of course not! Such a theory would eliminate the need for physics teachers! The multiverse theory could be used to explain any phenomenon, and it's no explanation at all! The multiverse theory was created to deal with the problem of the paradox. Has anyone heard of the grandfather paradox?"

One student in the audience offered, "Isn't that the problem that, if a time traveler goes back in time and kills his grandfather, then his father or mother doesn't exist, and therefore *he* is never born, and therefore he cannot kill his grandfather? The time traveler *must* exist, or there was no one to kill the grandfather. Yet the time traveler *must not* exist, because he was never born. Both answers can't be true, hence it is a paradox."

"Yes, you've got it! If we believe that a time traveler to the past *can* change the future, then he could easily change the event that caused him to travel back in time. Perhaps the time traveler met with his younger self, told him to buy Apple stock. The younger traveler gets filthy rich and has no incentive to travel back in time, again! Then who told him to invest in Apple? This is quite the paradox.

"So, whatever our theory of time travel is, the theory must prevent even the potential for a paradox. There can be no ambiguous actions! Surely, we don't know how a time machine would work, but you certainly cannot have a theory of operation that is inconsistent with itself. I, therefore, propose the following theory of operation:"

He put up a new slide:

Johnson's Theory of Time Travel

- Travel to the past is possible
- The time traveler is as capable of changing the future as anyone else
- These changes will replace the previous timeline
- The time traveler and his time trip are products of the previous timeline and are unaffected by the timeline change

"When a time traveler arrives in the past, the sequence of all events that occurred after his arrival is replaced with a new sequence. I call this sequence of events the 'timeline.' Once he arrives in the past, he starts a new timeline. The old timeline is a history that is no longer relevant, though there may not be much difference between the old timeline and the new timeline. The only potential for a difference would have to be caused by the time traveler's presence.

"Some people may be resistant to this theory since it sounds like an instantaneous change to many things after the time traveler's arrival in the past. It may seem like a lot of objects and people are suddenly created, or vanish, or move about. But from the viewpoint of those in the past, nothing unusual is happening. The time traveler has no magic—he is no more powerful than any other person in influencing the future—and no less able to influence the future, as well. We take actions and make decisions every day that can cause major changes in our futures, and we think nothing of it. We decide which college to go to, which person to marry, whether to study, whether to work out at the gym, whether to drive home after drinking—these are all things that can have a major impact on our futures.

"Now, how does this theory avoid the grandfather paradox, or any other paradox that I described earlier? I will invoke the most basic of physics laws: 'No effect can occur without a cause.' This seems reasonable enough, at least on a macroscopic level. What this means to a time-traveling scenario is this: A time traveler, his time machine, and the motivation to travel must first exist before there is any change to the timeline.

"Once he travels back in time, the timeline is reset to something new. If he shoots his grandfather, there will be big changes in the timeline. His father will not exist, and he will not exist. At least the person who would have been born with his name will not be born. But the time traveler himself is a product of the previous timeline. If he shoots his grandfather, his memory of his father and grandfather will not change. He will not vanish, and nothing he brought with him will change, not even a photograph of his father. He, and everything he brought with him, were products of the previous timeline.

"What happens if the time traveler goes back to the future?" a student asked.

"My theory avoids all the difficulties of assuming multiple universes—there is only one timeline, even if it is changed by actions taken, just as *your* future can be changed by actions you take today. So, things may be different if he were to return to the same date on which he departed. Even more shocking, he could meet up with himself, if, under the conditions of the revised timeline, his younger persona now decides *not* to travel to the past."

"If the younger time traveler decides not to travel back to the past, doesn't that create a paradox?" the hooded student asked.

"No. The original time traveler was from a different timeline, a timeline that no longer exists, so he cannot return to it. And his travels do not obligate his younger self, a different person, under different circumstances, to travel back in time. If *that* traveler were *forced* to travel, we would end up with another case of 'the Hand of God' getting involved.

"Consider a simpler case. What if, instead, the time traveler just parks the DeLorean behind a billboard and just lives out his life in the current, and only, timeline? Depending on how far back in time he went, he could easily meet his younger self. The time traveler can't force his younger self to go back in time as he did, and there is no need to. However, there is one problem with this theory that has to be resolved. I will get to that later."

Another question came from the audience, "So, Marty McFly travels back in time and accidentally discourages his future mother from even dating his future father. He struggles to get them back together before he returns to the future. Does the future change back and forth every time he succeeds and every time he fails?"

The prof answered, "Consider *your* future. One day you do well and your future, with your diploma, is bright. Another day you fail a test and feel like dropping out. Instantly, your future could change.

Which one is your future? Does your future keep changing every day? Yes, of course it does! Various people, careers, and spouses may appear and disappear suddenly from our futures. The concept doesn't seem strange to us. That's because our *actual future* is not determined until it happens."

A student interjected another question, "So, if a time traveler takes notes of the way things were in his future, then goes about changing the past, do his notes change too?"

"I have always had a problem with the physics of things morphing, vanishing, or fading away. That's magic, as these things can't happen in the real world. Take Marty McFly's photograph of his brother. It shouldn't have faded. We must assume that the time traveler, the time machine, and anything in the time machine are products of the old timeline, and remain fixed, even though the old timeline no longer exists."

Another student fired back, "Does the time traveler's memory of his pre-travel days change every time he does something in the past that affects his future?"

"No. If we assume that the time traveler is a product of the old timeline, then Marty should remember his life as it always was in the old timeline. Marty's brain neuron connections are just as physical as the photograph of his brother. Both should remain unchanged. It was quite appropriate, in that movie, that Marty was not aware of the changes he caused in the new timeline.

"Now, there are a lot of artifacts that Hollywood creates to make time travel interesting. Of course, any writer can claim that these ar-tifacts are properties of the time machine they just invented, but they are not properties required by a basic theory of time travel.

"For instance, the only reason that Arnold Schwarzenegger is naked when he travels back in time is so the producer can show off his muscles. Time travel in that movie wouldn't transport your clothes, only people. What's so special about cotton that differs from human flesh? There is no need for such an arbitrary rule. Even at that, we find out later in the movie that Arnold was no more flesh and blood than his clothes!

"And another artifact of time travel is the concern that time travelers should never interact with their future (or past) selves. But why should that matter? The real question is whether they can get along!

"Which brings up another problem I cannot yet resolve. There is a fundamental law of physics that prevents objects from suddenly appearing or disappearing. It's called 'Conservation of Matter.' You can't create matter out of nothing! And you can't destroy matter, either.

"For instance, what if you saved up and bought a brick of solid gold? Then you put it in the DeLorean and travel one day back in time. Now you have two gold bricks. Then you decide to never travel back in time again. Have you found a way to create two gold bricks from one? (Of course, you also have two DeLorean time machines, and there are two of you!) This cannot be, as you would be creating matter. Think of the impact if you did this a thousand times over. But matter cannot be created out of nothing! That isn't just a cute answer on an SAT test. If you are going to violate such a fundamental law of physics, then everything falls apart."

"What about mass being converted into energy? Then it could appear that mass vanishes," a student asked.

"You mean the old E equals MC squared? Do you have any idea from that equation how much energy would be released, just to consume a fully loaded DeLorean? But that doesn't matter, because energy is also conserved. You can't create or destroy energy, either. I do not have an answer on this subject, except that somewhere in the time-travel process, matter, and energy as well, must be rebalanced. There ain't no such thing as a free lunch.

"Now, there are a few other problems we have to overcome. Here goes: Almost every concept of a time machine assumes the machine will transport a person through time but keep them positioned in the same physical location on earth. This is convenient for a lot of reasons, especially for shooting movies with a limited location budget. But, while the movie scriptwriters don't propose that the time machine moves, the earth does. The earth rotates and travels around the sun. The solar system travels around the Milky Way galaxy, and the galaxy is constantly moving as the universe expands. Where do you put your coordinate system to measure this motion?"

These statements created a buzz of conversations among the students in the audience. They feared that these problems would challenge the possibility of ever building a time machine. A student shouted out, "Are you saying that time travel is not possible?"

The professor ignored the question and continued, "And let's consider the problem of instantly disappearing and appearing in a new time. Disappearing wouldn't be too bad—there'd be a rush of air into the vacuum where the time machine used to be—there would be quite a thunderous *bang* upon departure. The real problem, however, occurs when the machine appears where it didn't previously exist. Assuming we aren't appearing inside the ground or a building's walls, and we are at least outside. Even at that, what happens to the air that was there?

"In my thoughts, the time machine and all its contents would become permeated with a full volume of air molecules, except, of course, for the one-in-a-million oxygen or nitrogen atom that collides directly with an iron or carbon or whatever atom in the time machine. I don't know what the odds are or what the results would be, but 'splitting atoms' is not something you want to happen inside your gut. It's bad enough that every piece of the time machine and the time traveler's body would suddenly become an air-filled foam, and the body and machine would probably explode!"

The professor put up a slide, listing these impediments:

Problems of Time Travel

- Mass and energy are conserved
  - You can't create or destroy matter or energy through time travel
- The earth moves in space over time
  - A time traveler must consider the movement through space as well as time
- An object traveling in time cannot instantly displace an existing object upon arrival

The professor raised these objections to time travel and then could not suggest any resolution to the problems he created. I could see why the audience became disappointed with the seminar. They didn't want to go away and think up a solution. They wanted to be reassured that time travel was possible! People started walking out. Conversations started in the audience, without respect for the professor.

Maybe he planned to tell more, but the seminar had degenerated into arguments among the students, who reacted as though their favorite science was being attacked. The prof could not get the seminar under control or just didn't want to continue. He sat down and slumped in the chair. He seemed to look older than at the start of the seminar. His hair was white and thinning. His face was wrinkled. Academic study is the one place where old age is a compliment, but now he just looked worn out. He silently packed up his laptop and left the conference room.

This event was a touchy subject with the professor, and he refused my later efforts to get him to talk about it. Scientists have no access to power, rarely make much money, and are seldom recognized by the population at large. The attraction must be the thrill of achieving a major discovery and the resulting recognition of that achievement within the small community in that field. That day had to be the lowest point in Professor Johnson's career.

I sat in the back of the room and thought about his theory. What if you could go back in time and give advice to your younger self? Would you live a better life? Would you even pay attention to the "old man?" Would the only advice you could get from your older self be "I know one way to fail?" That didn't seem very reassuring.

CHAPTER 3

The Price for Grand Ideas
January 19, 2019, 12:45 p.m.

THE PROFESSOR'S CAMPUS OFFICE ADDRESS was available, and with a quick check of an app on my phone, I found walking directions too. After lunch, I thought I might find him at his office.

I hesitated at his office door. Office doors at MIT are made with a patterned glass that obscures the view inside the office. I could see a vague image of the professor thrusting about the office in abrupt movements and heard books being indelicately thrown into cardboard boxes. This would not be a good time to enter, and I thought I should probably wait till next week. But other events would change that timeline, and I never got to ask my time-travel questions.

I thought it curious, and later asked the professor about the seminar, but he would say very little about it, other than it upset him how the seminar had degenerated into a "misfits brouhaha."

I had to ask Hal about that phrase. Hal said, "It's not *misfits*. He must have said 'MITs-fizz.' The MIT Science Fiction Society members often engage in interminable arguments over elements of science fiction that can neither be proved nor disproved because it *is* science *fiction*!"

I looked up the professor's CV on the MIT website and asked some of his colleagues about him. I was shocked to find that he really wasn't even a tenured professor! He had somehow secured a temporary untenured position that was renewed each year. He might have been retained because of his expertise in real electrical engineering that was desperately needed by research physicists. It seemed most experimental physics projects were an endeavor to extract small, elusive signals immersed in high noise, something that required the professor's expertise.

Professor Johnson was an expert in the ancient art of nondigital electrical engineering—analog design, nonlinear effects, signal processing, extracting signals from noise, high-power electrical engineering, whatever. Most graduating electrical engineers were only interested in digital electronic designs. To them, circuits are on or off. But, in the end, all digital circuits are really analog. Voltages vary over time, noise is always present, and switching signals on or off doesn't happen instantly. One has to understand the subtleties of electronics to understand how things work at the limits encountered in physics experiments. This is especially the case when physicists are searching for extremely weak and hidden signals in massive noise.

Unfortunately, scientists often look down on engineers, just as engineers look down on nondegreed technicians like myself. I once overhead a student joke at MIT that I did not, at first, understand:

Question: What do you call a physics major who gets a B in 8.01?

Answer: An electrical engineer

The freshman physics class, required of all MIT students, was identified as 8.01, and was no simple science course. At MIT it included Newtonian, relativistic, and quantum physics.

Once, when we were recently working together, I told this joke to the professor. He did not laugh, and I felt embarrassed. What I didn't know was that freshman student Johnson actually had gotten a B in 8.01. Today, of course, any freshman physics major would opt to take the course *pass/fail* instead and avoid any potential embarrassment. He kept this a secret. His advisor tried to steer him to consider a different major, but he fought hard. Student Johnson attended every class session, deeply read every textbook, and did extra problem sets each week. He took copious notes. He worked hard through his undergraduate program and on through his doctoral work. So, while they did not consider Professor Johnson a true peer in the physics department, he had established a symbiotic relationship with other scientists and stayed on, even without tenure.

When I returned to his office the next week, hoping to discuss time traveling, I was disappointed to find his office vacant. "Had he been moved to another office? Was there a time-travel technology program underway?" I asked a teaching assistant who passed by.

"I don't know," the TA said, pressing his earbud. "He never talked openly about time travel, except for his seminar last week."

Could MIT be working, secretly, on time travel? I wondered. Why was time travel such a hush-hush subject, especially at MIT? Could this be because it's a DOD-funded program? Did MIT set up an off-campus site to study time travel, as it had with the first missile guidance systems and hypermagnetic research?

His office was empty and the door unlocked, so I entered to look around. Bookshelves still bore the dust shadows that outlined where books had been. The shadows of framed pictures remained on the walls. The desk was empty except for an excess of paper clips. It seems that the world has already produced more paperclips than will ever be needed.

The only unique items that remained were in the overflowing wastebasket. There was a dog-eared automobile dealer brochure for Jaguars; a tennis ball with ink markings on it, making for a miniature globe; and an old photograph of a much younger Professor Johnson, with an equally young woman. There was a faded copy of a journal paper about nuclear fusion, with an indecipherable two-line title. I finally found a clue to the professor's departure: a letter from the MIT Corporation notifying him of his COBRA rights to health-care coverage after termination.

CHAPTER 4

Sell What the Customer's Buying
January 19, 2019, 12:00 noon

MIT HAS A REPUTATION IN THE venture capital industry as a source for high-tech, innovative, and, incidentally, wildly successful startup companies. Whether the entrepreneurs were current students, former students, lab techs, or full professors, venture capitalists made big returns, entrepreneurs got well-funded, and the Institute collected its royalties. Hence, there was a lot of interest on all sides to support getting the technology people together with the money people. MIT put on forums throughout the world to do just that.

The story of what happened at the briefing has been retold many times, increasing in irony with each telling. It became part of the FutureView company lore. I will try my best to describe what I believe really happened, though I can't vouch for Hal's part. It may be tainted by revisions of the timeline with each telling:

Getting on the schedule to give a 15-minute pitch to a major venture capital company was a treasured opportunity for any startup, and Hal was determined not to squander it. Hal knew he could give a rousing presentation. I had to agree. But now his presentation would have to be so good that the venture capitalists would also want to cover his current payroll obligation up front. Even enthusiastic VCs would hold that first check until the venture is gasping for air and more willing to come to terms. Perhaps that was how they gained the moniker *Vulture*

Capitalists. Money wouldn't typically arrive in the bank account until the lawyers finished somewhere in time.

Hal could always give a good impromptu presentation. Even in his college admissions interview with an MIT alumnus, he answered their questions with swiftness and authority, and he embellished his answers with unauditable facts and figures. The way Hal described it was (with my apologies to Arthur C. Clarke), "Any technology, described sufficiently fast, is indistinguishable from genius."

Hal's having started a business in high school also impressed the admissions people. His first company had developed software that performed data transfer for early mobile devices, before the first iPhone. Back then, it was a struggle to get real-time interactive communications between mobile devices and client servers. Hal was good at rapidly developing new firmware that was state-of-the-art. He didn't even have a business plan and didn't need one. The venture became so successful that he dropped out of MIT, following in the footsteps of other great dropouts—Bill Gates and Mark Zuckerberg. He was on top of the world when he sold his company to a big tech firm for what seemed like a fortune at the time.

His success gave him the ultimate entrepreneur's prize: an open invitation to pitch his next idea to any venture capitalist, and sufficient money not to have to, at least until that money ran out.

He started another new company without a business plan or even a clear concept. At least he came up with a name for the venture: FutureView. With the name, he could then order business cards and reserve the URL. The name reflected his goal without committing to a product and was flashy enough to attract investors. A vague company name was in keeping with the latest trend of "agile entrepreneurship." According to that new-age business concept, the founder is expected to execute the "pivot." "Pivoting" is when you realize your product is a flop, and you desperately change the direction of the company while looking like a wise and aggressive visionary. You would then be recognized as an agent of change (or, as it turns out, an agent of time travel).

It took Hal quite a while to settle on the first product for FutureView, wasting a bit of time and money on false starts. In the end, the product of choice was a compact radio transceiver in the millimeter wavelength that could be part of the thousands of new cell towers needed to expand out the 5th generation (5G) cell phone networks. You would think such a product could have a sizable market, but this was a competitive field, and the product was only a short leap in technology. Hal danced dangerously close to the limits of the noncompete agreement he had signed as a condition of the sale of his last company, but he was not one to flinch at risk-taking.

I didn't realize that Hal's risk-taking had previously affected my life. I had once applied for a job at his company but had never heard back from them. Of course, that is the nature of electronic resumes today, especially for technicians without a degree. What I didn't know at the time was that resumes were not even being read, the cash was gone, the product was far from complete, and now, because of that poker game, I should probably move on.

A tech who had been laid off from the company gave me his own spin on it. "Where did all the money go? Hal's ex-wife was not so dumb. She took a cash settlement instead of stock in the company."

At that time, Hal was still making lease payments on his BMW and mortgage payments on their new condo. FutureView also consumed a lot more cash than his first company, especially after moving into flashy new offices in Waltham, on the Boston beltway. Perhaps he was living in the past, certainly not the future he had expected.

He often imagined how things would be different if he could go back in time and cut down on the expenditures. He managed to get the Beemer off lease and bought an old muscle car, a Plymouth Barracuda, instead. While it needed a little work, it was fully paid for. And it could accelerate faster than the Beemer.

The pressure was on for Hal to figure out how to present his "opportunity" to the VCs. I had seen Hal bluff at poker. He seemed to be energized by desperation and deadlines, not intimidated by them.

He had to snap out of it, as he had one more big bluff to pull off today. Managers from the New Horizons Venture Fund had expressed interest in his company, and he was going to meet with them today, at noon, in this very conference room.

He pulled out his thumb drive with his PowerPoint presentation, set it on the table next to his laptop, and dove under the table to plug in the power supply. He glanced at the room clock and figured that he was timebound but could still rush downstairs and get a Red Bull.

Hal sat down in the cafeteria to drink it and think over his presentation, how he could jazz it up some. He felt the pressure. But his efforts were interrupted by the conversation at the table behind him.

"Man, they really drill you…I wasn't expecting that," said the first voice, a male student. "I guess these guys are really dumb about engineering. Did I really need to explain to them what a thyristor is? Don't they even know the basics?"

(Note: Even I don't know what a thyristor is, but then, I'm not an electrical engineer, per se.)

"No," said a second male voice. "They don't have to be smart about engineering—they hire people, like us, to know about engineering. You were probably too short with them about thyristors."

"Yeah, and the conversation certainly veered off from our presentation—we may as well not have prepared anything but a term sheet!" said the third student.

Hal quickly concluded that these guys had just presented a business plan to some investors. Probably *his* investors! Hal thought about the beautiful presentation he had prepared. *Thirty-two slides and no term sheet! What is a term sheet? I thought that was something the VCs gave to the entrepreneur.*

"I don't think they even wanted a term sheet. That's something the VCs force on the startup," said the second voice.

Obviously, the leader, thought Hal. He now listened more intently.

"Well, they clearly were not interested in *another* 5G proposal," said a third person.

Hal said this last comment put him in a panic.

"That's right," said the leader. "Even though they have funded several ventures similar to ours, I got the impression that they came to MIT expecting to find hypersonic aircraft, invisibility shields, or some such shit! We never had a chance."

The clock in the cafeteria had its hands up. The future was present. Hal gulped down the last of his juice and headed for his inevitable destiny. Was it better to give a presentation just before lunch, when the viewers were hungry and eager to break for lunch? Or after lunch, when everyone was sleepy and uninterested in following the presentation? It didn't matter, as Hal had no choice. The timeline of events was fixed.

He still didn't have a solution when he got back to the conference room. Before he entered, he could see through the glass walls that the suits from Crandall & Jarvis, LLC, had already arrived—Dr. Dan Davidson and Mr. James Sizemore. He was good at bluffing his way. He just didn't have any idea how he could impress this audience.

Hal hobnobbed with the partners, using a measured smile and a firm handshake, being careful not to overcompensate for his impending doom. He could sense (and Hal felt he was good at sensing) that the VCs were tired—tired of hearing trite stories from egotistical student-geniuses who never had to live on PB&J, always asking for far more money than they needed. *Check. Be very vague about the money. Also, don't wow them with electrical engineering details*, he thought, mentally deleting half his slides.

Hal stalled, hoping he could come up with something, but he wasn't even "holding a pair." He introduced himself and the company name, FutureView.

This led to a poor joke from Sizemore, the junior partner of Crandall & Jarvis. "Does this mean you can view the future? That might be worth an investment!"

Hal feigned a laugh.

He caught Sizemore out of the corner of his eye indiscreetly looking down below the conference table, where he held his cell phone. They were not just tired—now the conversation was becoming less polite. Well, now he *had* to get started.

Hal plugged a tiny Bluetooth receiver into a USB port of his laptop, allowing him to advance PowerPoint slides from a remote controller—an advanced technology almost capable of replicating a Kodak Carousel slide show from 1955. He powered up his laptop, checked that the room projector was on, and plugged the projector into another USB port. Placing the thumb drive into a third port, he pulled up the first slide. He was working on how he could start off his 5G presentation with excitement. It was now getting to him; he had never been so speechless.

His hesitation only lasted a few seconds. Hal started talking, staring into the eyes of the two VCs, alternating between them. Hal has said this technique could make a corpse sit up and pay attention to his eulogy.

The VCs were whispering to each other when suddenly they both stopped talking as they stared intensely at the screen. His PowerPoint slides were good, Hal thought, but not *that* good.

Always alert to his audience, he was so confused by their reactions that he stopped midsentence. One of his presentation rules was to never look at the screen, but now he had to confirm what they were seeing. He was shocked. The slide read:

Is Time Travel Possible?

- Many theoretical physicists have shown that time travel is possible, but no one has had a clue how
- We all want time travel to the past for one purpose: to inform the past of the future
- There is now a means to achieve this end

Hal recognized the slide immediately—the font, the colors, the style were the same as the presentation Professor Johnson had given this morning. He must have put the prof's thumb drive into his computer instead of his own presentation! Hal didn't remember seeing this slide, but he could have missed it, considering. He grinned a little at his mistake but felt fortunate that the error had really woken up his audience.

Hal tried to press the electronic slide clicker to turn off the projector and the slide that was so distracting to his audience. But the "smart" controller only knew two commands: backward and forward. It advanced to the next slide:

There Is a Practical Concept that Avoids the Problems of Time Travel

- It is possible to build a real, practical time machine
- The solution is feasible using current technology
- While the costs are out of reach of garage mechanics, it is achievable with reasonable funding and development time

He was reaching for his laptop when he was hit with a barrage of questions he couldn't answer. Fortunately, he didn't have to.

"Are you telling me you have found a means for time travel to the future?" said Sizemore.

Hal didn't get to answer, if he even had a suitable response.

"Why, you could see the results of any investment!" Sizemore said. "You could see what's hot in next year's fashions. You could see who gets elected, what laws will get passed!"

"You could see which startups actually achieved their business plan!" said Dr. Davidson. "Forget long-range investments. If you can see the future, all you need to see is tomorrow's *Wall Street Journal* to get rich!"

Hal, remembering a few lines from the prof's presentation that morning, added, "Don't you really want to travel to the past, not the future? Then you simply tell yourself where to invest, and you would be instantly richer. No need to wait for the future!"

He set the hook. "Time travel can lead to considerable gains, well over development costs..." At least that was a safe boast since he'd presented no numbers.

Dr. Davidson stood up and rushed to the front of the room. "This is fantastic, Hal," he said. "This kind of machine would be worth anything! What will it take to develop this machine? How long will it take? What are the risks? What have you accomplished so far?"

Hal hesitated, hoping that he wouldn't actually have to answer these impossible questions.

He mentally created a politician's response, but before he could utter a word, Dr. Davidson said, "...*wait*, this has to be kept secret! Shut off the projector. Answer no more questions, and for heaven's sake, don't present this or talk to anyone else about it. We need to move to a secure building. We need to get the right people to see this."

Hal turned off the projector, though the last slide was still visible on his laptop screen. The VC reached for the thumb drive sticking out of the laptop, but Hal got to it first.

"I think you're right," Hal responded. "We have done a bit of work on this technology. There are risks in its development, but the rewards would compensate for any investment."

Hal, having sat through Professor Johnson's seminar, was sure the professor's slides were about how to build a time machine. Just as the venture capitalists were sure (and surely wrong) about what they were buying, Hal was sure (and surely wrong) about what he was selling. And this was not even what he was here to sell.

He had not forgotten about his urgent cash flow problem too, and remembered that line from *Glengarry Glen Ross*, "Always be closing."

"We do, however, need some small investment right now to maintain continuity in our staff and to secure our work," Hal said. "Not much."

The lead investor whipped out his checkbook and asked, "What do you need?"

With the check in hand and the thumb drive deep in his pocket, Hal knew the rest of the shtick. Vague words in small talk kept everyone thinking about what they heard and hearing what they wanted to think.

CHAPTER 5

Uncommon Goals

January 19, 2019, 1:00 p.m.

O F COURSE, HAL HAD NO intention of developing a time machine. Prior to FutureView, no one even had a theoretical concept of how to do it. Any physicist who could even show a nanosecond of travel through time would probably have won the Nobel Prize. The venture capital community, however, had higher expectations. And those VCs would be the ones footing the bill.

What became clear in Hal's mind was that he was going to perform a preplanned pivot. All Hal thought he needed to do was to keep the investors excited enough about time travel-research to continue to fund the development and demonstration of a time machine.

There would, of course, be an overhead charge applied to all labor and material costs of the project. The overhead charge would legitimately pay for management, the building lease, utilities, security, and…research and development. That last item would cover the entire development of his 5G transceiver. The more funds he could get for the time machine, the more he could charge to his 5G development. This was not illegal. It was even consistent with the Generally Accepted Accounting Principles (GAAP) of the Financial Accounting Standards Board (FASB) and the Federal Acquisition Regulation System (FARS).

Hal knew the VCs would eventually get antsy about putting in more money. At that point, he planned to offer them a demonstration test of the time machine. He would tell the time-travel staff that he *reluctantly* had to show the investors some progress in the development.

Then, of course, there would be a demonstration test that would surely not meet expectations. He would then say that the test revealed an unforeseen, fatal flaw in the theory, or an uneconomic, massive cost increase. Then Hal would offer a plan that would rescue their investment by pointing out that the work had helped them develop a better millimeter-wave transceiver that could be marketed to the cell tower industry!

With only a bit more money, he could then salvage their previous capital in FutureView and have a product ready for the market. That was the pivot plan.

While this may sound a little like the plot from *The Producers,* Hal consoled himself that this was a well-known and respected strategy in the tech startup community. He also knew that the VCs were aware that it also protected venture capital managers from being sued by their investors.

First thing he needed to do was to get Professor Johnson on his team. Since he was already on the MIT campus, Hal located Professor Johnson's office in the physics department and headed there. I must have just missed him.

I would expect that professors are usually lifers in the academic world. No MIT professor would give up his comfy, tenured, top-of-the-profession position unless dragged away by the Board of Directors of a booming business venture with an extravagant salary, *mucho* stock options, a title, an administrative assistant, a large office, and unrestrained research funds. Hal could not afford to offer any of these but was desperate to get the professor on board.

The professor told me about their subsequent encounter:

Hal started, "I attended your presentation this morning and, I have to say, Professor Johnson, you have certainly shown your tremendous capability and knowledge of a science no one dares to tread!"

The prof, quite leery of such a flowery introduction, cut him short with, "What can I do for you, mister?"

"Hawkins," Hal said. "I saw your excellent presentation this morning, and I was impressed with your detailed analysis of the physics."

The physics? the professor thought. *Who talks like that? This guy is probably from Human Resources and wants me to sign a termination agreement not to sue.*

Hal said, "I found your thumb drive—your presentation—this morning, and I just wanted to return it, that's all."

Hal offered him the drive, and the prof took it, throwing it into an open cardboard box.

"Your last slide especially impressed me," said Hal.

"You mean about the problems with building a time machine? It was just a conclusion from basic physics," said the prof, a little confused how that could be so brilliant.

"No," said Hal, "I mean the *last* slide. About your time machine design?"

The prof caught his breath. *That slide was among those I had not presented—the slides about my crazy design for a time machine,* he thought. This guy must have gone through all my slides!

The prof had to test him to see how much he understood. "What did you think of the circuit diagram, Mr. Hawkins?" asked the prof.

Hal was unprepared for that question but didn't want to let the professor know he was the guy who slept through his presentation. So he responded, "I was impressed with your detail."

The prof told me he breathed the proverbial sigh of relief. That circuit diagram was conceptual only and contained many "miracle occurs here" blocks in the diagram. *No one would answer the question with, "I was impressed with your detail,"* the professor thought. *I'm safe. Either this guy never saw the rest of the presentation, or he was too dumb to understand it!*

The professor turned away from Hal and worked on removing an automobile poster from his office wall. Hal could see that he was getting nowhere. He knew he had to cut to the chase, or this would all end badly. His plan for saving FutureView depended entirely on this professor taking his offer. There was no one else on the planet with any credibility in this field.

"I'd like to offer you a position to head up the development effort of a time machine at FutureView. I can offer you a 25 percent increase over your current salary…"

"I'll take it!" the professor replied.

"When you get the answer you want, stop talking," Hal had always said.

They shook hands and Hal left.

CHAPTER 6

Getting Hired
January 30, 2019

IT IS DIFFICULT TO APPRAISE company ads soliciting new employees. They all say the same thing: "Great place to work!" "Challenging opportunities!" "Great team to work with." They never say, "Dead-end project, everyone is fleeing," "Terrible management that will drop you in an instant," or "Work with assholes that will bad-mouth you to get ahead."

The FutureView hiring ad said nothing about a time machine. Nevertheless, I thought I would apply to this company to develop transceivers for 5G cell phone towers.

When I checked out FutureView.com on the internet, the company appeared to be in the business of making trade-show booths. That must have been a different company. The one advertising for new employees didn't seem to have a website. But what the hell, I thought. I sent in my resume anyway.

I'll admit I had been drifting from one job to another. I had not had the academic interest, nor the funds, to get a college degree, but thought I did better by learning hands-on. Unfortunately, not every technical manager agreed, so I had found the need to keep my LinkedIn profile updated.

I love working with technology. I have worked in electronics and in mechanical systems, and I am fluent in Python, C Plus Plus, and Ruby-on-Rails, as well as a variety of assembly languages. So many engineering college graduates want to work only on the latest generation of high-level artificial intelligence routines. In the real world, however, you have to know how computers execute basic machine instructions. You can get by knowing digital electronics, but when you push the limits, you better understand the subtlety of rise times, de-bouncing switches, and voltage thresholds. And, of course, impedance-matching and sneak-circuit prevention.

I wasn't sure FutureView would hire a nondegreed engineer, but I had been through the hiring process before, many times. The job description was typical—a lot of gibberish that meant nothing. I made sure that my resume contained every technical word and phrase that was in the job description so the automated search algorithms would find a high correlation. Once I got the interview, I knew my resume would be irrelevant. I never brought a copy to my job interview, only the customer's job description.

I dressed in the obligatory uniform: a white shirt and red tie, and a jacket that I kept in a dry-cleaner's plastic bag solely for this purpose. Upon arrival, I found the FutureView lobby in Waltham was decorated with modern art paintings and formless statues, but no products in glass showcases or photos of diverse, smiling actors working uncomfortably with hand tools, as you would find in most lobbies. The low coffee table contained only old copies of engineering magazines. The front desk receptionist, after some inquiry, knew a lot of detail about the people who worked there, but nothing about what it was they were building.

I recognized the professor as soon as he appeared in the lobby. The receptionist introduced me, and the professor led me to a glass-walled conference room next to the glass-walled lobby, where we sat for the interview.

I started off, "Professor Johnson! I attended your time-travel seminar at MIT! It impressed me how you had derived your unique theory of time travel."

"Well, yes. Thank you. We are here to talk about your electrical engineering experience."

He doth protest too much, I thought. Not even a word about something he worked on for years? Something he showed so much enthusiasm for at MIT? Like the poker player who suddenly stops talking after the cards are dealt, someone is holding aces. Could FutureView be doing something with time travel? I was suspicious but followed his lead and didn't bring up the subject further.

I started off trolling for a hot topic. "I have experience in microcircuits, in low-voltage power conservation, in analog and digital, in radio frequency, in high-power circuitry…" I kept listing topics, watching him for a tell. When his eyes lit up, I knew where to focus. "…in electric motors and magnetism, and in many other areas, but most-recently in high-power circuitry." I was perhaps stretching the truth but stretching in the direction he apparently needed.

"So, have you dealt with the degradation of insulation due to corona discharge?" he asked.

"Yes, that is one of the major problems I have had to deal with—corona."

I didn't even know what corona was.

"And have you dealt with the heating problem?"

"Yes," I replied, "heating is a real problem, especially with corona discharge."

OK, I thought, *I might have to deal with high voltage and time travel. Why not put them together?* "Of course, you can get away with some heating problems when you are dealing with high-power transfer in a short timeframe…"

His eyes lit up again.

You get the picture. That was how the interview went. That was how I got the job.

I had one advantage in applying for technology jobs. I used to get angry at my parents about my name—maybe my parents were drunk when they decided on it. But now it has opened many doors, and it helps people remember it, regardless of whether I said or did anything remarkable. My name also helps me get dates—even if I forget hers, she never forgets mine.

While the professor suggested that "they" were going to decide among multiple candidates, I sensed by the awkward questioning that the professor had little experience in hiring and not much taste for it. It was easy to slip in comments about how he should do "science" instead of waste his time interviewing candidates.

"So," I said at the end of the interview, "how many more candidates do you think you will have to interview before you decide…so I get an idea of how long it will be?"

"Oh, I don't know, maybe a dozen," he replied.

I knew that was an exaggeration—no one would interview a dozen candidates, not for a lab tech. So, I hit him with the next strike. "So, you will look at 15 or 20 resumes for each candidate—let me see, that's 240 resumes. I guess you will be at this for a while. I should probably keep my resume on the internet…"

"Well, I guess we'll have to part on that note. I'll be getting back to you soon, I'm sure," the prof offered, as he shook my hand.

From his expression, I would probably get a call in less than a week to start work. I figured I had better finish up the almost-final draft of my novel before I began the job.

***

The offer came a few days later. I doubted the professor had even interviewed another candidate. I felt confident from his description of the job that I could handle it, so I took the offer.

Sure, you may judge me. Perhaps I manipulated the situation on false histories, but you can see that neither Hal nor the professor was entirely honest either. It was all for the better, as we all struggled that much more to make FutureView a success. Isn't that how life works?

CHAPTER 7

Building a Time Machine
February 4, 2019

O N MY FIRST DAY, THERE was no training, familiarization, or even a mention of the time machine we were going to build. At least I assumed that's what we were building. I was given a name tag with my name in all caps, in case someone didn't know me. But after the first day, everyone knew who I was, and I dispensed with the name tag.

While the professor had suggested that we were at an early stage of development, and I was getting in "on the ground floor," it turned out that was literally the case. As soon as my first day, I spent most of my time on the internet buying tools, parts, and hiring subcontractors and job-shoppers. We were crammed into the first floor of the Waltham offices, with boxes of materials stacked in the hallways and delivery trucks blocking the only loading dock in the building. Hal wasn't too pleased.

Oh, the prof did take the time to introduce me to Hal. "Hal, this is my new engineering assistant, Thomas Edison."

Hal only responded with "Hi!" making no stupid reference to my namesake. I respected him for it.

***

I had been working at FutureView for three weeks when Hal marched into the prof's office, shut the door, and started up on the subject again. I was working behind a stack of boxes, trying to match up shipping numbers, so he didn't realize I was there. I kept my head down but couldn't help overhearing their conversation.

"You've got to get this stuff out of here, Sam," said Hal. He always called him Sam. "I'll gladly pay for a short-term lease…somewhere… somewhere else!"

"Actually, I'm going to need to move into a tall building with high electrical power capability," the prof replied.

I could see between the boxes that Hal was not pleased with the suggestion. He stomped around, struggling for words, or at least civilized words. "We can't afford to build a multistory building for the project! We just can't! Anyway, building even a one-story dedicated lab is out of the question—that would take too much time—you realize that VC money comes with an expectation of a return on investment? And it comes with an alarm clock! You need to get moving on this…this…project!"

"I have the perfect solution," the prof responded. "The Green Building."

"The *Green Building*? On the MIT campus? Why would you even consider it?" Hal said.

"First, the tunnels providing utilities to the building already provide the high voltage and high current electrical power that we are going to need. Second, the location on the MIT campus provides the cover we need for exotic science development. If we cause a blackout on campus from drawing down too much power for 'science,' who's going to complain? Third, the location on the 18th floor provides the best possible physical security and isolation from the public. The only way in is from the elevators—which we can easily control, without guards. Fourth, the lease cost is dirt-cheap, as the MIT Corporation is eager to see some revenue from this empty lab space, though it's only a six-month lease. Fifth…"

"I'll take it!" Hal said. "Get me the lease, and I'll sign it today!"

Hal smiled, turned, and hesitated at the door. There was no telling which feature had so rapidly convinced him to pivot.

"Good morning, Tom," he added, though I was still behind the boxes. He then walked out, more at ease than he had entered.

"When do we move?" I asked, stepping out from behind the boxes.

There was an unspoken reason Hal wanted us to move out—to keep the time machine development separate from the other engineers and staff working in the Waltham office—so there would be less disruption when it came time to shut our project down.

I asked the professor, "Is the Green Building one of those highly insulated, solar-powered buildings that requires zero energy to cover its own energy needs? If it is, we're probably going to shoot that to hell."

"No, it's not *a* 'green' building. It's called the Green Building because Cecil H. Green, an alumnus of MIT, paid for it. The building is an eighteen-story skyscraper designed by the famous architect I. M. Pei. Pei also designed the Prudential Building, once the tallest building in Boston. The Green Building was supposed to be a mirror-image of the 'Pru,' directly across the Charles River."

It must have been a carnival mirror, I thought, as the Green Building was only eighteen stories tall while the Pru was fifty-two!

"Another reason we need that building is because it was designed with a tall, open first floor," the professor said.

I found that strange. We were only using the top floors of the building, so I looked it up. When it was built, it was heralded as a brilliant architectural achievement. But they soon discovered that strong winds blowing through the open twenty-foot-tall first story caused such air pressure on the doors that they couldn't be opened. I still did not know what that had to do with our requirements.

Being on the MIT campus, the building became a target for hacks. Hacks like adding colored LEDs around each of the windows in the building and making the building into a giant video game screen for playing *Tetris* from the courtyard. On Halloween, the rooftop became a platform for launching pumpkins.

On top of all the work ordering parts and assembling assemblies, we also had to prepare the Green Building lab for high-power, high-cooling, high-noise, and everything else the professor could spec. One tremendous piece of equipment we needed was a gimbaled dish antenna, twenty meters in diameter. It had to be lifted to the rooftop by a construction crane. The union workers who operated the crane didn't work on windy days but charged every hour that they didn't work. There were a lot of windy days in winter.

The professor would design elements of the machine, and it was my job to get them built, delivered, assembled, and tested by sub-contractors and job-shoppers. By breaking up the work among the subcontractors, no contractor could either figure out the end purpose or duplicate the work done.

From the day I interviewed for the job, I knew we were going to build a time machine. I also realized that it was extremely important to keep that a secret. The professor was diligent in hiding or disguising anything that might suggest time travel. He was careful not to make any reference to time, even if it was, in fact, unrelated to time travel. "Time machine" was a phrase the professor never used.

He had once made the mistake of identifying a subsystem as a "time dilator." I was careful to never ask why it was called that. The next day I came in and saw that the circuit diagrams had been updated overnight, deleting all references to time—the subsystems were simply labeled "dilators."

There was always a lot of noise in the lab, coming from equipment and power tools, making it difficult to communicate. One day, I believe the prof said, "Tom, we will need higher voltage capability for these time circuits."

I thought it wise to ask, "What was that?"

He replied, "We need higher voltage capability for these *dying* circuits!"

I overheard the professor once responding to a question from one contractor, who asked what we were building. Hesitantly, the professor answered, "We are doing radio research."

That seemed to fit well with all the millimeter-wave radio-frequency equipment we were assembling and our location in an MIT laboratory. It was a good cover story, so I started using it too.

One day Hal came over from the Waltham office to look around, seeming to have no particular purpose. I was at the professor's desk, asking the prof for some clarification when Hal walked in.

"Good morning, Samuel. Good morning, Tom," Hal said. "How's the time machine coming together? Have you done any time traveling yet?"

Just like that, the charade was over.

"What! Is that what we're building?!" I asked as sincerely as I could manage.

"Yes, Tom, that's what we're building," the professor replied, also appearing to be sincere, but I could not be sure.

Now that the cat was proverbially released from the bag, I had a thousand questions about time travel. While Hal and the prof were willing to bring me under the tent, we still had to guard the knowledge of our mission from all the subcontractors, avoiding discussions in public. The professor continued to be tight-lipped about the science. I would have to ask time-related questions only when we were alone at night. After that day, the prof also seemed relieved and began confiding in me about many things, not just the "Big Secret."

The work was extensive and highly experimental. The professor would often come to me with changes that required throwing away obsolete components before they were even installed. This was very frustrating, but I knew the project would be historic, if it worked at all. I often stayed late into the evening since I had little else to do and no private life to speak of.

The professor also worked late into the evenings. He seemed obsessed, as if this project was his ultimate life endeavor. He often compared our work on the time machine development to his work on cold fusion.

The word "fusion" bothered me. It sounded "nuclear." Was I handling material that was radioactive? I trusted that the professor would have warned me. Or Hal would have.

Or would they? I finally had to approach the professor on the matter.

"No," the prof said, "the FutureView machine has nothing to do with cold fusion." He thought I was still apprehensive about it, so late one evening, he explained further.

When it had come time to select his thesis topic for his PhD program, and his future area of research, the professor selected a topic that was emerging as an exciting new field of physics.

Nuclear power in power stations or in atomic bombs releases tremendous energy through nuclear fission—breaking apart the excessively heavy atoms of uranium or plutonium and converting a small amount of matter into energy. A potentially more efficient process of converting a small amount of mass into energy is to fuse two very light atoms, like hydrogen. Hydrogen is the most abundant element in the universe. Hitherto, the only method of inducing the fusion of atoms in a chain reaction was by detonating an atomic fission bomb nearby. This is how a hydrogen bomb works. Fusion would be an ideal process for generating electrical energy. But detonating a nuclear explosion would hardly be acceptable to the EPA.

Early breakthrough work in this new science showed the possibility of inducing nuclear fusion in a controlled laboratory environment, in a process run at room temperature rather than temperatures of the surface of the sun. It was called "cold fusion," an ideal physics research domain that promised tremendous practical benefits—unlimited low-cost energy generated without significant fuel, no danger of radioactivity, no carbon generation, and no pollution.

Professor Johnson continued with this work in a research position at MIT. Unfortunately, after years of exciting progress in the field, the original discovery of cold fusion was found to be "suspect." This was a polite way of saying the science was bogus. Experiments could not corroborate earlier claims.

But Dr. Johnson hung tenaciously to the possibility of cold fusion, into which he had invested considerable research and theoretical and experimental work. However, scientific journals refused to publish developments on the subject, no matter how rigorous or valuable to science. Research funding dried up. No one wanted to be tainted with that brush.

The professor was unwilling to throw away the considerable work he had done in the field to start again in a new endeavor. He resorted to doing a lot of work on his own time with his own funds.

His stubbornness was not without cost beyond spending all of his savings. His career suffered. His marriage fell apart. The professor buried himself in his work, trying desperately to find hope. I think his greatest fear was that the time machine would be another dead end, a lost cause.

As we continued to build the machine, the complexity amazed me. The professor even tried to explain the operation of the machine, and once went to the whiteboard to derive his theory in algebraic terms. He may as well have been explaining to a hound dog how a shotgun worked. He could be assured that even under torture, I will never reveal how to build a time machine.

One interesting part of the FutureView machine (we eventually started calling it just "the FV machine") was a large steel chamber made from a tanker truck body. It contained a lot of uninsulated, high-voltage electrical circuits, and a steel hatch.

I discovered, working in this chamber, that I was claustrophobic, or electro-phobic, or both. There were a lot of high-voltage circuits in the chamber. At high voltage, it becomes ineffective to just rubber-coat wires—voltage potentials have to be separated and mounted on glass standoffs. The professor may have been an excellent physicist, but what we really needed was an experienced linesman who knew how to handle and protect these high-voltage circuits. More than once sparks arced between conductors and fried my work!

I convinced the prof that we needed to build in a few safety features in the chamber. We implemented a simple red flashing light to warn against turning on the high voltage when someone was in the chamber. I also installed a cellphone indoor antenna to relay cellphone transmissions to the outdoors since the chamber pretty much blocks all radio signals inside that chamber. Not only did this allow me to use the internet on my laptop inside the chamber, but it also provided for emergency communication in case someone was accidentally shut in the chamber or injured and needed help. I also added a small porthole that could provide a little light inside the chamber when the power went off.

One day I came in and saw that the prof had installed a wooden chair with the legs half trimmed off—inside the chamber. Did he choose a wooden chair to avoid electrical conductivity? *This chamber must be the capsule for the time traveler!* The thought scared me.

Who will make the first trip through time? I wondered. It would be historic!

Would the inventor be the first to travel through time, like in H. G. Wells' *The Time Machine*? Would the professor be his own test pilot? What if something went wrong, like it had with Jeff Goldblum in *The Fly?* You don't want to lose the only one who could analyze and fix a problem on your first test! If it failed, you don't want to lose the only inventor who could learn and make the next model succeed!

The engineer who designed the Bell X-1 rocket-powered airplane wasn't the one to break the sound barrier. They needed a steely-eyed test pilot, Chuck Yeager, not an engineer. Who could he ask to be the first test pilot for a time machine? What are the qualifications of a time traveler? There would not seem to be any physical conditioning requirement. Why not send a robot? But then, why did we need to send astronauts into space and to the moon, when it would have been so much easier to send a machine and a camera? We needed the ability to innovate, to recognize unpredictable problems and solve them. We needed technologists who know every detail of the spaceship. The time traveler would have to be a problem solver and a technologist with detailed knowledge of the time machine. The time traveler would be on his own, even more than a test pilot or an astronaut, with no remote support. The ideal candidate should be…me?

I would have to sit in that little chair inside the chamber! I have feared going in there, even when the power was off. Should I refuse? The professor would never force me to be the time traveler. So, should I volunteer? What about those problems the professor mentioned in his seminar, about being blasted into space, or being peppered with air molecules? I am going to have to confront the professor on this!

CHAPTER 8

Proof of Concept
April 13, 2019

I WAITED FOR THE OPPORTUNITY, LATE at night, when the prof and I were the only ones left in the lab, to ask him about those missing flaws in his theory of time travel.

"Professor?" I asked, "How do you solve the problem of a time traveler suddenly appearing in a place where there was already something there—if there is air, there?"

"That problem is easy," he said, wrapping his knuckles on the steel chamber. "We build air-tight capsules all the time, from space capsules to aircraft to submarines. That's not your biggest problem."

His answer did not comfort me, especially his last sentence, but I went on, "What about the problem of the earth being in constant motion, so time travel also requires space travel? How do you solve that?"

"I discovered, with more analysis," said the prof, "that we do not need to worry about absolute movement of the earth in the universe. The selection of an absolute center of the universe to define motion would be as arbitrary as selecting H. G. Wells' library as the location."

"That's good that we wouldn't go flying out of the galaxy if we went back in time. But you say we can't stay in the same place on earth, either?"

"The only relevant motion we have to account for is the movement of the earth relative to the local gravitational fields, driven mostly by the sun and the earth. That would be motion in earth rotation and in orbit around the sun."

"But isn't that still a lot of motion?"

"Yes, the earth travels in orbit at about 67,000 miles per hour."

"You would have to travel 67,000 miles to go back in time one hour? Isn't that pretty difficult to achieve?"

"Not if you're traveling at the speed of light!"

I was totally confused. "Wait a minute, professor! Are you saying that this machine will transport a time traveler at the speed of light?"

"No," he said firmly. "What makes you think we are sending time travelers?"

He looked at me with a puzzled twist in his facial expression, like I was asking a stupid question. At that point, I dropped the subject.

One amazing piece of test equipment we assembled in the Green Building was a complete radio-frequency anechoic chamber. Everyone knows what an acoustic anechoic chamber looks like—a room with every wall, ceiling, and floor covered with pyramids of foam rubber to absorb sound. If you have ever been in one, it's creepy. You would think the lack of sound would be just silence, but we are so used to some sound that we begin to lose orientation without it.

This was a radio anechoic chamber, designed to absorb radio waves. That made it possible to test equipment in an environment free of stray reflections of radio waves.

The supplier of the anechoic chamber carried it all up in the elevator, piece by piece, and assembled it in the lab. It comprised a rectangular enclosed room thirty meters long and ten meters wide, lined with one-meter-long pointy pyramids of blue, rigid foam plastic, loaded with carbon to absorb any stray radio waves.

The prof had the chamber set up with the rectangular room built diagonally across the lab. It would have been more space-efficient if it were aligned along one wall, but he insisted the chamber be aligned with the true east-west heading.

I came in one day, and the professor announced we were going to conduct the proof-of-concept test, or POC, to determine whether his theories were valid.

Most of the laboratory housed circuits for time travel, and a radio-frequency transmitter connected to a small dish antenna that was mounted inside the anechoic chamber at its west wall. I installed the antenna, aiming it toward the opposite end of the chamber.

"No, no!" the professor said. "Aim it the other way, toward the west wall!"

He had to show me, as it made no sense to aim the dish directly at the absorbent foam wall.

I thought we might be setting up to detect back leakage from the antenna, but we were not. The receiving antenna was a similar dish mounted at the *east* end of the chamber about thirty meters away. And the receiver dish antenna was also pointed *away* from the transmitter! It made no sense.

The professor had me connect both the transmitter signal and the receiver signal to an oscilloscope. Since the radio signal only had to traverse the thirty meters between the transmitter and receiver, I calculated that the transmitted signal would be received thirty-three nanoseconds after the transmitter signal. We were essentially reconfirming the speed of light, though both directional antennas were pointed away from each other!

The prof had me conduct a test run at close to noon. Looking at the setup, it did not surprise me when the scope reported only the transmitter signal. With the antennas pointed away from each other, the receiver probably never received a signal!

The professor seemed perplexed at the result. He went back and checked my wiring and settings, then said to me, "We are *not* measuring the speed of light!"

I'm not sure what his emphasis implied, whether we *did not* measure the speed of light, or whether we *should not* be measuring the speed of light. Either way, we got no results.

He then moved some of my wires, and I examined what he had done. To my amazement, he had switched my trigger wires so that the scope recorded the signals from both the transmitter and receiver but was now triggered by the *receiver*. We were now measuring how long *after* a signal was received it had been transmitted.

We reran the test. The oscilloscope recorded that the signal was received an unbelievable 0.95 milliseconds *before* the signal was transmitted. We were sending radio waves back in time!

"This is fantastic!" I told the prof. "I don't believe anyone has ever done this! I'm sure this is a critical first step to sending an object back in time. Will we be able to do that with this setup?"

"No," he said, "I'm afraid I don't know how to send an object back in time."

"I thought we were proving out how to build a time machine—a machine for traveling back in time?"

"Oh, no. I do not know how to build such a machine. Well, I have some ideas, but right now they are just notes on three-by-five cards. No, we are developing the ability to send data, to send information, to send *messages* back in time!"

The professor continued, "Sending radio signals avoids the problems of transmitting to where the earth was in the past, although our range into the past still requires a lot of energy to cover the distance the earth moves—67,000 miles for every hour in time range.

"Since we aren't sending objects back in time, it eliminates the problem of sending something to where matter already exists. Radio waves can easily appear without disturbing existing matter or existing radio waves.

"Sending only radio waves gets rid of the problem of conservation of matter, since we aren't creating more matter than existed before the transmission. There are other conservation laws we have to consider..."

I felt foolish and was still confused about the chair in the resonant chamber, so I had to ask, "I thought maybe that seat you put in the resonant chamber might have been… Why *did* you put the chair there?"

"I was getting tired working on the wiring in the chamber and needed a comfortable seat to sit in while doing it.

"What I've done," he continued, "is sidestep the problems of transporting a human being through time, and looked, instead, at a simpler problem: sending a message back in time. Isn't that essentially what a time traveler would do—carry a message back in time—anyway? You can send a radio signal at the speed of light, the secret to time travel—you actually have no other choice—and you can send it into a previous time.

"The test was conducted at noon because that was when the horizontal transmitting antenna would point directly back to where the receiving antenna was 0.95 milliseconds earlier, as the earth moved in orbit. In 0.95 milliseconds, the earth moves about thirty meters, the length of the anechoic chamber."

"What about the earth's rotation—doesn't that also affect the location of the receiving antenna?" I asked.

"Yes, but in 0.95 milliseconds, the earth only rotates less than a third of a meter. There is enough margin in the test for it to work, despite minor errors in pointing or timing. This proves my assumption that the only movement in time is that motion relative to the local gravitational masses—the earth and sun, in this case."

While this was an amazing achievement, I was unsure whether this was what the investors had in mind.

The prof went on, "Things will be more complex in the operational time machine. I think we have to be practical about how far back in time we transmit—you'll see why later. But let's look at only a few hours in time, for now."

That immediately dashed some of my expected ideas for such a machine. No going back to alert anyone about 9/11, Pearl Harbor, or Mount Vesuvius.

We continued our conversation in the professor's office. Hanging from the ceiling were two tennis balls on fishing lines hanging down to just above his desk. On each ball, he had penned in a crude outline of the continents. He used the balls to illustrate the movement of the earth. The prof had an old desk lamp—an accountant's lamp with a translucent green shade. While it was an antique lamp, it was fitted with a new LED light bulb. He tilted the shade out of the way and used the light bulb to represent the sun. The prof explained that the two tennis balls would represent the position of the earth at two different times—at the transmit time and at the receive time.

"We also have to consider that the earth itself cannot block the signal at transmission or reception, so we have to make sure we are pointing, without interference, at where the receiver *was*, at the time we want the message to be received, and where the earth *is* at the time we want to transmit. Since the earth rotates counterclockwise viewed from the North Pole, and our orbit around the sun is also counterclockwise, viewed from the sun's north pole..."

My head was spinning, trying to visualize this. But the prof showed me using the tennis balls.

"...which means we can only transmit in the afternoon and early evening, between noon and midnight, when we are facing backward in orbit, to where the earth was previously."

He grabbed the first tennis ball that was suspended at eye level above his desk and illustrated the time-of-day constraint by rotating the ball. Boston was marked on the ball with a green ink dot.

"The receiver antenna also has to be facing where the earth *will* be, so it can only receive in the morning, between midnight and noon."

He grabbed the second ball and rotated it to illustrate.

"The orbital movement is much greater. If this were to scale, the separation after two hours would look more like this."

He then stood up and swung the second tennis ball about two feet from the first ball, to illustrate.

"So, if we want to send a signal and can only transmit a limited distance, we should transmit a bit after noon, and receive a bit before noon. That also makes for a beam aimed low on the horizon. The line of sight might be blocked at such a shallow elevation angle, and we could suffer degradation of our signal skimming through a lot of the atmosphere. I've chosen a radio frequency in the X-band, where there is little spread of the beam, and at that frequency there is little absorption of the signal in the earth's atmosphere.

"X-band is what NASA uses to communicate with the Mars rovers, with very large antennas and powerful transmitters, which we cannot duplicate. But the dish antenna on the roof needs to be aimed almost horizontally, due east for transmitting, and due west for receiving. Since we have plenty of time between receiving and transmitting, we can use one gimbaled dish antenna to serve both purposes."

"So that's the fifth reason you wanted the Green Building!" I realized.

"Yes," the prof said. "The Green Building was designed in 1962. At that time, the city of Cambridge had a strict limit on the number of stories allowed in any new building. But the MIT Planetary Science Department needed a clean line of sight above all the other buildings in the city. So, the architect made the first floor a gigantic open atrium, two stories high, boosting the flat roof above any other building with the same limit on the number of stories. The university installed a radome on top to boot. It's still taller than most of the buildings in Cambridge.

"It's unfortunate that the rectangular building is skewed a bit from the east-west line, as it's lined up, instead, to be parallel with the other buildings on campus, and to the Charles River. That's why the POC experiment was mounted diagonally in the lab—to be aligned with the true east-west line."

Work began immediately on building the next version of the time machine, using a lot of off-the-shelf equipment. We also needed special electrical power connections to handle the power surge needed and dedicated power lines with slow-acting circuit breakers at the power substation to handle the expected sudden surge that would occur when sending a message. In addition, we had an array of ultra-capacitors to provide a peak power pulse.

"Now," the professor said, "if we aim carefully at where the receiver was, and we have a tremendous amount of power and antenna gain, we might send the signal about 134,000 miles, the distance that is required for a two-hour time range.

"With all of this, we will still only be able to transmit brief messages—that's the tradeoff for a weak signal at great range. A short digital message would have to include bits dedicated to error detection and correction, and some bits would be needed to distinguish the time message from every other radio signal that might be picked up. If we use the simple ASCII code to send an alphanumeric message, we might only get a handful of characters in a message."

ASCII encoding is the way characters are stored in most computers and displays. Each letter of the alphabet, caps and smalls, is assigned a 7-bit binary code, and an extra bit for redundancy, to detect errors. There are plenty of chips that directly convert these codes into the alphanumeric characters we see on a computer screen.

I was sure the professor felt that sending a few characters back only a few hours in time would be a monumental scientific achievement, but it seemed less than practical. I feared that this was going to upset many people, especially those who were putting up millions of dollars expecting to at least get a DeLorean.

This had to be the most feeble and ineffective time machine ever conceived.

CHAPTER 9

Meeting Expectations

May 31, 2019

I ENTERED THE PROF'S OFFICE TO pick up a small UPS order that had arrived earlier. He was engrossed in making an entry in his design notebook. This was a notebook that he kept very private, a notebook he opened to enter information about the time machine, and who knew what else, since he never shared the contents with me. I recognized the notebook by its distinctive cover—a photo of a rock formation in New Hampshire that looked like a human face called "The Old Man of the Mountain."

That was uncharacteristic of him; the emotional response, that is. He was like a spendthrift trying to balance a joint checking account. Abrupt in his movements, frowning, and making harsh cross-outs.

I attempted to leave quietly with my package, but he caught me and dragged me back to the Old Man. "Tom," he said, "my calculations show we are going to need considerably more electrical power than I had previously planned. We are going to need 500,000 volts and dedicated three-phase power lines with a rapid draw that must not trip a circuit breaker, despite our huge ultracaps. We are going to have to get a custom arrangement with the power company!"

The professor was not one to get mad about an electric bill. This wasn't the cause of his frustration.

I said, "Hal is good at getting partnership deals like this. Why not ask him to 'whitewash the fence'?"

"Whitewash? No, I'm talking about a very expensive power arrangement. Hal has already made threats about limiting our spending. This may be the voltage spike that trips the Zener diode."

I got his metaphor, though I thought he didn't get mine. I was worried about losing my source of income, as I was the one most vulnerable to a cutback in funding.

"Why don't you come along with me to see Hal? I could use the technical support."

I suspected that what he really needed was moral support; negotiating with Hal was like playing one-on-one with Stephen Curry at a dollar a point.

I, meanwhile, needed to be there for my own protection.

***

Now that we were working in the Green Building, I seldom spent time at the Waltham office, but it was always impressive. It was in an expensive technology industrial park in Waltham just off the tech-heavy beltway formerly (and presently, by the locals) called "Route 128."

The lobby and conference room were glass-walled, overlooking the Mystic Reservoir. Several young entrepreneurs had startup companies in the adjacent offices, and there was a college-like atmosphere in the compound.

Hal's receptionist was away from his desk, so the professor and I went directly to Hal's office door. An argument was going on inside. Even though we hesitated outside, we didn't have to strain to hear their voices.

"Our current prototype needs a lot of work, and it really should include the Mod Two features—we've *got* to have more time and the funds to cover this work!" said a voice I did not recognize.

"You've been burning your half of the venture funding faster than the Cambridge Project!" said a voice that was clearly Hal's. "Sorry, we are almost out of cash. I have barely $300,000 left. Don't worry about the added features just yet. There will be more funds available after the pivot."

Pivot? I knew nothing about the company's business strategy—I had, perhaps selfishly, assumed that our project was the primary focus of the company, and the investor funds were going straight to our work, which must be the "Cambridge Project." I had heard about pivoting in startup companies but wasn't sure what it meant.

I glanced at the professor, looking for an explanation. He looked at me for the same.

As Hal continued at a lower volume, we stood silently and moved closer to the office door to hear.

"The VCs will be here today," Hal said. "I will tell them the bad news that the Cambridge Project turned out to be unworkable. After they go through the five stages of grief, I will show them your prototype and explain how the X-band transmitter from the Cambridge Project could become a very competitive product useful in wireless internet connectivity. They will jump at it!"

"Is that what you call your 'pivot'?" the other voice questioned.

"In poker, it's called a bluff," Hal replied.

The prof's mouth hung open. It was the professor who went through the five stages of grief. He sat on a chair in the outer office and said, "It can't be happening, not now. I'll be damned if I'm just going to roll over!" He was already in stage two.

A man and a woman I did not know then entered the outer office. The woman, smartly-dressed in a business suit, carried a cell phone she obviously had to carry in her hand as she had no purse or pocket that could accommodate it. She held the front door for the man who followed her, then strutted ahead and offered her hand to the prof.

"Good morning!" she said to the professor and me. She waited for the gentleman to introduce her.

He realized his cue and stepped forward. "Sandy, this is Professor Johnson, the lead scientist on the Cambridge Project…"

"I am Sandra O'Brien, financial advisor to Crandall & Jarvis. I'm glad to meet you," Sandy said.

"Good morning, Sandra. Good morning, Dan," said the professor. "This is my assistant, Thomas Edison."

To complete the intros, I extended my hand to the gentleman, "Howdy! Dan, is it?"

"Dan Davidson. I am the senior partner at Crandall & Jarvis and manager of the New Horizons Venture Fund. We are the principal investor in FutureView."

I was glad I asked. We almost left out the most important person in the room.

"Professor Johnson, how is the FutureView machine going? Hal was going to brief us on progress, but I'm glad you're here to give us the details. Is Hal in?"

Hal must have heard us and opened his door. "Well, welcome, Dan, Professor Johnson, Tom…" He turned to Sandy, "…and I am Harold Hawkins, the CEO of FutureView, ma'am."

"Sandy O'Brien, Dan's financial advisor," she said.

Clearly, Hal must have been expecting the VCs. He certainly wasn't expecting the professor and me to be here, as we hadn't been invited. That alone made me suspicious.

Hal seemed interested in Sandy. She had her hair pulled tightly into a bun and was wearing an expensive professional suit and heels. She was no one's secretary or even a bookkeeper. She looked like the lawyer you didn't want your ex-wife to have in court—not one to be swayed by Hal's bullshit.

"Why don't we all go into the conference room? There's coffee in the dispenser."

We entered the room. Everyone got coffee and exchanged comments about the ducks in the reservoir.

I heard a comment from Sandy, speaking to Davidson in a private voice. "I trust you realize this is our *last* company."

She caught me listening and said to me directly, "We have visited each of the companies in our New Horizons Venture Fund, and you are the last one."

It seemed contrived. She'd felt for some reason that she had to give an explanation. All the more suspicious!

Hal came in, motioned for all to take seats, and immediately sat in the power seat—the front left side seat at the conference table, with a view out the glass wall to the Mystic Reservoir. The professor fell in line and sat next to him. Davidson moved opposite Hal, and Sandy was next to Davidson. I sat at the end of the table with a bagel. All we needed now was a deck of cards.

After a round of anteing pleasantries, Davidson started. "We have gone three rounds with you, Hal, and we have heard little. We need to get back to our investors, and we need to give them something about your progress."

Hal replied, "We have been struggling to build the machine. The expenses were greater than we had planned because we did not anticipate the cost of more expensive high-power equipment. Isn't that right, professor?"

The professor could only nod in agreement.

"Why don't you tell them about the proof-of-concept test you ran, professor?" Hal said.

"Yes," the professor began, "well, um, we were seeking to prove the concept of time projection, within a control volume, operating at ten gigahertz, and we were successful in seeing a 0.95 millisecond reversal, although we were hit by a power-time limit…"

"Thank you, professor," Davidson said before the prof could explain anything. I think the professor's description went over like a lead zeppelin.

Sandy asked, "And how much did that experiment cost?"

"I can't say exactly as to the capital equipment, and the chamber costs, and the power…" the prof replied.

"Approximately, including the equipment."

"Well, I would say…about…about $14.9 million. I don't know what the power bill for the test will cost us, as they have not invoiced us yet for the special charges on that, and…"

"You've been working on this project now for three months and running up considerable expenses," Davidson said. "We are at the point where additional funding will be very limited. Our investors are reluctant to go forward."

Hal stepped in at that point. "Dan, the work the professor has been doing has certainly exceeded our original expectations. While it may seem like wasted money, we shouldn't think of it that way. They have developed a powerful microwave transmitter that fits in well with our other work, our work in 5G cell technology…"

I now realized what "pivot" meant.

The prof suddenly interrupted and said, "Our test results have now firmly confirmed our theory of time. We are *now* ready for a fully operational demonstration of transmitting back in time. Would you like to see the demonstration?"

No one spoke. Hal appeared as shocked as the VCs.

The prof raised the bet. "All we need is support from the Mass Department of Energy Resources. We were just here to ask Hal to negotiate the power company's services."

Davidson's face lit up. "Of course, we will be here for the demo! Hal, can you get the services they need so we can have a demo next week?"

Hal replied, "You know these bureaucratic utilities—let's make it two weeks from today."

He looked at the prof, and the prof nodded approval.

"Let's meet here, at 11:30," the prof said.

I was puzzled why, or even how, we would do a demo in the Waltham office. I shrugged my shoulders and turned my palms up to imply to the prof, *Shouldn't we be running the demo at the lab in the Green Building?*

"I'll be bringing two investors along as well," Davidson said.

A flock of geese then flew low overhead and interrupted the conversation, honking loudly. It was quite a spectacular view through the glass walls of the conference room, though too much like a movie scene—it must have been an omen.

The rest of the meeting was anticlimactic. Sandy asked some probing questions of Hal but didn't get far. The VC team left and the rest of us sat at the conference table. Neither Hal nor the professor was ready to show his cards.

I had a dozen questions to ask the professor at that point, but I felt it best to wait until we drove back. The prof handed Hal a detailed list of our electrical power requirements and the contact information for the power company. Hal didn't even look at the paper; he knew he would have to get whatever the prof had written. We then thanked Hal and left.

As we drove out of the parking lot, I looked back at the Waltham office. It looked clean and high-tech—certainly like a place in which to invest millions of dollars. Maybe it wasn't such a bad idea to meet there instead of the noisy, crowded lab in the Green Building.

Perhaps it had to do with secrecy. The less that even the investors knew about the time machine, the better. "Vulture Capitalists" were known to invest in multiple companies in the same field, and some of the technology would find its way from the less successful companies to the more favored company, where they were placing most of their bets.

Then again, Hal might have wanted the VCs to see the 5G product and its progress in the lab in Waltham, knowing that the time machine demo would fail, or would at least fail to impress. He wouldn't want them to see how much equipment had already been sunk into the Cambridge lab, thus better convincing them of the pivot.

I was certain the professor hadn't objected because he had a plan.

"How, exactly, are we going to move the whole FV machine to Waltham?" I asked.

"We don't need to, nor do we want to move the machine. We just need a remote control and display connected through the internet to run the entire operation from Waltham."

I thought about it and agreed, suggesting, "We could do it all from a laptop, or an iPad…or even my cell phone!"

"No, no, no," the professor replied. He spoke enthusiastically, moving his arms about more like a marketeer than a professor. "We need to convince the investors that their money went into a high-tech electronic device. It needs to be heavy, so put a few large batteries in it. It needs to heat up, so put some heater coils powered by those heavy batteries. It needs to have two screens, one for the transmitter, and one for the receiver, oriented opposite each other so that neither operator can see the other screen. And yes, it needs a Wi-Fi internet connection…and put some solid handles on it."

"Would you like a Jacob's ladder on top?" I asked. The prof frowned at my sarcastic offer.

This would not be so much an engineering project as a marketing project. I gritted my teeth in disappointment.

CHAPTER 10

The Card Demo

June 13, 2019

WITH ALL THE WORK WE then had to do, it took two weeks to be ready for the demo, including a lot of late nights. Though we couldn't run any tests until power lines were installed, we were now ready for the first test of the FutureView machine.

The professor and I worked feverishly all morning to finish the electrical power connections. I was angry at the bureaucracy of power companies that had been in the same business too long and seemed to drag their feet whenever a customer had a critical deadline. On the other hand, you sure don't want to rush when dealing with voltages high enough that you would be dead before the shock would reach your brain.

I just had time to change my shirt and wash up before leaving for the Waltham office.

I grabbed the new remote terminal and threw it in the back of the prof's Honda Civic hatchback. The passenger door wouldn't open until the prof rolled down the passenger-side window so I could reach in and open the door from the inside handle. The prof cursed his car, but cars were not the issue this morning.

On the way over, the professor said, "Please do not interrupt the demonstration. The investors, and even Hal, may have some false ideas about the FV, but let's not enlighten them today, OK? We can straighten things out later."

I certainly had been in marketing presentations before where you over-promise performance, but I had also learned to keep my mouth shut, as difficult as that was. I just did not know why he requested that.

As we arrived, a limo pulled up at the FutureView office and the entourage filed out. This was comprised of the VCs Jim Sizemore and Dan Davidson, their financial advisor, Sandy O'Brien, and two others, introduced as investors—Messrs. Kevin Brayton and Ronald Fox. Yes, *that* Kevin—the big winner of that poker game at MIT. Hal led them, the professor, and me into the conference room. Pleasantries were exchanged, and Hal welcomed Kevin without showing his enmity.

The professor and I lugged the remote-control box from the car to the conference room. The separate transmitter and receiver screens and keyboards were mounted on opposite sides of the box, as the prof had requested.

Since this was a marketing machine, I had added a few "marketing devices"—a couple of old milliammeter dials and a circuit late one night. The circuit was triggered whenever a message arrived. The circuit sounded a *ding* from a piezo buzzer recycled off an old Maytag washing machine. Then a capacitor discharged into the meters, so they swung wildly for a second. At least it added some excitement to receiving a message.

One person could carry the whole thing much like a suitcase, using the double leather handles on one side. I had even attached casters so it could be wheeled through an airport like a piece of luggage. It could probably even pass through an X-ray machine.

Mounting the screens on opposite sides made it difficult for one person to check out, but the prof had insisted it would be important in the future to keep the person operating the transmitter from seeing the results in the receiver. I did not appreciate the significance then, but I would soon learn why the hard way.

The professor carefully placed the box on the conference table. He asked me to sit directly behind the transmitter side of the box, and he sat on the receiver side. Everyone else took seats around the conference table.

Dr. Davidson, looking over the remote box, did most of the talking for the venture capitalists. "This is amazing! I assumed you would not be sending a person, or even a live animal, back in time—but probably a small object—right? But I am amazed at how compact the whole device is! It can fit here on the table!"

Hal looked at the prof. The prof looked at me. I could only shrug, thinking, *I hope this isn't what I'm supposed to be mum about!*

"No, we will not send a time traveler to the past," Hal said. "Maybe you were expecting a time machine that looks like a swamp boat? Or a DeLorean? Maybe a British phone booth? It would be dramatic, but what would be the business value of sending a person a short time into the past? If we accomplished that, what would we expect him to accomplish during the time traveler's brief stay in the past?"

No one answered his presumably rhetorical question.

"There is nothing he could learn from a quick trip to the past that would be any better than books, newspapers, YouTube videos, or even our own memos and memories. No, the *only* thing he could do that would be of any exclusive value is to leave some information about the future with people in the past! So, why complicate things by sending a very-expensive messenger? What we really want to do is just send information! Just like Alexander Bell, Guglielmo Marconi, and Al Gore, we have simply developed a revolutionary means of communication!"

Davidson asked, "You mean this is a device to only look at the future?"

"Yes, in a sense. This is a device for looking at information *from* the future! It appears on this screen in front of Professor Johnson! The way we transmit from the future is through this station, on my right, in front of Mr. Edison. While we cannot yet transmit videos or images, we can send text messages—and that's what we intend to demonstrate today!"

Davidson looked perplexed. The investors looked stern. Hal read his audience and moved on quickly.

"I think things will be clear when we see the demonstration. Now, I have to caution you that this is only a developmental test, so we may have more work to do to make it work. While we expected to be at this stage six months ago, your $31 million investment has not gone to waste. In the future, this will produce something more practical. Let me now hand off this demo to Professor Johnson."

I thought the introduction wasn't a ringing endorsement of the technology. Was Hal working for us, or against us? The investors became even more stern.

The prof picked it up at that point. "We call this the FutureView machine. It can send a message from this screen, in one time period"— he pointed to the transmitter computer—"to this screen"—he gestured to the receiver computer—"at an earlier time. Essentially, a message is received before it is transmitted. At this time, we can only send brief messages, but that will be sufficient for this demonstration."

"How short? A five-minute compressed video?" Davidson asked.

The professor responded, "Well, the message size is inversely related to the distance in time that we want to traverse and is really limited by the electrical power we can apply to accomplish the time translation. We are talking about short text messages."

"How short?" Kevin Brayton asked.

This question led to an immediate drop in expectations, clearly visible in the corresponding facial expressions.

The prof continued without stopping, "For this demonstration, we will send two alphanumeric characters displayed on the screens."

"Really, Hal? Is that all you can do for $31 million?" Kevin said.

The VCs' mental gears seemed to be recalibrating their expectations downward.

"Why not just string together a bunch of messages to get a longer message across?" Sandy asked.

"Unfortunately, we can only send one message today," the professor answered.

I knew a few reasons why that was the case, the most important one being that we would draw so much power that the cooling system back in the lab would melt down if we made a second run sooner than thirty minutes after the first. I hoped no one would challenge him on it.

"How far into the future can you view?" asked Mr. Fox.

Obviously, he wasn't listening.

"It's more a transmitter into the past," said the prof, "not a viewer into the future, but the effect is the same. When we send a message from the transmitter, we specify how far back in time we want to transmit. When the receiver receives a properly encoded packet, it filters out most of the radio-frequency noise, autocorrects errors using the redundancy in the message, and decodes the message into ASCII characters, which are then displayed on the receiver screen. For now, the FV machine can send a message from a few minutes to a couple hours back in time."

Sensing more disappointment, he added, "Theoretically, we could go a lot further, given sufficient power."

I realized he had just spoken the ultimate engineering lie, *"Anything is possible, with enough power."* That line had been used to justify overloaded container ships, poorly performing airplanes, and losing NASCAR race cars.

The prof continued, "Here's what we will do to demonstrate the system operation. I have here a deck of ordinary playing cards. At precisely 11:30 this morning, we should see a message arriving at the receiver display. Then, at precisely 1:30 p.m., Mr. Brayton will shuffle the deck, select a card without looking at it, show it to Thomas here, then place the card face down on the table.

"Thomas will transmit a message through the FV machine. He will enter a two-character code for the card. For instance, if the card is the seven of hearts, he will enter '7H.' If he draws the king of hearts, he will enter 'KH.' Of course, a ten card would be a 'T,' and an ace would be an 'A.'"

The prof and I individually powered up the two computers and sequenced through some flashy startup screens and a log-in screen that added to the excitement. The professor gave me a memorable password, "chronothon." I entered this on the transmitter side. The unique password added to the aura of the machine, as the message, surely, would not be very impressive.

Then the prof double-clicked on an app icon identified only with large letters "FV." A new window opened up, displaying the date and a running digital clock. Half the people in the room instinctively checked their timepiece against the displayed time, but I was sure it was correct, at least to a billionth of a second.

The flashing cursor then moved to the next line and stopped. Everyone gathered around the receiver display and silently watched the displayed clock. I couldn't see it from my side of the box, but at 11:30 a.m. we all heard the automated sound device *ding*. I later found out the receiver apparently displayed this simple message:

6S

Of course, by the professor's strict protocol, I was not supposed to know the message received. No one spoke the card out loud; at least that part of the test was run correctly.

Everyone sat quietly and watched the clock, sneaking an eye at their emails.

Around 1:20 p.m., Mr. Brayton then picked up the deck of cards and shuffled them several times. We may have started a little late, and Kevin kept repeatedly shuffling and cutting the deck. I worried we might miss the professor's timeline, but Kevin finally put the deck down on the table, drew the top card, and showed it just to me. He buried it deep in his hand and then placed it face down on the table.

Despite the professor's plan, Davidson impatiently grabbed the card off the table and turned it faceup.

It was the six of spades!

There was a gasp from the group. Hal was bug-eyed. For once, even he was speechless.

Everyone started talking at once. First congratulations and shaking of hands, then talking about applications. They talked like the remote box *was* the magical FV machine, not thinking about all the blood and sweat—well, at least sweat—and money that went into the Cambridge lab to make the demo work! So *that* was why the prof wanted me to not tell them too much.

Kevin suspected the card demo, as he was distrusting of Hal, especially with anything involving cards. Kevin scanned the ceiling, probably looking for a camera, even though he knew (and I knew he knew) that the card was never exposed, or even selected from the deck, before the message appeared. Heck, Kevin hadn't even drawn it from the deck when the message arrived!

In all the excitement, I looked at my watch and saw I was close to missing my critical time window. The FutureView machine was set to transmit to 11:30 a.m. I nervously approached the keyboard and quickly entered the 6S, an index finger on each key. I noted the clock time when I entered the digit and letter—it ended precisely at 1:30:00!

The extent of the audience's enthusiasm puzzled me, and I thought, *This seems like a neat trick, but this is hardly traveling into the future. What use is it?*

Mr. Brayton asked for some privacy for a moment, so our team left the glass-walled conference room and stood outside. Hal still seemed in shock. The prof and I were pleased with the operation, but mostly we were pleased that they were pleased.

The investors looked highly animated in the conference room. Kevin was apparently doing most of the talking. He moved his hands about like he was speaking Italian and seemed to be positive and enthusiastic about the demo. Mr. Fox was listening attentively to Kevin.

Dr. Davidson seemed to be upset, probably over the time and money spent for such a minor accomplishment, with such a small device, but he was in the minority. And they all apparently believed that the time machine itself was sitting on that conference room table.

Sandy appeared to be trying to open the box. Fortunately, I had assembled the box enclosure with flush rivets to prevent anyone from finding out how empty it was.

Mr. Brayton motioned us back into the conference room.

Davidson spoke first. "Congratulations to you, Hal, and to Professor Johnson and Thomas. You have really done something here. The demo was excellent! We will definitely be interested in going forward!"

I supposed Davidson knew who buttered his bread.

Hal, always closing, said, "We are always ready to take the FV machine to the next level."

"I'm sure…" Davidson started.

But Hal interrupted, "We need an additional tranche before we can make much progress, though. Is there any chance we might get another round in the bank before the end of the month?"

Kevin stepped in. "I think we can write you a small check now and follow it up with another round of investment after another little demo. But next time the message should be a stock market symbol— maybe four characters, sent from an hour in the future. I think we all want to be here for that test."

Dr. Davidson said, "And I would like Sandy, our accountant, to check your books and audit the demo, if that's all right with you?"

Hal, of course, responded in the affirmative, while shushing the prof. My head was spinning with what these seemingly simple requirements would take. I would definitely be working long hours to comply with the requirements.

Hal sometimes seemed like he was working against us, and sometimes for us. Now that we had shown that the FV machine could work, I wondered if he was fully behind us. I questioned everyone's motives.

As we drove back to the lab, I thought through what had happened. Everything seemed in order. I was pissed at myself for almost missing my target time—but what would have happened if I were a little late? The message was received on time, I thought, but I hadn't checked or recorded the time of receipt. I needed to make a note that the system should record those times automatically.

Something was wrong, though.

I retraced my steps. In all the excitement, I had been anxious about sending the correct message and sending it exactly on time. To do that I didn't touch-type with ten fingers like I usually did. I didn't use the number pad on the keyboard. I just hovered over the "6" key and the "S" key with my two index fingers, and pressed them, in rapid sequence, exactly at 1:30.

But I hadn't hit the "return" key! The message was never sent!

CHAPTER 11

The Audit
June 29, 2019

HAL HAD ASKED ME TO come to Waltham and assist Sandy in auditing FutureView. He thought if I could do some blocking, it would allow the work to go on in Cambridge without her interference. It also stopped me from getting my work done, but at least it was a break from all the work the prof had piled up for me.

Sandy arrived on time as Mr. Brayton had insisted to audit FutureView, and probably to poke around for the VCs. Hal was eager to keep tabs on her and had mentioned having some concerns about her snooping into the financials.

She wore a professional skirt and jacket and carried a laptop computer in a Gucci bag. Visible in the side pocket was a red notebook, though not a tall, lined ledger book an accountant might carry. It was more the composition type that students in an English literature class would use to write their exam essays.

Hal and I both became curious about that notebook, as she often took it out to make entries after receiving hesitant answers to her technical questions, auditing our books, and conducting our demo test. She never opened it after writing to reveal the contents and didn't provide many clues to its purpose.

"Let me show you what we have set up for you," started Hal. He took her to the conference room, recently renamed the Godel Conference Room. "We have provided a computer for you with access to our financial files. Everything we have is digitized and on our server."

"I'll just set up my laptop here," she said.

That was his plan to keep her at the Waltham office, away from the Cambridge lab, where there might be too many questions about what we were building.

"Thanks," she told him. "I will also need access to the original paper files…and I am particularly interested in the development costs for the time machine."

I could tell that she might be a problem.

"When you're through today, perhaps we could have dinner this evening?" Hal asked.

"I'm afraid I have to decline. I will have to go back to the office and finish some other work later this evening," she said.

Hal tried repeatedly to ask her to dinner, then backed off to lunch, and then to coffee and a donut. The donut was probably inappropriate, so he tried again with croissants, pronounced with a "Q." I thought her rejections were probably professional and not personal—well, the last rejection might have been personal.

Hal was getting nervous about leaving her alone and tried to engage Sandy in some conversation. She had been looking through the general expense accounts at our financials and had even opened boxes of invoice copies from suppliers.

"Did you need my help in explaining any of the financials, Sandy?" Hal asked.

She opened her red notebook. I could see a lot of writing, and she had added a few tabs—the stick-on kind—to the pages.

"Well, I was having trouble understanding your account numbers," she said. "Here we have an account number 112 entitled 'Test Equipment Rental'…"

"Yes, that covers any rented or leased test equipment used on the project. Is there something wrong with that?"

"No, but here's another account, number 253, entitled 'Equipment Rental.' What is the difference between these accounts? They seem to be redundant."

Hal knew the answer, as did I. He stumbled a bit, then answered, "I believe…yes…that 112 is for laboratory equipment, and the other account…did you say 255?…may have been for other company equipment, like copy machines, et cetera, et cetera…but I can look into it for you."

"There appear to be two rack-mounted digital counters leased from the same company, on two different invoices—one recorded in account 112, and the other recorded in account 253. It doesn't sound like office equipment. Can you explain that?"

"Well, it could easily have been a mistake in recording, given the titles of the accounts being so similar…"

Sandy cut him off. She opened her notebook and looked down at it, then slammed it shut and said, "The shipping addresses for the two counters were also different—are you running two labs?"

Hal, in full poker bluff mode, offered, "Yes, we have two facilities, but one counter probably got delivered to our warehouse. Let me take the action to look into this. I'm sure we can straighten it out. I'm writing a note on it right now."

He motioned like he was writing on a Post-it note, but the ballpoint pen he was using refused to leave ink.

Looking again in her notebook, she said, "On this issue, I have already checked it out with the engineers who ordered the equipment at both your lab facilities. I also figured out that the time machine project used the 100 series of accounts, while the 200 series of accounts are for purchases for the other lab…the one that appears to be working on a 5G cellphone transceiver."

Sandy paused. Hal had no response, so she added, "So, are you squirreling away funds to support the 5G effort instead of putting it all into the time machine?"

It was as if he were bluffing with a pair of fours and accidentally dropped his cards. There was no way out. He said nothing and looked at me like a quarterback tossing a lateral pass while being sacked. But I had nowhere to run with it.

Sandy continued, "Since you have no other source of income, I assume we alone are funding all of your development work. Despite the card-trick demo, there is still a lot of risk in that project, though it might become extremely profitable. No one has ever done anything like what Professor Johnson proposes to do, nor has anyone even conceptualized a method of doing it. You, running the business, aren't sure he can do it either, so you're covering your bets by also developing a less risky product, a transceiver technology of value in 5G networking."

Hal let her talk. What else could he do?

"Don't worry, I won't tell the VCs. I think Davidson believes too much in his own marketing hype. They have too many other problem companies trying to develop gee-whiz technology with no backup. The New Horizons Venture Fund only has one company left with any viability, and that's FutureView.

"I think you're doing the prudent thing. That's what I would do if my company totally depended on a high-risk new science. I wish some of the other companies we invested in would have done this. FutureView would have been a good name for our venture fund. Any profits are always in the future.

"Also," she said, "I see you're almost out of cash."

"Yes," replied Hal. "I guess I'm planning on your boss coming through with something now that we have had the demo."

"I guess the time machine is in the Cambridge lab. Davidson and Sizemore think it's all in that little box you had at the demo! All of those parts you have bought would never fit in that little box, and your need for massive electrical power is what you would need to run an entire factory! I would like to visit the Cambridge lab this afternoon. Would that be acceptable?" she asked.

I looked at Hal and was about to offer to take her over to the Green Building, but Hal was already ahead of me.

"Why, yes," he answered. "I'll take you there—we can get lunch on the way."

CHAPTER 12

Preparing for the Next Test
June 29, 2019

THE DAY AFTER THE CARD demo, I could see that we would have a load of work to do before the next round. The investors were not completely convinced that FutureView would work and wanted an assuring demonstration.

I started a list of the changes needed, not the least of which was improving reliability. There were just too many failure points in the chain of events. We were lucky that the card demo had even worked. Or maybe it hadn't? I was pretty sure I did not hit the "return" key.

I got back to the lab shortly before Hal and Sandy arrived from the Waltham office. When I told him, the prof had been amazed that Hal had even agreed to let her come over.

I heard the elevator and held the lab door open. Sandy asked to first take a walk around. The prof and I weren't sure what we needed to keep from her, but Hal nodded approval from behind her back—so we just let her go into the lab.

"I just have a few things I want to check out, then maybe we can get together and talk about the next demo," Hal said to her.

We went into the prof's office while Sandy explored. Hal seldom got into the technical weeds, so to speak, but he now seemed very inquisitive about every detail.

"Let's look at the remote controller," Hal said. "I want to walk through all the details of both the transmitter and the receiver, and I'd like to see the software source code for the remote controller computers."

I pulled up the source code on the remote controller transmitter computer so we could walk through it. The bad news was that Hal *was* technically competent…sort of. He seemed suspicious of the card demo, but I wasn't going to mention the problem with the "return" key until I had time to discuss it with the professor.

I brought up the FutureView display on the receiving computer. It still showed the message from the card demo: "6S." I didn't think this was unusual. "Yeah, the old message is still in the received-message buffer. The message buffer is cleared when a new message is received," I said.

If he thought that the prof had somehow inserted the correct message into the receiver, he would be wrong. How would the professor have known which card would be drawn, and when would he enter it?

Hal, Sandy, the prof, and I sat down in the lab to go over the requirements for the next demo.

Sandy began, "We need to assure the investors that their money is invested in a reliable tool that can generate profits. For the demo, you will need to send a four-character message over a one-hour time period, when the stock market is open. We want to show how we can make a profit from that bit of viewing the future.

"I will work with Hal on developing a method of selecting a profitable stock trade that will increase in value over the time range of the message. That way we can assure the investors that there will be a profitable application of the machine and some return on their investment."

The professor responded, "Going from two characters to four characters is a factor of two increase in message length, which would require as much an increase in power."

It seemed like a reasonable requirement, requiring only a little tweaking. That, of course, would be in addition to patching the leaking water-cooling system, increasing the noise resistance and recovery from transmission bit errors, checking on overheated circuits, and any other fallout from the last test.

CHAPTER 13

The Options Demo
July 16, 2019, 11:45 a.m.

THOUGHT WE HAD AGREED ON the test starting at 11:30 a.m., but our investors had not yet arrived. I started getting nervous about another rushed demo. By noon, however, everyone had arrived at Hal's Waltham office again for the second test of the FutureView machine.

It was not apparent that any of the VCs or their investors knew yet that the box on the conference room table was only a remote terminal and the big machinery was elsewhere...except, of course, Sandy, who appeared to have kept quiet about it.

Hal stood up, welcomed everyone, and they all reintroduced themselves, the same group that had viewed the first demo.

Hal then said, "I think we have a demonstration that meets Mr. Brayton's requirements."

He didn't get any further than that when Sandy took the floor from under him. "I think we have established a significant demonstration test of the FutureView system. This test will also show how quickly there could be a return on investment."

The audience seemed pleased with her approach, so Hal let her continue. Then again, she knew too much for him to stop her.

Sandy continued, "Now, Mr. Brayton has asked that we set up a prediction that will yield some financial gain using the stock market. We needed to find where a short-range view of the future produces some significant financial gain.

"The price of any stock moves rapidly, and somewhat randomly, up and down during the day. These changes in price are clearly not because of anything the company does—if you could even measure that on a minute-by-minute basis. These changes are because of breaking news that affects the market or the industry. Sometimes it is only the result of the selling or buying of large blocks of shares by an institutional investor, or by computer algorithms suddenly deciding to load up or unload certain stocks based on predicted correlation with outside events."

"What events?" Kevin Brayton asked. "Something we can detect?"

Hal replied, "Events like the word choice of the CEO after a few drinks at a conference or how the Fed Chair is feeling today. The stock price movements are almost random and hard to predict. All that matters is knowing whether the stock price goes up or down. FutureView can do an excellent job of that!"

Sandy continued, "Stock options are contracts that give you the right to buy—a 'call option,' or to sell—a 'put option,' a particular stock at a particular 'strike' price. The prices of stock options are even more volatile than the price of the underlying stock. The options expire at preset deadlines—weekly or monthly, and there are longer-term options. Most option holders do not exercise these rights. Instead, they sell their options back to the market before the option expires, providing an opportunity for a large gain in a short time period.

"We have equipped Thomas with a program that monitors the price movement of near-term option prices and selects the stock with the greatest movement over a one-hour time period. Thomas will watch this program, and at 1:30 p.m. today will enter the stock symbol in a FutureView message. He will indicate whether to buy calls with the letter 'C' if the stock is going up or puts with the letter 'P' if the stock is going down. The message should arrive at precisely 1:30 p.m. We can then buy the option, then sell it after the price changes."

Dan Davidson asked, "Is this legal?"

"Like the stock markets, gambling casinos would like you to place your bets and win or lose based on luck," Hal replied. "But there are blackjack players who know more about the game than others and win more than they lose, and there are investors who know more about stock trades than others and gain more than they lose. Neither is illegal. We can be one of those winners."

I placed the remote controller box on the conference room table, as I had for the last test. I then sat on the transmitter side, this time with a Bose noise-canceling headset, playing Van Halen rock music from my iPod. Hal sat on the receiver side. The observers gathered around the receiver station.

"This reminds me of an old story…" Hal said.

This seemed like an opportune time to put on the headphones. Hal powered up the receiver computer a little before 12:30, our planned receive-time. Almost immediately, a message appeared:

CRMP

The message flickered a bit, and I heard the message alert *ding* despite my headphones. The following was told to me later by the professor:

Kevin was already on his cell phone with his brokerage app running and entered the stock symbol.

He said, " 'CRM' is the symbol for Salesforce.com, a rapidly rising successful management automation company. I would have suspected that to be a potentially rallying stock, but the letter 'P' indicates we should buy puts, as the stock price is about to drop."

Kevin asked, "Who's in? I can buy the options right here. You can cover me later."

I could see that the investors, the ones who were probably the most familiar with stock options, were not speaking up. Since this was a sure thing, if you believed in the FutureView machine, their reluctance *must* have been because of concerns about FutureView itself!

Hal realized this too. He stepped up, as the others expected he should, and said, "What do you have, Kevin?"

"The Salesforce stock put option with a $114 strike price, expiring this week, is 90 cents a share. How many contracts do you want to buy, Hal?"

It was just like Kevin to intimidate Hal by forcing him to put money on his word. But here the stakes were higher than in their poker games. While it seemed Hal had doubts about the FV machine, he knew (and I knew, from Sandy) that our company was broke. If the bet was good, he could generate some cash, save the company, and he would look confident in front of eager investors. If the bet went bad, we would be bankrupt, but we would not be much worse off than we already were.

"I'll take 1,000 contracts!" Hal said, nodding positively with his head up. He was betting all-in, again.

Kevin stepped back, likely unsure whether Hal was a winner or a bluffer. He had to raise or call. He couldn't fold.

"I'll buy 1,000," Kevin said. It was probably more than he was planning to buy, but he was now forced to at least match Hal's bet.

The game was on! Now the other investors shouted out their bids. Kevin took them down on a notepad and entered the final numbers on his cell phone.

For the next hour, we all sat around watching the clock. I knew nothing about the FutureView message that arrived or the buying of options since I was listening to Eddie Van Halen, per the prof's orders.

Everyone slowly drifted over to my side of the table and watched my computer screen. At precisely 1:29, I pulled up the special spreadsheet Hal created for this test and read off the stock symbol at the top of the spreadsheet and the option type. The spreadsheet showed:

CRM P

Eyes widened throughout the room. I focused on the computer screen and tried to ignore the people watching me. I was committed to following the directions the professor had laid out to the letter. I set the arrival time for the message to 12:30 p.m. and prepared to enter the message. At precisely 1:30 p.m., I transmitted the message and was certain, this time, to press "return."

Kevin had been monitoring the price movement in the options on his cell phone and had already sold the put options. "I sold out all of our positions," he announced.

Kevin tried to hold his poker face, but his eyes were too wide open to look calm. He announced, "The stock price plummeted, and the value of the put options grew rapidly. I sold out after a gain of $1.42 per share."

"Congratulations, Hal," he said in a muted voice. It was hard to tell with Kevin whether he was happy with his great winnings and his ownership of stock in FutureView, or whether he would rather have seen Hal fail.

I could see from the faces in the room that the lightbulb had finally come on for the investors. Sandy was pleased. Professor Johnson was pleased. I was pleased. Hal was very pleased that everyone was pleased. The only time it's bad that everyone is pleased is when you're playing Texas Hold'em and everyone is pleased with their cards, as I'm sure Hal recalled.

Kevin then turned to the venture capitalists and said, "We need to talk." He and the VCs then thanked Hal for the demo, thanked Sandy, and abruptly left.

Sandy went to Hal and said, "Congratulations, Mr. Hawkins! You seemed to have quite the confidence in your people and your machine. I see you bet big when you have the cards."

Hal looked pleased yet puzzled.

"How much did you win, anyway?" I asked him.

Hal pulled up the company bank account on his phone and looked at the last transaction. I saw it showed the transfer from Kevin's account a few minutes earlier. I was shocked!

Hal cornered Sandy. "That's twice now that we've shown we can get the right answer. Don't you agree?"

"I haven't reviewed the details of the run, so I can't say yet," she replied, always the skeptic.

"Since I have made a little money on this, how about I treat you to dinner?"

"I have some work to do, to evaluate this test," was her nonanswer.

We all went out to the parking lot, feeling pretty good, while Hal locked up the office. As we went to our separate cars, I said to Sandy, "Hal is pretty good at knowing when to bet big!"

She replied, "I'm pretty sure that Hal wasn't aware that a standard options contract is for 100 shares per contract."

On the ride back to the lab, there was an issue that was gnawing at me. "Professor?" I asked. "Weren't we supposed to transmit only in the afternoon, and receive only in the morning? Wasn't there something about earth blockage?"

"What I said," the professor explained, "was that we needed to straddle the midday. Transmit when the earth faced backward in orbit and receive when the earth faced forward in orbit. Midday is, of course, close to 1:00 p.m., during Daylight Savings Time."

That seemed to make sense.

CHAPTER 14

Tail Chasing

July 31, 2019

MEMORY DUMPS ARE JUST A display of the data stored in segments of computer memory. They have looked the same since the days of old IBM mainframes with magnetic core memories.

They aren't of much use today, as memories are far too large and data stored is too complex for anyone to read and interpret the contents of computer memory. The format has become standard. Displayed on the left two-thirds of the screen is the binary data, displayed in groups of bytes in hexadecimal format, something few people today can or want to read. But on the right one-third of the screen is the same data converted to alphanumeric characters, using the standard ASCII encoding. If the memory contained any text characters, the text would jump out on the right side of the screen.

After the demo, I did a memory dump of portions of the FutureView computer memory. Sure enough, if you looked carefully at the right-hand side, mixed amid random symbols, was the simple message:

CRMP

There also was a lot of random data in the memory allocated for the process of time messaging.

"I see our short message. But what is all the rest of this stuff?" I asked the professor.

The prof responded, "In developing the time-transferring process, there's a lot of intermediate data being stored here even after the message is transferred. Some of it has been useful, but now it is much too overwhelming to deal with."

He pointed to a page of the display as he scrolled through dozens of pages. "This is data that is actually input to the process…"

He scrolled through more pages. "…and this is output data."

The pitifully small size of our "messages from the future" never ceased to embarrass me. Hal even considered calling them something other than "messages." We thought up names like "tokens," or "keys," or "watchwords." But we still call them "messages."

I was curious about all that data that was created in the computer memory when only a tiny message was transmitted. There was, perhaps, an opportunity to send a far more substantial message through time by using this data. I tried various means of adding additional message data to input memory cells and looking at the corresponding output memory locations after a FutureView run. Because it seemed to be affected by sending a message, I came to call this data the "message tail."

The professor saw me manipulating some of the memory from the options demo and asked, "What are you doing with these massive memory dumps?"

"I have seen some large patterns of memory change after we send a message, and it seems to reflect input memory data."

"Have you found any correlation between input and output?" he asked.

"Yes!" I said, "but it's not reliable. This could become a means for sending much longer messages through time."

"Thomas, you are just dealing with data noise! There are theoretical bounds on the amount of information that can be transferred. Messages are information, and there is a price to pay, in terms of energy, to transmit more information. It's limited by the conservation of entropy!"

He seemed a little too self-assured in his theory. *"The arrogance of the PhD,"* I called it.

He seemed to dismiss my idea too quickly, even though I was a little fuzzy on the conservation of entropy. I didn't bring up the idea again, but I was determined to continue my experiments, which mostly amounted to trial-and-error with each run of the time machine. I kept the results to myself.

CHAPTER 15

Jakarta

August 10, 2019

WE LIVED IN THE REAL world. There were no government science grants where we might operate for years and produce nothing but published papers and conference talks. We knew we had to meet the requirements of the investors, as making money, in the end, is what drives new technology.

Ironically, it was Kevin Brayton who seemed to have the greatest interest as an investor in the company. It made for strange bedfellows with Hal, but "money is money," as Hal used to say.

One day Hal called and asked the professor to come over to the Waltham office. I feared it was another financial issue—as the money ran out, the meetings were more often to make "suggestions" to the professor, who often, in turn, held his ground. This time, the meeting would be in Hal's office, where we knew Hal had a greater psychological advantage.

"I need you to come with me for this meeting," the prof said.

I did not have to ask why.

When we walked into Hal's office, my apprehension grew when I saw Kevin sitting in the back of the room.

"Kevin would like another demonstration," Hal said. I frankly couldn't tell whether Hal was OK with this or whether he was bluffing his support for a demo to please Kevin.

"I would like to see a larger message size," Kevin said. "Twelve characters at a minimum."

I whispered to the prof, "Twelve *ASCII* characters? There are 128 combinations of seven bits used for an ASCII encoded character. If he only needs numbers and capital letters, there are only thirty-six of those. We could be a lot more efficient if we invented our own code."

"It doesn't matter," he whispered back. "I think we can get twelve full ASCII encoded characters with the latest changes."

"What else?" Hal asked.

"I would like to conduct the demonstration at night," Kevin continued. "I have interests in the Far East and need to receive a message at 9:30 p.m. that is sent at 11:30 p.m., eastern time.

"And the most important requirement is that this demo needs to be completed on October first, in two months. I cannot be flexible with the date, as I will have others with me. And I will transmit the message myself. Can you do it?" he asked, looking at us.

I knew all our funding was tied to this demo. Hal looked firmly at Kevin, then said yes, in so many words. Actually, he said "yes" in one word. He glanced away from us when he said it because there was no other answer that would have been acceptable.

Hal let the acceptance sink in, then added, "In order to achieve this, we are going to need more funding, and our cash flow situation is going to require that funding immediately."

"How did I know that was coming, Hal?" Kevin responded. "What are you going to need?"

"One point two should be enough," Hal said. I assumed he meant millions of bucks. "As a loan." Hal knew how much he could raise the bid in poker, regardless of the cards he was holding.

"I can loan you the money," Kevin said. "I'm going to have to insist on stock warrants on this."

"Draw up your terms," Hal said.

A short time later, I saw Kevin leave after the two shook hands.

"Warrants" are the ability to convert outstanding debt to shares of stock. Warrants would allow Kevin to invest without taking risks, whether FutureView succeeded or failed. He would collect interest on the loan, even if the machine never worked, but if the company ever became profitable, he could convert the loan to stock shares.

This perfectly fit Kevin's conservative nature, and the Golden Rule: "He who has the gold makes the rules."

I heard Hal on the phone that afternoon, explaining it to Sandy.

"Yes, I think we have a solution for our cash problem," Hal said. "We got a loan from Kevin that will carry us through the next demo. …Yes, that Kevin. Kevin Brayton. …Interest is Prime plus four percent. …Well, he also wants stock warrants. …Calm down! Even if he converts all the debt, he still won't have more voting shares than I have."

I heard Sandy hang up her phone.

"And I love you too," Hal said.

***

The professor and I headed back to the lab. "I don't think Kevin totally believed the previous demos," I said.

"Do you?" he asked. "Let's take the requirements one by one. First, the twelve-character requirement will be relatively easy to meet. We might do even better.

"The two-hour time range requirement will require a signal to travel the distance the earth moves in orbit, around 134,000 miles. It will require four times as much transmission power, but also a lot more power for the time circuits. That's going to affect everything in the power train, but it's theoretically doable."

"Does your car handle OK?" I asked.

"Seems OK. Why do you ask?"

"Because there's an 800-pound gorilla in the back seat."

"Oh, you're worried about how to receive a time message at night, when the past earth is facing away from the future earth?"

"I guess transmitting is no problem between noon and midnight, but yes, how do you propose we receive a message at night?" I asked.

The professor answered, "Do you realize that all the time-shifting functions are performed before the signal is transmitted? The receiver antenna and signal processing are ordinary radio reception and filtering equipment in the X-band. We could just use any antenna and receiver in another time zone where it's still morning. Could you build up a signal processing unit that we could install at a leased antenna site?"

He continued, "We will also need an antenna-pointing capability that is aware of where the receiver is located."

"I have been developing a universal pointing software algorithm, using NASA ephemeris software available on GitHub so that the receiving antenna is always pointed to the transmitter location, when it might receive a two-hour time-shifted transmission," I responded. "It takes into account the earth orbital motion, rotation, wobble, and tilt, and determines acceptable windows in time when the receiver is available. I call it 'The Ephemeris Program.'"

"That sounds good," said the prof. "The same program should work here in Cambridge and anywhere that we locate an antenna. One question: what is GitHub?"

"I've just looked up the world map of time zones on my laptop. If we located our secondary antenna on the exact opposite side of the earth, we could receive at any time of day, though we would still be limited when we can transmit to about sixteen hours of the day! That would be fantastic!"

"And where should this antenna be located?"

"Jakarta, Indonesia."

"Hal is going to have to handle that one."

CHAPTER 16

Self-Fulfilling Prophecies
August 20, 2019

W E HADN'T COMPLETELY SOLVED THE problem of increasing the message size and time range, but we could compromise and send a one-character message back as far as three hours, using the Jakarta antenna. The full capability required to send twelve ASCII characters would require much greater electrical power and the ability to dissipate proportionally more excess heat. We could, with our current power capability, test the system and see some demonstrated progress. The opportunity to send one-character messages came up sooner than expected.

Sandy had been spending a good deal of time in the FutureView lab. Hal never failed to try again to ask her for a date. After we all worked late into the night, he asked her, "You must be hungry now. How about we get some dinner?"

It seemed a little edgy since Sandy had already rejected his advances so many times. The prof overheard and grimaced, but he said nothing.

I was amazed when she responded.

"That would be fine. Give me a few minutes with the professor," she said.

Perhaps, I thought, she accepted the date to press him on the problem she'd found with the options demo. It would almost be like an unstoppable force hitting an impenetrable object. She was an unstoppable force, but Hal was not impenetrable. He was, however, good at dodgeball.

Sandy turned to the professor and asked, "Now that you have tested the Jakarta antenna, professor, would it be possible to run another short test message?"

The prof was hesitant at such a sudden request. He fumbled a bit and responded, "I am worried about the system power drain and overheating from the last run. Each run draws considerable electrical power. Like all machines, any inefficiency in the system turns the lost power into heat, and there are plenty of inefficiencies at this point."

I thought it would be good for an independent and authoritative person to conduct a test of the machine, so I said, "I checked on the machine and the cooldown went well. There should be no problem making another run!"

The prof looked at me and pursed his lips. Perhaps I was a little too eager to please.

I added, "We don't have to worry about accidentally overloading the machine. As a safety measure, I have implemented both time and temperature tests to prevent sending messages sooner than thirty minutes apart or if the machine is still recovering from a previous run."

"It's a good safety measure," the prof added. "There is only one rare case that the software won't protect."

Sandy said, "Well, I won't need to transmit until around ten o'clock this evening. I understand that you're now capable of sending a one-character message three hours into the past, using the Jakarta antenna. That is all the capability I would need."

"I guess we can probably do it," he finally conceded. With the new receiver antenna in Jakarta, it would now be possible to transmit in Cambridge in the afternoon or evening, noon till midnight, and receive a message at any hour, using either the Jakarta antenna or our original receiver antenna in Cambridge—limited only by the time range from the transmit time to the receive time.

The prof said, "Let me finish up my data analysis from today's run. I am concerned that we may have damaged some components in the run. If everything checks out, we might get the machine ready again before ten." He turned back to the FutureView computer terminal. "Tom, could you please turn on the remote controller receive terminal?"

Sandy asked, "Professor, what time do you have?"

"It's 7:03 p.m."

When I turned on the receiving computer, it immediately sounded a distinct *ding*. I was shocked. "Who would call at this hour?"

I was also surprised that Sandy was *not* surprised. "I'm sure that message is for me," she said.

All three of us rushed to the monitor.

The only symbol on the screen was a single letter:

N

"I guess we will be able to send your message, after all!" the prof said.

Sandy looked sternly at the screen but said nothing. She picked up her red notebook and walked to the elevators. Hal met her there, and they both departed.

Twenty minutes later, I also left the lab to grab something to eat. As I walked to the parking garage, I caught a glimpse of Hal and Sandy speeding out of the garage in his 1972 Plymouth Barracuda. You knew it was a 1972 Barracuda, because the license plate said "72 CUDA."

Older men admire classic muscle cars from the 70s, more out of reliving their youth than any respect for the metal. Younger men drive classic cars because younger women admire a young man with enough money and machismo to drive an overpowered one. It was a real "chick magnet." But, unlike Hal's previous passengers, Sandy didn't seem to be impressed.

I noticed that the passenger-side window was open. I remembered Hal had mentioned something about needing to replace the window crank, although I wasn't sure what that was. It also had rained earlier, and it was getting pretty chilly. All of that probably didn't start the evening off well.

The professor continued into the evening checking out the FV system and the results of the options demo run. Our relay link to Jakarta worked well. He had me jumping to check out circuits that may have overheated during the last run and to repair some water leaks in our rapid-cooling system that only became evident after the run, when the lines were put under pressure.

A bit before 10:00, Hal and Sandy returned to the lab. We were still working when Sandy came in. She was tense, spoke few words, and walked in long strides. She did not look happy, and she was on a mission.

I had checked on the cooldown of the FV machine, and it appeared to have handled the burst of power more favorably than the professor had feared. It was ready to go for another run.

The professor offered her the remote controller. The transmit computer was already booted up. She entered the one-letter message, punching the "N" key firmly, followed by the "return" key.

She left without confirmation of the system operation. Of course, the virtue of a time machine is that the confirmation occurs *before* the system is operated! She had departed the lab immediately, taking the elevator down.

Being in the lab when a message was transmitted can be a bit nerve-racking. The power draw dimmed the lights. The cooling system pumps started up, creating a racket. The room grew noticeably warmer. The professor's idea of using the remote controller to operate the machine from the Waltham office for the demos was definitely a good idea! I stepped outside the lab until things cooled off a bit.

The professor's office provided some isolation from the noise, and the air conditioning was better. Hal was hanging out there, talking to the prof.

I asked, "OK if I come in?"

They both nodded approval.

Hal looked depressed, seeming to hang around to find a friendly ear to talk to. He didn't know that the professor and I had finished the work for the evening. I was only feigning work as they spoke.

"Can't live with 'em, et cetera," Hal said.

"Date didn't go well?" the prof asked.

"Yeah, it seems anything I said either came out wrong or was taken wrong."

"She seemed like a nice girl. Pretty damn smart. And she can't be BS'ed—she sees right through that."

"I hope I haven't endangered the company. She could do a lot of damage with our investors."

"I don't think she would do something like that. She's already had the opportunity to have us cut off, if she wanted to. Maybe she was just having a bad day. You should try again. You know she really believes in us—I mean, she believes in the FV machine," the professor said.

"Really?" Hal remarked.

"Yes, and I think if the machine told her there was a bright future with you, she would believe it."

"You think that if she got a positive message about an upcoming date, she would be motivated to make it a positive date? Sort of self-fulfilling prophecy?"

"Absolutely! Especially if the prophet is herself. You know, maybe there is something we can do. I could convince her to send a FutureView message tomorrow."

I left the office a bit confused about the idea of a FutureView message being a self-fulfilling prophecy. I could see now why the prof was so insistent that the person sending the message be separate and isolated from the person receiving the message.

Does a message mean anything if it is only a repeat of itself?

The next day, Sandy finished up her financial review in the Waltham office. The company was solvent enough to continue but was not generating any revenue from the FV machine or any other business, so it was only a matter of throttling the cash flowing out. There wasn't much to say about the financials, as they would not drive the decision on continued funding of FutureView. The success or failure of the FV machine itself would determine whether this was a lost investment or a goldmine.

In the late afternoon, she came over to the Cambridge lab to finish her write-up on the options demo. The professor struck up a conversation with her.

"Judging from your one-letter message yesterday, I guess your dinner with Hal didn't go too well?" he asked.

"No, it didn't. But Hal should be happy."

"How's that?"

"Well, that message I sent yesterday was the confirming test that reinforced my belief that the FutureView machine really works."

The prof responded, "Too bad we can't document that test. I never told Hal about it. If you would like, you can run another private test. We are ready to run this evening as well. If Hal asks you for another date, you're welcome to check out the results with the FV machine, without Hal being the wiser."

"Why, thank you."

Hal came over to the lab in the evening "serendipitously," meaning "just per his plan." I do not know what transpired between Hal and Sandy, but they sequestered in a corner of the lab and had a quiet conversation. He must have asked her to dinner again, as Sandy came directly to me after that and asked to look at the receiver on the controller. I powered up the controller.

"What time do you have, Tom?" she asked.

"It's 6:53 p.m.," I said, knowing full well why she asked. There was a *ding* from the remote controller and a one-letter message appeared:

Y

Neither Sandy nor Hal returned that evening. We shut down at 10:00 p.m. anyway, after we could have transmitted such a message.

As I drove back to my apartment that night, I wondered whether the FV machine really worked. I thought that Sandy seemed sure it did. Hal, not so much, and I was confused myself. The only one who really knew for sure was the professor.

CHAPTER 17

The Truth

August 22, 2019

SANDY DID NOT APPEAR THE next morning. Around eleven, the prof called over to the Waltham office to see if she was there, but neither she nor Hal had come in. Her Mini Cooper was still parked in the garage at MIT.

Around noon, when returning to the lab from lunch, I heard the Barracuda pulling into the parking garage. It must have been another twenty minutes later, after I had returned to the lab, that I heard the elevator door open as Sandy and Hal arrived.

I glimpsed them breaking off an embrace when the elevator doors opened. She was wearing the same outfit she had on yesterday. So was Hal, but that wasn't unusual for him. They both seemed quite upbeat. I guessed the date had gone well.

Sandy greeted me at the lab door. Was she drunk? No, she didn't slur her words, and she walked reasonably straight—and she was wearing heels. She greeted the professor and engaged in some meaningless small talk. I became less worried about the "second date message," since it apparently didn't bother her, and she had other interests to attend to.

She said pleasant goodbyes to Hal, the prof, and me, then headed back to the elevators. I was relieved that we didn't have to explain anything.

As they waited for the elevator, she turned around, Columbo-like, and said to the prof, "Just one more thing…I would like to thank you for taking care of that message thing."

He smiled and nodded. Hal pretended to ignore the statement.

The professor should have left it at that, but he responded, "Yes, you didn't show up in time, so I sent the message myself."

I knew that was a lie. The professor did not send any message, but maybe he thought that would be a quick answer to end Sandy's inquisition. It did not.

The elevator arrived and Hal and Sandy entered. The door closed, then opened again, and she stepped out to let Hal have it.

"How would you know what the right message was to enter?" she asked the professor. "Did you just assume to transmit what was received?"

To no one in particular, she said, "If you already know the answer, the question doesn't matter?"

Hal stepped out of the elevator and let the door close. Everyone stood in the lobby.

"Yes, just like the options demo message?" she said with an upward pitch as if it was a question. She pivoted toward Hal.

I could see her thinking through the logic of FutureView, and I was sure that this would not end well.

She looked at Hal. "I did some research on the options demo. The reason the price of Salesforce.com stock dropped so drastically had nothing to do with the performance of the company. It was entirely due to a speech by a member of the Federal Open Market Committee, the 'Fed.' The speech was scheduled weeks ago, and there were many stocks affected by his comments. Salesforce.com was sensitive to actions by the Fed and would be guaranteed to move significantly up or down in value. It would have been easy to preselect that stock and a 50 percent chance that the stock would either go up or down significantly.

"With a little knowledge, you could increase the odds of a profitable bet to 60 percent. You might think 60 percent odds would not be worth risking the entire company. But the company was going to go broke for sure without a successful demo. Sixty percent odds sound pretty good, under the circumstances, and Hal certainly has shown that he is willing to make that kind of bet."

She thought more about it as we nervously waited, all eyes on Hal.

Hal hesitated and looked down at the floor. He then slowly responded, "Well, I couldn't depend on the FutureView machine to work perfectly for this demo. After all, the entire future of the company depended on this test! So, I wasn't trying to fake the test. It was only insurance in case there was no message from the future. I noticed that the software never erased the previous message until a new message arrived. I simply inserted the message 'CRMP' into the receiver message buffer, just in case no message arrived."

Sandy responded, "Well, I guess this leads to questioning whether the FutureView time machine really works at all!"

"Wait a minute!" Hal said. "We still have the card demo as a valid test of the FV machine!"

Although Hal's reference to the card demo was an attempt to support belief in the machine, I'm not sure he really believed in the card demo. I had my doubts about the it, too. I felt it was now time to tell the truth.

"I have a confession to make," I said.

Hal cringed.

"During the card demo, after we received the FutureView message and everyone was so excited that the message matched the card—the six of spades—that I got a little flustered. I almost missed my cue to transmit the message. I hit the '6' key and the 'S' key with my two index fingers. Now I realize I didn't hit the 'return' key. The message was never sent!"

We all looked at each other. *Did the FutureView machine* ever *really work?* I wondered.

"I was aware of that, too," Sandy added. "My concerns about both tests are fully documented in my notebook."

No one spoke.

Hal broke the silence. "I guess it doesn't matter whether the machine works. I'm sure that Davidson is looking over that red notebook right now. If there's any question about the validity of our tests, Davidson will hesitate to put any more money into the venture now. You may not realize that we are out of money. We've been out for some time, and we're living off our unpaid accounts payable."

Sandy stepped forward and pulled her red notebook from her bag.

"No one has seen this notebook…yet," she said.

Hal reached for it, but she deftly returned it to her bag.

"I've never told this to Davidson nor to anyone at the venture capital office. Frankly, I believe you all are doing a tremendous job in developing such a revolutionary machine, and you need to continue. It will be well worth it.

"However, Davidson and the New Horizons Fund will not give you any more money. Not because of my reports—the fund is out of money. Every other venture they invested in is already bankrupt or heading to it. You are their only hope."

The professor then took the floor, and well he should have. "Now, everyone, wait a minute. Let me explain what happened," he started.

"First, let's talk about the options demo. Hal admitted he filled the FutureView message buffer with the message 'CRMP,' knowing that Salesforce.com was a volatile stock, and he might have done something with the app that he gave Tom to select the winning stock symbol, so that Tom would also attempt to transmit the message 'CRMP.' You're right, in that Hal might have chosen a particularly volatile stock that would either go up or go down significantly during the day. However, Hal's plan was only a backup, in case FutureView didn't work. And it was a pretty poor backup at that, with only a 60 percent chance of working.

"But the only question is whether FutureView worked. Can we determine that? We all heard the *ding* of the computer when the message arrived. That means that a real FutureView message arrived. There is nothing else in the software that could trigger the piezo sound generator to make that sound unless the routine is called, and the routine is called only upon receipt of a decoded message. No matter what value Hal might have stored in the message buffer, if a new message arrived, then that message would replace whatever was in the buffer with the actual message. If FutureView didn't send a message, we would never have heard the *ding*. If the FutureView message got scrambled or was different from what Tom transmitted, we would have seen that in the message.

"Therefore, Tom must have transmitted a message from the future, and that exact message, '*CRMP*,' was received in the past. QED.

"Now, let me explain some details of the time-messaging process, based on my time-travel theory," he continued. "There is a fundamental principle of physics that is so fundamental you may not even realize that it is an assumption, but it is an assumption that must be true, as it would affect everything else in physics if it were not true. That principle is: 'Nothing in the universe can change without there first being a cause.'

"In terms of time messaging, all the requirements to transmit a FutureView message—the transmitter, the operator, even the motivation for the operator to send the message must exist even though no message had yet been received. Then, because a message is now transmitted and received, the timeline will change—it must change. There is no need, in this new timeline, to transmit the message again.

"As you know from my time-travel seminar, this action is an essential element of my theory, otherwise there would be unexplainable paradoxes whereby the message might have to both exist and not exist.

"Don't get me wrong here. You must be fully capable and committed to transmitting the message, or it will *never* be received. Once the message is received, any action resulting from receiving the message becomes part of the *new* timeline. If, for instance, you become so flustered by people excited about *receiving the message* that you are asked to transmit, that you forget to hit the return key. That does not change the fact that you've already received the message, and that message must have been already transmitted in the previous timeline."

"So," I said, "the card demo really worked!"

"That is why, for a 'clean' test, I have harped so much about keeping the person who is to send the FV message, Thomas, here, from being involved with the received message. That's why I asked that the remote controller be built with separate screens for the receiver operator and the transmitter operator. We need to limit the interaction of the received message with the person who will send the message."

"What if," I had to ask, "after receiving a message from the future, a person attempts to transmit that message, again—so to speak? At the least, wouldn't that cause twice the power to be used, and totally overload the time machine?"

The prof replied, "There might be some complications, but I think you have already prevented that from occurring."

"I did?"

"Yes. It has to do with the First Law of Thermodynamics. Remember back in my seminar on time travel, that I said there was a problem with sending a time machine back through time—that, if you did so, you would duplicate the time machine and create matter. That's against the law! Specifically, it is against the Law of Conservation of Mass. Only God can create matter!"

"But," Hal exclaimed, "we aren't sending a time machine through time. We're only sending massless radio messages, pretty thin ones at that!"

"There is a similar law of physics to consider. We have already seen that it takes a massive amount of energy, with some of it wasted as heat, to send a message back in time. If all that energy was required to do the transmitting, and the transmitting only occurred in the first timeline, then in the second timeline we receive messages from the future, and since we never have to transmit them, then who pays the electric bill? Energy must also be conserved. That's the First Law of Thermodynamics. You can't get something for nothing. At first, I was puzzled how we seemed to get away without paying the energy cost, but we weren't. At the time the message is to be transmitted, whether it is in the original timeline or in the post-received-message timeline, the FutureView machine draws power and heats up. *We* pay the electric bill in either timeline! Even if we aren't transmitting the message in our timeline. It is spooky, for sure, but that way, no laws of nature are violated."

"So," I said, "if we tried to send the message in our timeline, too, then there would be twice as much energy consumed—we would blow up the time machine! Holy shit!"

"Wait, Tom," the prof responded. "You have already written the software to protect us from that—don't you realize? Your software prevents sending a message too soon after the machine is already in heat, and it certainly stops you from sending a message while the machine is heating up because of a message sent in a previous timeline! You have actually stopped anyone from repeating the trans- mission in the current timeline. Thank you for your great foresight!"

I had to think about all this. I realized, in all outward signs, it would appear as though the message was transmitted, but it was really the message sent in the original timeline that was drawing the electric power and turning on the time machine!

Sandy asked, "What happens if you don't let the machine draw energy to complete the process at transmission time? For instance, what if you just pull the plug?"

"I suspect what would happen," the prof responded, "is that the timeline would revert to the previous timeline where no message was received. But I'm not sure. It would be an experiment that could never be conducted, because all electronic records, video recordings, notepads, and memories of the participants would be changed. Hard to run experiments like that."

"Actually," I said, "this may explain some of my earlier tests I conducted where the machine just didn't seem to work. I wondered, but found no bug in the system. The reason the test might have failed was because of my own action! I was turning off the power to the machine too soon after receiving a message!"

Sandy was ahead of us, and already on to the next problem.

"What about those two date messages that I received? Were they meaningless because they were self-fulfilled prophecies?" she asked.

"*Two* messages?" Hal asked.

The prof ignored him and replied to Sandy, "Those two FV messages about your dates with Hal were real FutureView messages, but they were definitely *not* self-fulfilling projections of the future. Let me explain.

"Remember the theory of modified timelines. First, there must exist a timeline where *no* message is received, only transmitted. In that timeline, you freely decided, after the date and without having received any previous message, whether the date was good or bad. That must have represented your true, unbiased feelings about the date. They were not 'self-fulfilling prophecies.'"

"But," Sandy said, "I…we…never returned to the lab last night. In the first timeline, where I didn't receive a message, I would assume that even then I wouldn't have returned to the lab either. So, who sent that message?"

The professor said, "I can only surmise what happened. You probably called me and asked me to send the 'Y' message. That would be the only explanation since you definitely received the message. But we will never know, since that timeline has been replaced, and none of us has any memory of it.

"Because of Tom's simple overheating prevention software, the secondary message you sent after your first date never got transmitted. Admittedly, you already sent that message in the first timeline.

After your second date, there was no need for me to send a message, because I knew that message too would be blocked by Tom's anti-heating algorithm.

"Since the only messages that got transmitted were the ones you created without being influenced by first receiving a FutureView message, those messages were your unbiased feelings. There was no self-fulfilled prophecy!"

Sandy and Hal looked at each other. Maybe they could figure that out, but I was still confused.

Sandy started to say something but cut herself short. Hal rushed her to the elevators to avoid any further discussion of the matter, thanked us, and closed the elevator doors. I thought I saw them approach each other as the doors shut.

"So that's your theory of how Sandy got the 'Y' message last night," I said to the professor, "That's as good as any theory, except for one thing."

"What is that?"

"There was no power blast on the FV machine last night. No message was sent in the previous timeline or in the current timeline. So, how did Sandy get that message?"

The prof said, "I lied. There never was a FutureView message last night."

"So, Sandy never really expressed her own feelings about Hal and their date?" I asked.

"No, but Sandy didn't object. Therefore, she must have felt that the second date went well, and she had no basis to think that I was lying."

"And Hal thinks the same?"

"Actually, Hal knows I was lying. He asked me to fake the message."

CHAPTER 18

Preparing for the Big One

August 24, 2019

A S THE DEVELOPMENT WORE ON, Hal seemed to take on a different approach to our development of the time machine. When investors came by, he only had praise for our efforts and confidence in the machine. Hal definitely delegated the work on the machine to the professor and provided materials and funding whenever the prof asked for it. There was no sign of any attempt to pivot.

Hal spent more time in the Cambridge lab, keeping tabs on the progress. On the few occasions where I had to go to the Waltham office, I noticed fewer people in the hallways and fewer pallets on the loading dock. The FutureView machine seemed to be the entire future of the company.

I noticed a change in Professor Johnson, as well.

"I regret we rushed into this, without a real understanding, either of the engineering or the physics, in order to show investors some magic," he said to me in the lab.

"But without the investors on board, we would never have gotten this far!" I said.

"That may be true, but what if the machine had not worked? How quickly would the investors have vanished? Now that we have some breathing room, we need to make sure every element works properly. We have to make sure we aren't slowly destroying the machine with all the overheating."

"I guess so. I guess we need to go back and look at all the stuff we threw together!"

"And I think we ought to look at more of that high-voltage wiring. How quickly would this project end if the machine develops a massive short-circuit?"

"Or one of us is electrocuted," I added, from personal experience.

"I'm still not sure of some of the timeline effects. The problem with running experiments in time travel is that you can't rely on video records, notes, or even your memory when history changes."

The professor was pleased with his authority to conduct proper tests and apply true scientific rigor. But it came at a cost—a financial one. Hal was often agitated by the delays and resulting costs, and the cost of expensive test equipment. Still, to his credit, he held true to his promise to allow the engineering to be completed with proper quality control and reliability.

Over the next month, we were extremely busy. This time, we ran many progressive tests to prove the hardware and software.

On the spooky side of the technology, the professor was fanatical about requiring complete isolation of the person sending the message from the information in the received message, so I became the stooge for sending messages. The professor, though, maintained strict control of the runs. He expressed some concern about changing the future. While we were still operating from the remote controller box, the prof locked up the transmitter with a password that he kept only to himself.

Neither the professor nor I heard much about the "other half" of our company—the team developing the 5G cell tower transmitter in Waltham that was supposed to bring in the revenue to sustain the company.

Hal seemed to spend more time at the Cambridge lab, I thought because he was taking a greater interest in our work. I only discovered later that Hal had thinned, then totally frozen any further work on "5G," to divert all funds to our project. I'm sure that hurt him greatly. Sandy, of course, was aware, but he never talked about it to anyone on the time-machine team.

To help me analyze the results of experiments, I equipped my personal laptop (with a cell data link) to duplicate both the receiver and transmitter remote controller functions, as well as the ability to examine the FV computer memory for my tail message work. While I couldn't transmit FV messages without the prof's password, I could look at the results of our runs at my leisure, back in my apartment. My laptop was a lot easier to lug around than that remote controller box, too!

The professor kept a list of improvements and verification tests that he wanted to have done on the machine. But we had to put a lot of these plans aside to get ready for this test. We had to make sure the FV machine would work reliably. We could sure have used more time, but Kevin was firm about the date.

While the professor could always think of improvements, Hal reminded both of us, "Anything that takes us beyond October the first is too late!" That was the deadline we had to meet.

CHAPTER 19

Solving the Tail Question

September 15, 2019

URING THE FURTHER DEVELOPMENT OF the FutureView machine, I was determined to follow through with my investigation of the "tail"—the memory that seemed to change in a weird way, perhaps allowing much longer messages to be sent back in time. After the professor pooh-poohed my ideas, I kept this work pretty much to myself.

I needed to try inserting messages in the tail memory, to see if they also got sent back in time. After the embarrassing situation during the options test, in which the message buffer was not cleared, and it was difficult to assure anyone that a message was really sent back in time, I decided I would run tests of the tail message in a more controlled manner.

Knowing the professor's penchant for Shakespeare, I thought it might excite his interest, should my experiments work, to use lines from *Macbeth* for my messages. I copied a page with the soliloquy from act five of the play, as the lines seemed appropriate to time travel:

Tomorrow and tomorrow and tomorrow

Creeps in this petty pace from day to day

To the last syllable of recorded time,

And all our yesterdays have lighted fools

The way to dusty death. Out, out, brief candle!

Life's but a walking shadow, a poor player

> That struts and frets his hour upon the stage
>
> And then is heard no more. It is a tale
>
> Told by an idiot, full of sound and fury,
>
> Signifying nothing.

We were running tests of the FutureView messages every day, transmitting at 1:30 p.m. and receiving at 11:30 a.m., using only the antenna on top of the Green Building. With each day's FutureView test run, I inserted a line from the play into the tail input memory of the FutureView computer. Then I would cross that line off the printout, so that I was sure not to use it again.

After I received the short FutureView message in the morning, what I also hoped to find was the next line from *Macbeth* in the tail message area of the computer memory.

But it never worked.

I could never find a memory location that transmitted the *Macbeth* line back in time. Perhaps the professor was right in his theory about entropy—that only our very short messages could be sent back in time.

Then something strange happened. It was so strange that I had to get the professor involved.

"Yes, so your lines were not getting transmitted back in time?" the prof asked following my explanation of the experiment.

"That's true, but something weird happened," I said. "I worked my way down through the following line: 'And all our yesterdays have lighted fools.'

"I crossed that line off my list. I was planning to insert the next line into the tail memory before the next transmission, but I got too busy analyzing the FutureView message we received this morning and ran out of time before the 1:30 transmission.

"This afternoon, to make sure I had cleared the tail message memory, I checked the tail output memory and found the following message: 'The way to dusty death. Out, out, brief candle!'"

"So," the prof said, "isn't that the next line in *Macbeth*?"

"Yes, but I never typed in that line!" I said. "It was not crossed off my list!"

"Hmm. That's very interesting," is all he said.

He had me repeat the test the following day with our next FutureView run. As before, I left the old line from *Macbeth* in the tail memory, and did not enter the new line, then checked the tail memory after the FutureView message was transmitted at 1:30 p.m.

But this time there was no new line in the tail! The tail memory still showed the old line from the previous day: "The way to dusty death. Out, out, brief candle!"

We repeated this "tail" experiment again the next day. Again, nothing happened. I was losing confidence in my memory! I wrote careful notes and meticulous experiment directions, but I *could not* duplicate the original strange behavior.

The obvious explanation for any strange phenomenon that cannot be repeated is to assume a failure by the technician in execution. So, I must have screwed up. But how could a misplaced keystroke, a rushed movement, or *anything* I might have done, or done wrong, have caused an entire line from a Shakespearean play to jump off the paper and appear on the FutureView computer?

Sandy overheard our discussions about my dilemma and offered her own explanation. "In Shakespeare's time, the *Macbeth* play was considered being cursed, and actors refused to speak the name of the play aloud. Perhaps you have awakened the ghost of Macduff, the king of Scotland, who Macbeth murdered!"

I was not amused.

Hal was in the lab that day, helping me replace a pump, and was handing me tools while I lay on my back. I handed him back a screwdriver, but he dropped it. Taken by Sandy's line, he said:

"Is this a screwdriver which I see before me,

The handle toward my hand? Come, let me clutch thee.

I have thee not, and yet I see thee still!

Art thou not, fatal vision, sensible

To feeling as to sight? or art thou but

A screwdriver of the mind, a false creation,

Proceeding from the heat-oppressed brain?"

"So, you know some Shakespeare," Sandy said to him. "Do you know what Macbeth is about?"

"Isn't it about how Macbeth was pussy-whipped by Lady Macbeth to murder Macduff so she could become queen?"

"Actually," she replied. "Actually, it starts out with a covey of witches who can see the future. It's about the failure of a man who thought he knew what they predicted. But messages from the future are always cryptic and can lead you to your own death."

One day in the lab I remarked, "How strange it was for there to be two timelines. The first timeline occurs when no message is received. Then, the transmission of the FutureView message disrupts the chain of events, and a new timeline occurs."

The prof explained, "That logic satisfies the principle of all principles, that nothing in the universe changes unless there is a cause for the change. There first has to exist a timeline that results in the transmission of a FutureView message. Then receiving the message may cause a different set of events to follow.

"That is also why there is no paradox. Since no event can prevent itself—sending a message, or a messenger, back in time cannot influence itself, so we can never experience an impossible situation where a message prevents its own existence!"

The professor paused, then said, "I think I know how your 'dusty death' tail message occurred."

"You mean back to my tail message problem?" I asked.

"Yes. The person who entered that 'dusty death' line was *you*!"

"No way. I don't remember *ever* typing that line! And I never crossed it off my list!"

"Here's what happened. You were planning on typing that line into the computer to test your tail message *after* receiving the FutureView message at 11:30 a.m., and *before* transmitting that FV message, at 1:30 p.m."

"Yes, that's right, but I got distracted and never entered the line."

"There was an original timeline where we *didn't* receive a FutureView message. In that timeline, because there was no FutureView message to distract you, you had plenty of time to type in the next line from *Macbeth*."

"So, I entered the line in a timeline that no longer exists?" I asked.

"The tail memory, as you call it, must retain information from the previous timeline. That was the only time when the line was entered."

"But why couldn't I repeat the experiment?" I asked.

"Well, in our subsequent attempts, we set up the procedure so that you would *never* enter the line from *Macbeth*, regardless of the situation. Because we set that as a rule for the experiment, you wouldn't have entered the *Macbeth* line in either the first timeline or the second timeline, so the line never appeared!"

"Wow," I said. "The tail message apparently doesn't appear until after the FutureView message is transmitted. It doesn't go back in time with the FutureView message. Too bad. It's no better than writing the message on a pad of paper."

"Well, for one thing," said the prof, "we now have a way to know what happened in a previous timeline—information that currently gets lost as soon as a FutureView message is received."

I realized the professor was not wrong in his theoretical assessment—in fact, the tail message would not be a means of sending longer messages into the past. I should have respected his opinion.

I realized, though, the perfect application for tail messages. If I wanted to keep a journal of what happened, but my journal was rewritten as soon as a message was sent, I had to store my journal in the tail message memory. That way, even though I have to wait until the FutureView message is transmitted, I would have a bona fide record of what happened in the previous timeline.

At that point, I started putting my automatic backups of my journal directly into the FutureView computer's tail memory.

CHAPTER 20

Hiring a CFO
September 17, 2019

E VEN THOUGH HAL WAS SPENDING more time in the Cambridge lab, he still maintained his "castle" in Waltham. His glass-walled office there, in the heart of successful high-tech companies along the famous Route 128, was a status symbol of his success. But now the lease was an unneeded drain on cash.

I overheard him reluctantly telling the landlord that he would not be renewing our lease. There was still time left on the current lease for us to do the next demonstration run in the Waltham office, and Hal could still spend his mornings there until the end of the year, enjoying his office space.

But he knew the future. Hal had a contractor come in and build a room within the Cambridge lab that had sound and thermal insulation, an independent air conditioning system, and plush carpeting on the floor. He offered it to the professor and me as an office, to provide relief from the noise and heat of the machine, and we graciously accepted.

It became obvious, however, that there was more than enough room for our desks, and Hal himself took a cubicle in this new office. It was clear what Hal was planning when we discovered he had transferred the main company phone number to his cubicle phone.

While there was some privacy within the five-foot cubical dividers, it was not like the Waltham offices—every phone conversation could be heard throughout the room. I was working on my laptop in the office when I overheard Hal picking up a phone call. It was Dan Davidson, the venture capital guy, so my ears were up and my typing slowed, even though I could hear only half the conversation.

"Dan, thanks for the callback. Did you see my progress report? … What about my proposal? How soon can we get the next tranche? … Sorry to hear that. I'm sure it's tough to be in your business. But—we are certainly developing a high-risk technology, but I think we are certainly over the hump, with our last demonstration proof. … Oh, that's too bad. Is she OK? I'm sure she has other clients to keep her busy. … Of course, I can see what we can do for her! But we really depend on your funding. If you could, could you at least look at my summary? … Yes, Kevin and I go way back. … Really? Well, that's good news! … Thanks! OK if I call you next week, just to update you? And yes, I will give Kevin a call! … Thanks. Goodbye, Dan!" After a moment of silence, "Damned!"

"Bad news?" I asked.

"Well," Hal said, "the VCs are out of money, and they sold their share of our stock to an interested investor."

"That doesn't sound too bad. So, we have an enthusiastic investor?"

"The investor is Kevin Brayton. He and I go way back," Hal explained. "We were students together at MIT—actually, we were room neighbors in the same dorm—East Campus. Not that we had the same tastes or background. No, we were quite the 'odd couple.' The dorm room assignment committee put us next to each other as a joke to see what would happen. They weren't disappointed.

"Kevin wore a jacket and tie to every class he attended, and he never missed a class. He has had a lifetime plan since he was in high school to get a bachelor's degree in economics at MIT, then move upriver to Harvard Business School. But his father ran out of money, or influence, or both. But he has done well since investing in commercial real estate. I admire his patience.

"I was, perhaps, the opposite of Kevin. I *never* wore a jacket and tie. I missed a lot of classes and dropped out my junior year. There were a few pranks that he might have blamed on me. Kevin left the campus on Christmas break our freshman year. When he returned, all of his room furniture—his desk, chair, bookshelf with books, lamp, and fully made bed were all glued, upside down, to the ceiling of his room! He has resented me ever since."

***

Not much later that day, Sandy walked into the office to see Hal.

I looked over at his cubicle and saw he had left. "I'm sure he'll be back in a few minutes," I said. "He said he had to run out to the auto parts store." That was our code that we told visitors when we didn't know where the hell Hal was and didn't want to explain further.

She did not look well. I knew why, but it probably would not be a good idea for me to bring up the subject.

It was just before eleven-thirty in the morning, so I told her, "We've been running tests transmitting at 1:30 p.m. and receiving at 11:30 a.m. If I receive a message, then I know the test worked, and I am on the second timeline, so there is no need to transmit. If I don't receive a message at 11:30, then either the test failed, or we are on the first timeline. If we get a power draw in the machine at 1:30, then I know the message was transmitted in the previous timeline, but not received, so the test failed. I then break down the machine and investigate what might have failed. If we don't get a power drain, then we must be on the first timeline, and I should transmit the test message."

"Oh, really," she said.

Without questioning her about being fired, I attempted to circle the subject. "Since you were set up as a contractor, you work for many companies, right? Not just New Horizons?"

"Well, actually, most of my time has been with the New Horizons Venture Fund. They have been having a lot of financial issues lately."

"Oh, really?" I said.

"Yes, and now they can no longer afford me. I thought I would check with Hal to see if you guys needed some financial support. You don't seem to have much of a support organization left."

"I guess in your business you are always having to be marketing yourself."

"Yes, but I don't do well in that part of the business. I guess I just have a negative feeling about myself when I try to interact with other people, especially men. My ex used to say that about me."

Her eyes were looking down as she spoke.

"Oh, really?" I said, surprised she was confiding in me.

Another unexpected guest then arrived—Kevin Brayton. "Good morning, Mr. Ba…" I started.

"Sandy! How are you doing this morning?" Kevin said. He didn't wait for an answer but continued talking. "I'm just here to check up on my investment! I heard Hal is getting tight with money again. You must be pretty familiar with the finances here at FutureView? What do you think?"

"Well, I can't really discuss the finances, since I provided information about FutureView in confidence just to Davidson. You'll have to check with Hal," she said.

"I see. By the way, I understand you may be looking for additional business. I wonder if you might want to provide some support to my real estate organization?"

"What can I do for you?" she said.

"Oh, our financial department is always in need of some help. Why don't you stop by my office sometime, and we can come up with something, I'm sure."

"Thank you, Mr. Brayton."

"Thomas, can you fetch Hal? I'm here with a check we talked about. I'm sure he could use the cash now."

Sandy's posture stiffened. She inhaled like she was going to say something, but her lips were tight.

"I'll go find Hal," I said. Actually, I couldn't stand listening to any more of his BS.

I left the lab and took the elevators down to get a cup of coffee, meeting Hal at the elevators on my way back. "Hal! Kevin is in the lab, waiting for you."

"Thanks, Tom," Hal said as we rode up together. "I guess I'll have to force a smile and pat him on the back to reach his wallet!"

"I'm sure you could sell a get-rich-quick book to Jeff Bezos. Oh, and he's in there making a deal with Sandy," I said.

"Oh, really?"

"Oh, and Sandy is here too. I guess you heard? Sandy was laid off. Kevin is offering her a hefty salary to come over to his side of the Force. She was very interested in the position he offered her and was about to close on the deal just now."

"Well, we certainly can't compete with Kevin on salary."

"Yeah. About the only thing you can offer people to work for FutureView is a top-level title and a view from the 18th floor—figuratively speaking, that is. Actually, she might go for that!"

"Oh, really?"

"Yeah, but you would have to give her the role of Chief Financial Officer. Is that even legally possible?"

"Thanks," he said and darted for the lab ahead of me.

I figured I had better stay out of the lab in case someone wanted to catch me in a lie, so I stood there for five minutes, checking on my Facebook newsfeed.

Sandy came out. She smiled at me and said, "Thanks, Tom. I will see you tomorrow morning, to see what we can do about our accounts payable."

"Oh, really?" I said.

She summoned the elevator. It arrived obediently, and she left.

Kevin came out a very short while after, gave me a terse "Tom," and left.

CHAPTER 21

Sandy's Birthday
October 1, 2019, 9:00 p.m.

"WHERE THE HELL ARE YOU guys?" Hal said on the phone. "It's getting close to the message time, and you need to be here and set up."

"We're heading out right now," the prof responded.

Hal was not one to complain about timeliness. After months of additional engineering and testing, tonight was going to be the final, shining demonstration for the investors. We'd even made a last test run this morning, using our Cambridge antenna, and everything checked out.

The prof and I rushed down to the parking garage with the remote controller and a box of party favors in hand. To make sure that we beat Sandy there with enough time, I called all the elevators and sent them to the lobby with the prof and me, leaving her standing outside the lab.

She was none the wiser about our prank. As the prof and I hurried out of the parking garage, she was just walking in. I saw her in my rearview mirror and almost ran into a pair of black Chevy Tahoes with tinted windows coming up the ramp.

"Is the president having a drink on campus tonight?" I quipped to the prof on my cellphone as we both passed the SUVs.

After working so many long days and nights, we had finished and were ready for the evening test. We arrived early at the office with the remote controller to set it up in the conference room, and also to prepare the room for a small party—both to celebrate the completion of the FutureView machine and this final test, and to celebrate Sandy's 29th birthday.

Sinatra sang "My Way" on the conference room speakers. She had been kept unaware until she entered the room with Hal (and keeping Sandy unaware of anything is difficult). We sang an off-key rendering of "Happy Birthday to You" on top of Sinatra. It made for an interesting tune.

In place of a traditional birthday cake, I had arranged a collection of cupcakes in a circle on the conference room table next to the remote controller. The cupcakes were frosted half black and half white, representing the earth in positions in orbit around the sun. There were candles on each cupcake, but the candles were, of course, not combustible, containing multicolored LEDs, a lithium battery, and a Bluetooth receiver. There was plenty of food and drinks, and a good time was had by all.

In all the singing, no one noticed the banging at the front door until Hal rushed to the lobby to escort Kevin and his party into our soiree, quickly offering Kevin a Sam Adams.

Kevin introduced his associates and their titles, a strange mix of people I had not seen before. His associates looked like they never refused cake, and they didn't. None of the usual suspects showed up since the venture capital company had sold out its interest to Kevin Brayton. Mr. Fox was the only other person I recognized; I presumed he was still an investor.

"I would again like to thank this team for their hard work and excellent achievements at FutureView," Kevin began. "I would like to congratulate Sandy on her birthday and everyone on the success of the FutureView machine. Also, after the party and the machine demonstration tonight, I have an important announcement. Sandy, why don't you tell us what we're going to see today?"

"Since this is a demonstration of the time messaging machine," Sandy said, diplomatically handing the meeting back to Hal, "Mr.

Harold Hawkins, the president of the FutureView Corporation, will describe what we will see tonight. Hal?"

Hal looked miffed by Kevin, but immediately took command of the meeting. "Thank you, Sandy. What we will see this evening has been a challenge. First, we have had to extend the message size to twelve characters. I believe the team achieved the ability to actually send messages of thirteen characters. Well done! We are also extending our nominal time range to two hours—so we should receive a message at 9:30 p.m. that will not be sent until 11:30 this evening. And executing this message at this time of day may not seem to be significant, but it has been a major technical challenge. Since it is almost 9:30 now, we had better get ready to receive the message."

I thought about the limitation of thirteen characters and a time range of two hours. *That is really embarrassing.* If the laws of physics limited our range and message content, as the professor had said, then I had to think that FutureView would be of little practical value.

The receiving computer in the FV remote controller booted up smoothly, passing quickly through the startup screens for Windows 10. After booting up, it displayed the time: 9:28 p.m.

We watched until the display read 9:30. I keep feeling that there was something special about the FV messages always being on time, but computers can read clocks better than humans, and it is only humans who miss deadlines.

Almost immediately, the receiver *dinged*, and we saw the message appear, just as Kevin had requested—twelve digits:

224195180468

Kevin wrote the numbers down carefully in a small notebook that he returned to the inside pocket of his suit coat. The professor then shut down the remote controller and pressed the button on a small electronic box on the table, lighting up the LED candles on the cupcakes.

Sandy blew out the birthday candles as if they were real. They flickered under her breath, then died except for one candle that remained lit a few seconds longer before joining its mates. I had to take credit for that simulation, executed in an Arduino processor.

The professor commented, "You know, we are transmitting this message in ASCII format, which requires seven bits per character. If we were just going to send decimal digits, we could do that using binary-coded-decimal encoding, in only four bits per digit."

Neither Hal nor Sandy appeared interested and drifted away.

I asked Hal, "What information is Kevin sending in these twelve numbers? What is this for?"

"I have no idea," he said.

"Maybe he'll let us know when he transmits this message later tonight," Sandy suggested.

"Well, that may not happen," the professor said. "Remember, there is no need for Kevin to send a message at all. This message has already been received. That means it was already destined to be sent from a timeline that no longer exists."

This logic always disturbed me. I added, "I always wondered how anyone could assure that a message would be sent, when it comes from an alien world with a different sequence of events, different priorities, and maybe even different people."

The professor replied, "You assure everything is in place so that, even in the timeline where no message is received, the equipment, the FutureView machine back in Cambridge, and the operator are ready, and that the operator has the *intent* to send the message. If all that is in place, then the message will be received. So, everything must…I mean, *will* operate just fine, since we *received* Kevin's message already. I have insisted in the past that Tom go through the motions and send the message even after it is received, anyway, as there is no harm done, and it assures that you would have sent the message in the previous timeline as well. All that is unnecessary, but it provided me confidence in the results."

Hal, Sandy, and I stood around and chatted, while Kevin drew the professor away in a separate conversation.

As the evening wore on, aware of the 11:30 deadline, Hal was getting nervous about Kevin's promise to make an announcement, something Kevin hadn't bothered to reveal to Hal in any detail.

Kevin finally rapped with his fork on his beer bottle, silencing the crowd to make his announcement.

I shut the lid on my laptop.

"Since we have already received the digital message, I must congratulate the team on the proof of the success of FutureView. To commemorate this achievement, I have had engraved plaques and photographs of each of you made that will be mounted in this conference room, as we move into Phase II."

Phase II? I thought. I'd never heard of any phases on this project.

I looked at Hal to see if he had taken part in this plan. His mouth hung open. He looked as perplexed as I was; actually, more so. *That's not good!*

Kevin continued, "And I want to announce a more practical reward to each of you in recognition of your outstanding achievement."

His associate then passed out envelopes to each. They were windowed business envelopes with the name exposed in the window—the colored pattern of a check was visible. I ripped open mine, revealing a check and a tri-folded paper. The others followed suit.

Hal nervously read the paper before looking at the check. "What is going on here?"

He immediately interrupted Kevin, saying, "You're taking over the company? You're taking over the company!"

The room became very silent. The music from my iPhone ironically disconnected from the conference room speakers.

"Yes, since I have now acquired a majority share of the company stock by purchase and execution of my warrants, I now have controlling interest in the company, and as the self-appointed CEO, I am terminating all current employees, immediately, as allowed by our at-will employment agreement, under state law."

As if to defend his statement, Kevin handed a single-page printout to Sandy. Sandy scanned it over and gave Hal a shallow, vertical nod. That was not what I wanted to see.

"Those papers included with your severance check are a copy of your own employment agreement that you signed, and the penalties for violating protection of the company's trade secrets and intellectual property."

"You mean we're all fired?" I asked no one in particular.

"No, you are just laid off," Kevin responded. "Now that the FutureView machine is operational, we are moving into Phase II, and you will no longer be needed. We can certainly provide you with a good reference for your fine work at FutureView."

It finally hit Hal in the face. "You son-of-a-bitch! You've just been waiting until we perfected the machine. Then you take over and make yourself rich!"

Kevin didn't respond, and he didn't have to. His "associates" had well-developed upper body strength and physically escorted each of us to the door. I grabbed my laptop and the last cupcake.

The professor, Sandy, and I stood in the parking lot, each thinking about our future.

"Why don't we get together at my apartment? It's close to here," said the professor. "I guess Hal has more words to say to Kevin."

Just then, Hal was physically dragged out the door.

The professor, Sandy, and I got into our cars. Sandy and I followed the prof to his apartment. I had told Hal where we were going, but he just sat in the Barracuda, in the dark—probably the wiser thing to do.

We parked in the apartment lot and headed up the stairs to the professor's place on the second floor. On the way up, my cell phone rang. I saw it was Hal.

"Do you have the message?" he asked.

"Yes, I have the message on my laptop. What's up?"

Hal continued, "I know what the FutureView message was for. I followed Kevin, and we are here at the Waltham Quickie Mart. The message was—that is, it will be—the *winning lottery numbers* for the Massachusetts Millions Lottery jackpot this evening. It all fits. The drawing will be at 11:00 tonight. Kevin's now in line to buy a lottery ticket. I'm behind him at the back of the line, so he hasn't seen me yet. Give me the lottery numbers, and I will also buy a ticket. I'd buy more, but the store has rationed the last tickets to one per person. At least Kevin will have to split the winnings with us!"

My hands were full, but I had plenty of help from Sandy and the prof, who also heard the phone call, as we rushed into his apartment.

I opened my laptop and looked at the message. The twelve-character message would provide six two-digit numbers, exactly what is needed for the five winning number-pairs and the bonus number in the lottery. I cursed myself for not recognizing it and read the numbers aloud to Hal.

Sandy turned on the prof's TV and flipped to the local news channels, stopping when she saw mention of the lottery. The station was presenting a dramatic preshow on the lottery number drawing.

The announcer said, "There has been tremendous interest in the state lottery tonight after quite a promotion in the local market by the Mass Lottery Commission. The governor has called on the Mass National Guard to protect the lottery, and we see them here at the commission headquarters in Dorchester, guarding the ball-drop machine. I think maybe this is a little over-the-top! The grand prize is now up to $52 million, but I don't think they're keeping it here in a bag under the stage. What do you think, Amanda?"

Amanda took the mic. "They're going to draw the winning numbers—actually it is a ball-dropping machine, like all the lotteries—at 11:00 tonight! You can still get a lottery ticket until 10:30 this evening, though the lines are getting long! Everyone's out buying lottery tickets!"

I checked my watch. Yes, Hal could still make it!

This was the first time I had been to the professor's apartment. I glanced up from my laptop to take notice of it; it seemed rather sparse but utilitarian. I immediately noticed the Apple IIc computer, powered up in the corner. A tiny square monitor, limited to displaying only characters in a green font, showed a single line in the middle of the screen:

HELLO WORLD!

The professor had a more practical PC sitting on his desk. On the wall was a framed 1968 poster for the Jaguar XKE. The poster was in excellent condition and was probably worth more than the professor's Honda Civic.

I brought up my laptop app, where I had duplicated all the functions of the clunky remote controller box, except, of course, I needed the password to transmit a FutureView message. That brought an obvious question to mind, so I asked the prof, "How did—I mean, how will—Kevin be able to send the FutureView message without the transmitter password?"

"I gave it to him," he replied. "Well, he asked for it, and he *was* going to transmit that digital message tonight. Obviously, he will be successful!"

My cell phone rang. It was Hal. I put him on speaker.

"I'm having a problem," Hal said. "The third number pair is 95. Number pairs on the balls only go up to 70. There can't be a 95 in the lottery number!"

Before I could double-check the number, the prof interceded.

"Kevin must have planned to apply some simple cipher—just complex enough so that no one else who saw the FutureView message would know how to convert it into a lottery number."

Sandy added, "I guess Kevin doesn't even trust his own crew with the real number."

Hal replied, "That fits. That's why he's buying the ticket himself. He can't trust anyone else. I guess he's going to be very rich very soon."

"Well, what can we do?"

"Perhaps I should have done something in the past. There's nothing we can do now. Kevin has control of the future—his and ours, and there's nothing we can do."

With that, he hung up.

The professor responded as if Hal were still listening, or perhaps speaking only to himself, "The deed is done."

We talked about telling the Lottery Commission, the police, the FBI, the Boston Mafia, or some other authority, but it always came back to believability.

Sandy said, "And you would do this at the last minute, over the phone? And would you mention the use of a time machine? And, even if we stop Kevin from winning the lottery, he still legally owns FutureView, and we will still be unemployed."

On the television, the lottery drawing was being shown, live, at 11:00. A cute young lady came on stage to release the numbered Ping-Pong balls from the ball tumbler. She was introduced, but I didn't record her name. They were obviously trying to make a show of it, but drawing the numbers would take only half a minute at most. Five individual white balls rolled down to the display chute, each with a two-digit number printed on all sides.

The young lady's job was to release a ball, then rotate it slightly to orient the printed number. After the five white balls, a yellow bonus ball rolled down, also with a two-digit number on it.

Hal called the professor back. "I'm on my way back to the Waltham office. I am going to stop Kevin from sending his message!"

"Wait!" the prof shouted into the phone. "It will do no good. The message has already been received, so the message has already been sent!" His words fell on a deaf cellphone.

"Kevin is probably sitting in a bar somewhere, laughing," Sandy said.

"What about stopping the machine itself? Can I just shut off the machine in Cambridge?"

Now I realized why there were two Chevy Tahoes in the MIT parking garage when we'd left this evening. "I'm pretty sure Kevin has seen to protecting that asset, immediately," I said. "I saw his muscle men ready to move in when we left the lab."

I could only assume at this point that there was no need, now, to transmit the message. We'd already received it! That means that the remote controller would work, the professor gave him the correct password to the transmitter, and everything would work out well in the Cambridge lab where the veritable time machine sat.

The 11:30 late evening news came on. The newscast led with a story on the Massachusetts Millions Lottery. They announced that there was only one winner of that lottery, and the winning ticket had been bought at the Quickie Mart in Waltham, Massachusetts.

The professor's cellphone rang. Hal's name showed as the caller. He put it on speaker.

"This is Hal. Hey, I've been sitting out here in front of your apartment for the last fifteen minutes, watching a couple of mean-looking guys in a red Ranchero who are looking at your apartment window. They have weapons and might be ready to break in. I would recommend you all get out of there and go down the west stairwell. Leave your door unlocked if you don't want it destroyed. They have tools to break in. I don't think they're jewel thieves. I'll call the cops, but they will probably be in and out by the time the cops arrive."

"What do you think they want?"

"It's too coincidental that they're here tonight. They probably want *you*! Or, if you're not there, they want whatever they can find about the time machine."

We all left by the west stairwell, and just in time. I was the last one down the steps and looked back to see and hear the apartment door being pried open.

CHAPTER 22

The Mercedes
October 2, 2019

THE NEXT MORNING, WE ALL dragged ourselves down to the IHOP next to the Motel 6. Hal had said to meet there at 8:00 a.m. As expected, he was the only one not present. We took a booth and ordered coffee just before he arrived.

"Who were those guys?" the prof asked him.

"I'm pretty sure those ugly dudes would have done some harm. Maybe they were just waiting for the rest of us to leave—didn't want to deal with too many bodies," Hal responded. "They could have just come to search your place, but since they were waiting for your return, I think they had something more sinister in mind."

"Now that you mention it," the professor said, "I think they were there before I came back last night. My apartment did not appear to be looted, but some things were not where I had previously put them. I thought maybe I was unsure of my memory, but now I am certain someone was in my apartment. Who are they? Kevin's muscle?"

"I don't think so. It's not Kevin's style. Anyway, Kevin has what he wanted—total control of FutureView. Why would he bother sending thugs after you?"

"So, was the attack unrelated to FutureView?" I asked.

"No, it may still be related to FV—I think that's the only thing the prof has that's worth major illegal activity," Hal said.

Sandy looked at him.

"Well, that's true," added the prof.

"What about any notebooks, schematics, drawings of the time machine—did you have anything like that in your apartment?" Hal asked.

"No, I would keep nothing like that at home."

"How are we going to find out who those thugs were working for?" Sandy wondered.

"I've already got a trace going," Hal said. "I stuffed my iPhone in the back of the Ranchero. I tracked where they drove to last night using my laptop and the Apple Find-my-iPhone app. Turns out they ended up in the Shangri-la Motel, just down the street. I went for an early morning run by there this morning."

"Did you call the cops? Did you get a good look at them?" I asked.

"There's probably little to tie them to any crime. If they found nothing related to FutureView at the professor's place, they probably took nothing that would tie them to the break-in. And that's if they didn't already give whatever they found to their employer."

Hal continued, "But there's more. I saw a late-model Mercedes sedan parked next to the Ranchero at the motel. Not what your typical Shangri-la patron is driving these days."

"Did you get a look at the model number?" the prof asked.

"Yes, I got the license number, thank you. It was 791ERB. Model number? I think it was S-something. Is that important?"

"The S-class is top-of-the-line, well over $100,000."

"I didn't think you were in the market for high-end automobiles, professor! I suspect a meeting was going on in a motel room nearby. The Mercedes driver is who we want—so I retrieved my iPhone and mounted an Apple tracker with a rare-earth magnet under the side of the Mercedes. We can track it from my laptop right after we order breakfast."

Sandy put down her coffee and said, "That means someone with lots of money probably wants more of it. I doubt they were only after the professor—we're just second priority. All of us here know about the FutureView machine. I doubt any of us are safe going back to our apartments right now. And we have no way to control the use of the FV machine—it's entirely in Kevin's hands."

The professor asked, "Who else knows about FutureView?"

Hal pondered, "Well, the venture capital guys—Davidson and Sizemore. And the only investors who were aware of the program—Kevin Brayton and Ronald Fox, as far as I know. There are other minor stockholders who invested in the New Horizons Fund and held FutureView stock, but they think we were developing a 5G transmitter for the cellphone industry."

"I don't think Davidson and Sizemore even realized the potential of FutureView, and they're out of the picture now that Kevin has bought most of our stock," Sandy said. "Fox showed some interest. Kevin may think he has taken over, but clearly someone else now wants in. Kevin may not be aware that he could also be a victim here. Then there are the people that these guys might have told."

Hal responded, "I don't think Kevin trusted any of his 'associates' well enough to tell them about a time machine. After all, he couldn't trust anyone to even buy him a lottery ticket. Since those guys in the Ranchero were already in action last night, they had to be working for someone who knew about FutureView before yesterday."

"Then, what are we going to do, besides hide out?" I asked.

"Kevin had to put out a lot of cash to gain a controlling interest in FutureView," Hal replied. "He probably needs the lottery win to pay back short-term loans as his money is tied up in long-term real estate assets—assets you can't, or don't want to, sell quickly. We aren't totally powerless. Maybe we can delay Kevin's lottery win and keep him from making any more money from FutureView. If he's under a lot of pressure, maybe we can make a deal with him about getting back into the company."

The professor added, "We also need to follow that Mercedes, and find out who is sponsoring those guys."

"Sam," Hal said, "I think the one thing that would cripple Kevin's use of FutureView is something he doesn't actually appreciate right now—the ability to operate at almost any time of day."

"Well, half a day, anyway," the prof said. "The remote receiver allows transmitting in the afternoon and early evening, because we could receive in the morning on the other side of the earth."

"We never really set up a permanent link with Jakarta," I said. "We don't have to do anything. Kevin is unaware of the importance of a remote receiver, but he cannot replicate his lottery win without it!"

"Tom never was very good at documenting his software," the prof added.

"But let's not kid ourselves," Hal said. "Kevin could still employ experts who could reverse-engineer the machine, create a new receiver processor using the signal processing employed on the Green Building receiver, and build a receiver antenna in another time zone. Then he could operate without time-of-day limitations."

"He could also expand on the capability of the machine—build a next-generation time machine, with even more capability," the professor said.

"That's as good as it gets, for now," Hal replied. "Heaven help us if Kevin gets to do that. We need to regain control of the machine before he can get to that level."

***

We all got together again the next morning for breakfast, and to report progress. This time, Hal was there on time.

Sandy said, "Tom and I shut down the Jakarta operation. Kevin is stuck doing 'nooners' with the FV machine, at most."

Hal said, "One thing I did right away was email the Massachusetts Lottery Commission to suggest that Kevin may have manipulated the lottery. It may only slow down the payout, but it will also make it look awfully suspicious if Kevin wins big in another lottery."

"Since Kevin knows he can make good money in short-term movement in stock options," Sandy added, "I alerted the SEC and the major stock exchanges that that there is some suspected insider trading going on in short-term stock options."

"Bureaucracies move slowly," Hal said. "Kevin could get rich and retire before they take any action."

"Just in case, I sent a notice to Kevin and to Kevin's brokerage as well, warning them of the ongoing investigation and the potential criminal penalties."

"I don't think Kevin is going to be frightened by your threats!" Hal declared.

"I helped Sandy with those notices," I said, "so they are indistinguishable from official legal correspondence from the SEC."

"Oh," Hal said. "Good work."

"You may be concerned, Hal, with stopping Kevin from making money," Sandy said, "but I am more concerned about the long-term problem: If the wrong persons are in control of FutureView, it could become much more powerful, providing detailed forecasts of the future and therefore powerfully directing efforts to prevent ever being put out of business. FutureView is the perfect tool for control of the future."

Hal replied, "On a practical level, this device is valuable enough that people will kill to get it. We are in real danger. We don't even know who is after us. The important first step is to make sure Kevin doesn't get a lot of money—it will be a lot harder to stop him if he's rich. Then he could start reverse-engineering the machine and building more of them. That's why we need to stop Kevin now."

"So," Hal started, "can we figure out where Kevin will be next? Mostly, he needs cash soon—lots of it. He has to stay hidden—mostly from us! The FV remote controller allows him to use the FutureView machine from anywhere while it remains secure and locked up in Cambridge."

The prof was the first to respond. "Well, he can't win local lotteries—because without a receiver antenna in a distant time zone, he can't send a FutureView message in the evening. Lotteries typically draw the numbers late at night."

Hal suggested, "What if he bets online in some of the European lotteries? It's legal to bet online in many European countries, and the time zone difference would allow sending a message in the afternoon."

Sandy responded, "But you also have only two hours between when bets can be placed and when the winning number is announced. The Eurozone Lottery, for one, requires betting to stop twelve hours before the draw. I think they all have rules like that. It helps prevent other forms of fraud."

I was at a loss to know how or why she knew that.

***

I later looked online and discovered that Hal's email also had its effect. I told our team, "The Massachusetts Lottery Commission put a temporary hold on awarding the jackpot prize from last night's lottery and was conducting an investigation."

Sandy replied, "That will only provide a temporary delay, though, since they will find nothing unbecoming in the lottery, and they will have to pay up, eventually."

"In the meantime," Hal said, "where would Kevin go to get money to pay back his 'investors' in FutureView?"

"Kevin is not that experienced in options markets," Sandy said. "I think my emails will keep him away from the stock market for now."

"What about schemes outside of the stock market?" the professor asked. "I think Kevin may also want to remain anonymous."

The question seemed to be posed to Hal, for obvious reasons.

Hal stuttered, "W-well…card games are out—too hard to get a message in or out in time, and if you could do that, you might as well cheat by traditional methods, using an associate with binoculars, or with a computer with AI."

I started to ask, "How…?" but Hal cut me off. "It would be like playing *Jeopardy!* with an iPad on Google," he said.

The breakfast food arrived, and we continued our conversation as we ate.

"What did you find out about the Mercedes, Hal?" the professor asked.

"I followed the car's movement into Winchester, to a commercial area where it appeared to stop for a long time. I drove out there this morning, expecting to find the car, but all I found was a car wash. I went inside and found my tracker."

"Are you saying the tracker fell off in the car wash?"

"I found it in the car wash. You know, I think that's what you would have thought. But the tracker has a strong rare-earth magnet on it. I put it on the side panel of my own car and drove through that car wash, too. The tracker held fast. There is no way that tracker just fell off the Mercedes."

"Let's look at the route the Mercedes followed," Sandy said.

Hal pulled up his laptop and opened an app for the tracker. The app displayed a familiar map of the Boston area. Everyone looked carefully at the trace of the Mercedes' location.

I looked at it and asked the obvious question. "Why drive all the way to Winchester to go to a car wash? I'll bet there were plenty of car washes along this very route."

"The Mercedes owner was not staying at the Shangri-la Motel, Tom," Sandy added. "He was probably headed somewhere in Winchester and stopped off at this car wash. Perhaps he goes there regularly."

"No, Tom's got a point. Look at the route he took. It's not even the most direct route to that car wash," Hal added.

"Some of these apps allow you to connect the dots, so to speak. Can we actually watch his progression through this route?" the professor asked.

I offered, "I think I can make it display position in time." I pulled down some menus and found the right display option. Since Hal had emplaced the tracker long before the Mercedes left the motel, I manually adjusted the pace until the car symbol appeared to move.

We watched the Mercedes pull out on the map display, staring at the screen while the car stopped and started in city traffic, probably at stoplights.

"Tom," Hal asked, "could you speed it up until he gets near Winchester?"

After a few moments, Sandy said, "Stop! Go back a little and let it run in real time."

I did that. We all watched intently. The car seemed to back up for a few seconds. I thought it was just a noisy signal.

"There!" the professor said, "The Mercedes parallel-parked on the street, in the middle of the block. It sat there for a while, then moved on."

"Exactly!" Sandy said. "What I suspect is this: the driver arrived at his destination and parallel-parked on the street. When he got out of the car, he saw the tracker, and figured he had better take off again."

"Exactly!" Hal said, "What would I do in this situation? I would at least drive far away and ditch the tracker before returning to my destination. When he saw the car wash, he figured out how he could make it look like an innocent failure of the equipment. We wouldn't suspect a thing! You can bet he will check his car for trackers in the future. Tom, can you pull up Google Maps at that location on your laptop?"

Before I could bring it up, Hal said, "Oh, my God!"

I zoomed quickly in Google Maps, to the location, and entered street view mode, showing a video simulation of driving down the street.

"Look to your left," Hal said. "Stop!"

We watched as a professional building came into view on the screen. I moused over to the left side of the street.

"That's my lawyer's office!" Hal said.

"What does that mean?" Sandy asked.

"Damned if I know."

CHAPTER 23

Trip to Holland
November 2, 2019

Staying in the Motel 6 was already wearing on us. I asked Sandy, "Why is it called 'Motel 6'?"

"It was originally called Motel 1, but it got downgraded."

After almost four weeks had gone by since Kevin's takeover, we hadn't seen a single FutureView message, and we couldn't imagine why.

While Kevin would have very likely changed the transmission password so we couldn't transmit messages, he didn't know about my laptop implementation of the remote controller box, so he didn't have any reason to shut down the internet output. He probably wouldn't want to disable his own remote controller, either, by pulling it off the internet—so we *should* have received FutureView messages.

We got together for our breakfast meeting at the IHOP.

Sandy said, "I saw a brief item in the *Globe* yesterday that you might be interested in, Hal. It announced the winner of the grand prize for the Massachusetts Millions Lottery—the winner was a guy named Kevin…Kevin *Mahar.* Kevin Brayton must have set up an alias in advance—avoids a lot of questions."

"That may be true," Hal said, "but the Lottery Commission ought to have someone tell them that Kevin Mahar is Kevin Brayton!"

Sandy replied, "Lotteries frequently deal with false names—typically people avoiding overdue debts, alimony payments, and friends who think they're owed something. But sometimes it's more serious fraud. The Massachusetts Lottery Board probably doesn't care so much—to them, it was just another name they can use in their promotion of this vice. But it really matters to the lottery insurance business. Yes, there is a lottery insurance business. If somebody wins the big one, that can make the difference between a large profit and a large loss. These companies have to pay off if there's a big win. And this was a big win. If there's some fraud involved, they might not have to pay up.

"By the way, I called the Lottery Commission, and they said the payout was on hold right now. I mentioned Kevin was a good friend of mine, and how he always used that phony name to pick up girls. I told them what his real name was and gave them the FutureView office address. They're going to check it out."

Hal smiled "Thank you, Sandy. I am worried, though. We can keep the pressure up by delaying the lottery, but I'm amazed that Kevin has not tried to use the FV machine. He must be hurting for cash to pay back his takeover of FutureView. We need to see what's going on."

"Anything further about the Mercedes, Hal?" the prof asked.

"Yes, here's what I'm thinking. The Mercedes indeed stopped at the office of my lawyer, Orson Greenbaum. He didn't park in the reserved parking spaces for the office workers. He parked on the street. So, he had to be a client, not a lawyer from the office. But how did Greenbaum become my lawyer? He was recommended by Dan Davidson, the venture capital guy. Davidson recommended him because of the work he did for Kevin Brayton!"

"So, what does that prove?" asked Sandy. "He could represent everyone who invested in the New Horizons Fund and knows about FutureView."

"Well…" Hal said. "I guess so."

***

It had been another month living in Motel 6, afraid to go home and unable to find Kevin. The Waltham former offices of the FutureView

Corporation were now abandoned and up for lease. They'd made the Cambridge lab even more physically secure and under guard 24/7. The elevators could not access the eighteenth floor without a key. The only staff seen coming and going were maintenance and security personnel. Since Kevin could operate anywhere using the remote box, there was no need for him to show up there at all.

The operation must have still needed money to keep running, with the lease, utilities, and all the technicians and security guards. It was strange that there had been no activity in terms of FutureView messages. At first, we feared Kevin had disconnected or changed our access to the FV messages, but I could still remotely examine the FV computer memory and set up tail messages.

There was another possibility—that Kevin was operating the FV machine directly in the lab or in some other way was locking us out of receiving FV messages. To verify whether this was happening, we would draw from a deck of cards every evening. The loser would have to drive out to the MIT campus around noon the next day, observe the Green Building, and watch for steam escaping from the cooling system on the roof.

We never saw steam.

"Where could Kevin be holing up? Is he hiding in cheap motels like us?" Sandy asked.

Hal knew more about Kevin than any of us. We looked to him for an answer.

"First, I know for sure that Kevin would not be hiding in cheap motels, like us," Hal answered.

"We know he's not at the FutureView office or at the Cambridge lab. He would definitely avoid his own office in Wellesley," Sandy added. "And he would also avoid his residence in Medford."

"Let me think. Kevin used to describe spending summer vacations at a cottage on the shore in Holland..." Hal said.

"In the Netherlands?" Sandy asked.

"No, no. Holland, Massachusetts. It's a resort town, with lakes… near the Connecticut border."

"It's probably a nice hideout, except a little cold in the winter, I'm sure."

"Speaking of hideouts," Sandy recalled, "I remember that people in the office would whisper about a real hideout condo that Kevin called 'Quantum.' He kept that location secret even from his own staff, and his wife, when he was married."

"And have you been there?" Hal asked.

Sandy gave a wan smile, then said, "Maybe it was called that referencing the Bond film *Quantum of Solace*, a place where Kevin could take refuge from the world."

I had to correct her. "You're thinking of Superman's *Fortress of Solitude*, where Superman could take refuge from the world. Actually, the title of the Bond movie *Quantum of Solace* was taken from another of Ian Fleming's writings and refers to the minimum amount of compassion a man could give his unfaithful wife—only a *quantum* of solace."

"Nevertheless," Sandy said, "I think it is some kind of fortress of solitude."

"So, the most likely places for him to hang out would be first Quantum, and second, some cottage in Holland," the professor said. "We don't have a clue as to the address of either."

Hal said, "Well, if Kevin is in Holland, at least that's a location, and a small one at that. If he's at someplace called Quantum, we do not even know where to start. Is there any way we can narrow this down, professor?"

The professor seemed distracted and didn't answer immediately. Then suddenly, he said, "I think we are about to get a clue. Tom, what time do you have?"

"It's 11:22, but why…?"

Suddenly, there was a *ding,* announcing a FutureView message.

I checked my laptop for the message. It read:

NOQUANTUMNOW

It was chilling. Was somebody listening to us? And how did the prof know?

"Does Kevin know we're receiving FV messages?" I asked. "Has he bugged this motel room? Is he warning us to stay away from Quantum, wherever it is?"

"That's a little far-fetched, don't you think, Tom?" Sandy asked.

"Wow, maybe the bad guys have staked out Kevin's Quantum, and Kevin desperately sent himself this message, warning himself to stay away," I said.

"Or maybe Kevin is already there, but things go bad this afternoon, and it's a warning to himself to get out!" Hal suggested.

"How lucky for us!" Sandy said, "Just as we needed it, now we can eliminate Quantum and concentrate on just the Holland location."

Hal looked perplexed, so I asked, "What's with you?"

He answered, "Maybe it wasn't just luck."

"Huh?" I said.

"I was just thinking how, if we still had access to the FV machine, we could send a message like this," Hal said. "It would keep Kevin away from Quantum and probably allow us to find him in Holland. And Kevin would assume that *he* sent that message to warn himself. He wouldn't even suspect us."

"But didn't Kevin immediately change the password?" I asked. "It's been an entire month since he took over, and I'm sure he doesn't trust us."

"He thinks he has the only remote controller, and access to the lab is locked up tight, so he might think there's no need to change the password."

There was a long pause as we all tried to digest this theory.

"Well," Hal added, "wouldn't it be easy to see, right now, whether the old password is still in effect?"

"Unless Kevin is going through the same thoughts we are," Sandy said.

At least I could quickly answer that question. I got on the FutureView transmitter function on my laptop app and attempted to log on using the professor's previous password.

"I have some bad news. Kevin *has* changed the password," I said. "So, *he* must have sent that Quantum message."

"Unless," Sandy said, then hesitated. "Unless he saw the message come in and was unsure whether he sent it or we sent it. What would you do? First thing I would do would be to change the password on the FutureView transmitter, just to protect myself from those bastards!"

"I know who sent the message," I said. "It was the professor."

We all looked at the prof. He smiled and said, "How did you know?"

"You knew *exactly* what time to send the message to," I said. "You just asked me for the time, and that's when the message arrived."

"We need to go to Holland," Hal said.

***

The next morning, we were finally going to *do something*. We all packed into Hal's Barracuda and drove back to Cambridge. I had mentioned that I had a DJI drone I enjoyed flying and spying with, so we drove back to my apartment to get it.

Hal first circled the parking lot to make sure there was no stakeout. He then dropped me off to run in and get the drone and its transmitter. Only upon leaving did I notice the new camera mounted above my apartment door.

We then headed back out onto the highway. If anyone was following us, Hal would have certainly lost them, so there was no need to speculate. Hal drove out the Mass Pike past the Boston beltways to Route 84 toward Hartford. We were almost to Connecticut when Hal pulled off at the exit for Holland.

It was a simple task to fly over the lake, looking toward the shore for a black BMW. There were no trees, power lines, or buildings to avoid, no elevation changes, and it was pretty easy to see and follow the shoreline around the lake.

As it was November, there were no leaves on the trees, and few of the cottages had garages. There were barely any cars at all, since this was mostly a summer resort. It didn't take long for us to find the Beemer.

We noted the location, and I flew the drone down to sight the street sign. It was getting dark and cold, so we headed back to the hotel.

The next morning, we drove down to Kevin's street and stopped a distance away but in sight of his cottage.

Hal and Sandy hiked up the street to check it out. We saw the Beemer, parked on the side of the road. Sandy remembered his license number and confirmed that it was Kevin's car.

We all got back in Hal's car and warmed up. Hal and Sandy sat in front, and the prof and I sat in the back. Sandy turned and looked toward us, then out the rear window.

"Duck!" she shouted.

CHAPTER 24

Cicero

November 3, 2019, 8:32 a.m.

A S SOON AS SHE SAID that, Sandy ducked down in the car. Hal and I were facing her, and we ducked too.

"Kevin just got in his car! He's got the remote box with him!" she said.

Kevin zoomed by, his windows still covered with frost except for a small hole he had cleared on the driver's side of the windshield. He probably hadn't seen us.

Hal paused for a moment, then kicked up mud from the snow-covered dirt road as he whipped the car around and followed, fishtailing on the way out. We caught up to Kevin as he made it onto Route 84, then to the Mass Pike, heading west until we reached Springfield. Hal followed Kevin down an exit and slowed to stay back.

Despite the narrow, crowded streets of this old city, Hal seemed to have a knack for tailing others while staying back far enough to avoid being discovered. Then a large semi, backing onto a loading dock in the narrow streets, cut us off from Kevin and ended our tail. Hal pulled to the side of the road.

Before we could figure out what to do next, we got a *ding* from my laptop. I looked at my watch, then pulled up the message:

CICEROWAHOTBD

"It's 11:32 and this is the message," I said, holding up my laptop for the others to see. "Cicero…Washington…Hotbed?" I said.

"I don't think so," Sandy said, "and you forgot to set your watch back last night. It's only 10:32 a.m."

"Cicero, wahoo, to be determined?" the professor suggested.

It also fell flat.

"Tom, google 'Cicero'!" Hal shouted.

I found an entry on Wikipedia and read part of it aloud. " 'Marcus Tullius Cicero was a lawyer and consul in the Roman Republic'…" I paraphrased a bit. "…who got on the wrong side of Mark Antony… who then had him beheaded. It is also a small suburb south of Chicago, famous for being the home of Al Capone. Named after Marcus Tullius Cicero."

Since none of us could make sense of either, I then googled 'waho.'

"WAHO: West African Health Organization. Also, World Arabian Horse Organization."

Hal responded, "Wait a minute! Horses…yeah…*racehorses*! These sound like racehorse names. Check today's horse races. Go to DRF.com."

I typed in that URL. It came up as the *Daily Racing Form*. I guess Hal knew the site. I had to register for their newsletter, but after another search, the site confirmed Hal's idea.

"Yes," I said, "Cicero is running in the first race, and Wahoo in the second, at Tampa Bay Downs. That must be what TBD stands for."

"Isn't there a casino in Springfield where you can do sports betting?" Hal asked.

"I thought sports betting was illegal in Massachusetts?" I said.

"Yes," he said, "it's illegal to bet on football players, but apparently it's OK to bet on horses, like they're more ethical."

"But it's only legal to bet on horses from another horse track," I said.

"But it's remote betting! Who's gonna know? The horses?" said Hal. "Look for any casino in the area."

Sandy had the directions to the Springfield Starlite Casino pulled up on her cell.

Hal glanced at the map and peeled out. Within minutes we caught sight of the casino.

Hal pulled the car up to the red curb and jumped out, shouting, "Stay here!"

Sandy reached over and turned off the ignition. We sat in the car. It was now 10:52 a.m.

After a minute, Hal called. I put my phone on speaker and mute and lodged it under the driver's headrest so everyone in the car could hear. That freed up my hands to allow me to type into my journal. I felt like a 1940s newspaper reporter covering a boxing match.

Hal said, "I checked out the offtrack betting lounge. Kevin has already left…one moment…yeah, I see that the first race at Tampa Bay has already finished, and Cicero won! I'm going to look around for Kevin."

A few minutes passed, then Hal continued, "Kevin just collected on the second race and is now in line at the registration desk. He's with some leech that, I'm sure, is *quite curious* about the remote control box he's lugging around! Kevin's probably planning to send the Cicero message from his room. I will try to follow him."

Hal's voice went on, though more distant, "Hey, kid, want to make twenty bucks? Here's all you have to do: See that guy in the gray suit? When he gets in the elevator, you rush in and see what floor he's going to. Then push a bunch of the buttons and run out of the elevator. Come here and tell me what floor he's going to, and I'll give you the twenty. Got it?"

Some time passed. We heard a few elevator *dongs*. I had to ask, "Hal, are you still there?"

Hal came back on. "Yes, I'm now in another elevator. I'm going up to Kevin's floor. I will try to keep out of sight until he enters his room. He's probably going to be distracted by that other gambler, who's now stuck to him like glue."

I heard the elevator door open. I did not hear it close. Perhaps Hal was hiding in the elevator.

Half a minute passed. Then some distant voices. One that must have been the gambler said, "Let me come in for a second, I have something important to tell you…"

Kevin, in an irritated tone, said, "How about we get together at the bar this afternoon, instead? About three?"

I heard the *clunk* of an electronic door lock click open, followed by the sound of a door opening.

The gambler said, "Naw, I'll just be a minute. You need to show me…" His voice drifted off.

I did not hear the door latch close. I assumed Hal must have had a foot in the door, literally. The voices of Kevin and the gambler drifted off.

"Who the hell are you?" demanded the gambler.

Hal responded, "I'm the hotel security. Is there a problem here?"

"Yes, Officer," said Kevin, gladly playing along with Hal's bluff. "This *asshole* forced his way into my room! Please get him out of here!"

"Sir, could I see some identification?" Hal said sternly.

"You sure can!" the gambler said.

"Now, there's no need to use a gun," Hal said, perhaps to let us know.

The gambler continued, "Both of you get over there or you'll be bleeding real soon! Now hand me that bag of money…and the box!"

Kevin responded, "That box is nothing. My network provides me with the winning tips! That box is just how they send me the names of the horses to bet on."

"Do I look like an idiot?" replied the gambler. "That's got to be the largest damned cellphone in the world! No, asshole, you're going to show me how you won this morning, or neither of you is gonna leave this room on your feet!"

Sandy stepped out of the car and dialed 9-1-1 on her cell phone. I realized that would be futile, as we didn't know what room, or even what floor, they were on. We couldn't even be sure that Kevin had registered under his own name. The operator seemed to ask questions that Sandy couldn't answer. She must have backed out of the call as she got back in the car.

Hal then began, "Well, Tex, you're absolutely right. That ain't no cellphone. You're never gonna believe me when I tell you what it is. How do you think this guy could win on two horses in two bets? How could he possibly know that Wahoo was going to win at Tampa Bay Downs when the horse never won a race in its lifetime? No, even with a fixer at the track, you can't make a glue factory like that into a winner!"

The gambler responded, "So, what's in the box? What does it do?"

Kevin interrupted, "Don't, Hal! You can't tell him…I know that too many people are already willing to kill for it!"

"Well, Tex, it's a time machine," Hal said. "I knew you weren't gonna believe it! This is a simple time machine. It doesn't send people into the future—it sends messages from the future to the past. Here is how it works: You open this side of the box…"

I heard a *beep* from the remote controller booting up.

Hal said, "You pull down this menu. Before you can do anything, you enter a password. What is the password, Kevin?"

"You son-of-a-bitch!" said Kevin.

There was the sound of someone groaning with strained breaths.

"You'll only get one chance to give him the right password. Understand?" said the gambler.

Kevin, under strain, shouted, "The password is…*timescape*! *T, I, M, E, S, C, A, P, E!*"

Hal resumed, "Now I enter the time the message is to arrive. Let me see. I am pretty sure that was 11:05 this morning."

I checked my watch. It was now 1:02 p.m., which means it is really 12:02. If Hal was really sending a message, enough time had passed since the last FutureView message, so the system back in Cambridge could handle the power load. I remembered that we had received the

Cicero message at 10:36 this morning. So Kevin was in the casino then but had just arrived. *What is Hal trying to pull off?*

Hal continued, "Now, we enter the name of the winning horse."

"How the hell are you gonna know who will win?" the gambler asked.

"The race has already happened, Tex! We know who won. You enter the name of the winner from the third race at Tampa Bay. This machine sends the message *back* in time. Remember when you saw Kevin downstairs in the offtrack betting lounge? If I enter the name of another winning horse, Kevin here will probably place a bet on that horse, too. Now, you know Kevin won two bets at Tampa Bay. If I enter the name of another horse, you will see the results of Kevin betting on *three* horses. Got it?"

The gambler replied, "I don't know what the hell you're saying, so I'm gonna start shooting if I don't get a better answer."

Hal continued, "Let me put it this way: if this machine really sends information back in time, we should see that bag of money get a lot fuller, as soon as I send the message."

It was certainly an intriguing story to Tex, but it had so many flaws, I knew it would not happen. Even if it happened, Tex would notice no difference. The bag of money would never be perceived as changing, even if it contained more money!

"Go ahead," Tex said. "What's the name of the winning horse?"

"Well, the winner of the third race was something like 'Run for the Money.' No, more like 'Run for Me!' No, it was 'Run for It!' That's it!"

I knew one thing. If Hal was about to execute a real transmission from FutureView, I had better end this text and save it in the tail message.

CHAPTER 25

Cicero 2

November 3, 2019, 10:52 a.m.

H AL PULLED THE CAR UP to the red curb and jumped out, shouting, "Stay here!"

Sandy reached over and turned off the ignition. We sat in the car. It was now 10:52 a.m.

After a minute, Hal called. I put my phone on speaker and mute and lodged it under the driver's headrest so everyone in the car could hear. That freed up my hands to allow me to type into my journal. I felt like a 1940s newspaper reporter covering a boxing match!

Hal said, "I checked out the sports betting lounge. Kevin has already left…one moment…yeah, I see that the first race at Tampa Bay has already finished, and Cicero won! I'm going to look around for Kevin."

My laptop then *dinged*. It was 11:05. I stopped entering the journal and pulled up the FutureView message:

RUNFORIT

"Is this message from Kevin? Or from us, to warn Hal?" I asked.

"Or is it a message to all of us to get out of here?" Sandy said. She slipped into the driver's seat and started the engine.

I shouted into the phone, "Hal, get out of there! We just got a FutureView message. It just says, *run for it!*"

"Sounds like a message Kevin must have left for himself! I'll just be a minute."

Almost immediately, we saw Kevin come running out of the casino, lugging the remote controller.

I said, "Hal, Kevin has just left the building in a hurry!"

"Got it," Hal said.

A few minutes later, Hal walked out of the casino and got back in the car. By then, Kevin was long gone.

We drove home at a reasonable speed, stopping at a diner for lunch. It was 1:02 p.m., so I downloaded the tail journal from the "RUNFORIT" message. While we ate lunch, I read my journal entry from the last timeline. After that we all cheered Hal for his quick thinking.

I finished my Impossible burger and said, "All-in-all, it has been a good day. I have proved out the value of the automated journal backup, allowing me to save a record of the timeline that no longer exists…"

Sandy added, "We have found Kevin's lair in Holland, and we learned Kevin's secret password for FutureView transmissions, while he remains unaware that he has given it to us."

The server dropped off the tab for our meal. Hal grabbed it, drew a large roll of bills from his pocket, and laid down enough of them to generously cover the tab. He then dealt out the rest of the stack to each of us like he was dealing a poker hand.

"We also did well today," Hal said, "thanks to a horse named Wahoo."

CHAPTER 26

Asteroid Hits Cleveland
November 4, 2019

T HE NEXT MORNING, WE WENT back to Kevin's place in Holland. There was no car in the carport or beside the road, and no lights were on. Hal parked his car out of sight.

"Let's go look," he said.

The snow was mostly gone from the street, and only patches of melting snow remained in the shadows of bushes and the north side of trees.

I looked through the windows and saw that the refrigerator had been turned off and its door wedged open to air out. While the snow under an outdoor spigot appeared to have been penetrated by a spray of water, Hal turned the spigot to find that the water had been shut off, probably to prevent pipes from freezing and bursting during the winter.

We went back to the porch. Sandy noticed a note on the door that spooked her:

THANKSFORALL!

"It could have been left here for the neighbors," Hal said.

"Isn't it strange that the note is exactly thirteen characters long, and there are no spaces between words?" the professor said.

"But then again, that could just be because the person who wrote it realized there was barely enough room to fit in all the words!" I said.

We could only speculate about how Kevin knew we knew about Holland, if he knew that at all.

As we walked back to the car, Hal suddenly said, "I know exactly where Kevin is!"

When we got back to the car, the professor finally asked, "All right, Hal. Where's Kevin?"

"Kevin's at his Quantum of Solace."

***

Sandy said she thought it would be better to move out of the city and convinced Hal to use the Wahoo winnings to move up to the Sheraton in Framingham. Actually, the hotel was my idea since it was built like a castle. Definitely an upgrade from the Motel 6.

We all had only the clothes on our backs when we left Cambridge, but bought some at the local Walmart, enough to last the week between washings. Hal tried to sneak back to his apartment but discovered a new camera overlooking his front door. He didn't dare set off any alarms, so there was no going back yet.

We all agreed not to go back even to pick up the mail until we knew who our adversaries were and had some defense. We bought disposable cell phones, would drive out to other towns to use the ATMs for cash, and seldom used credit cards. Fortunately, Hal felt guilty enough, and had enough money, to cover our hotel bills.

We intercepted a few FV messages, but they just contained cryptic letters and numbers that must have had some meaning for Kevin— maybe midday stock moves, or more sports betting, who knew.

The professor kept detailed records of each message. "The key to breaking a code is keeping all messages, even if you can't decode them at the time," he said. Perhaps Kevin might have even made a little money along the way.

Then the most disheartening news story appeared in the *Boston Globe*. Kevin Brayton (actually Kevin's pseudonym, Kevin Mahar) was finally awarded the Massachusetts Millions Lottery grand prize after the investigation ended. *I'm sure his lawyer's threats may have influenced the decision,* I thought. Kevin might still have some problems laundering the money, but I was sure he wasn't hurting for cash now.

***

Being on the run was not all that exciting after the chase ran cold. We had not seen a FutureView message in weeks and didn't know for sure whether Kevin had found out we could receive FV messages, whether he had left the country, or even if he was still alive.

It was Sunday, so we all met as usual in the laundry room to share the large bottle of Tide that the professor had bought. There were some other long-term tenants of the hotel, but they all seemed to wait until Sunday night to do their laundry and fill up the few washing machines, so we knew we had to get it done early in the day.

Sandy came down first to wash her clothes while reading a paperback romantic mystery. The professor had somehow gathered a pile of science journals when we'd left and read them intently, using a yellow Sharpie to highlight the important text. I usually set up my laptop to work on converting the journal in the tail messages into the story that you are now reading.

Sandy's wash finished, and as there was no other open washing machine available, I asked, "Sandy, are you done with your wash?"

"No, Tom, I wash my white clothes separately from my colored clothes—you're just going to have to wait!"

I saw that Hal's washer was almost done, and he was nowhere in sight, so I removed his clothes and set them on the worktable.

"What the hell are you doing? Can't you wait? I'm right here!" came Hal's voice as he entered the laundry.

The clothes weren't the only things getting steamed.

We all sat in silence, having run out of decent conversation. Only the FutureView team was in the room, but the only sound was the drone of the dryers.

Sandy broke the silence. "Why are we here?" she said aloud, not obviously directed at Hal, except by context.

158

"We're after Kevin," Hal started off, "to confront him, to negotiate with him, to threaten him…"

"Threaten him? With what?" the prof asked.

"We can threaten him with going public about FutureView. That would really throw a wrench into his 'future' plans," Hal said.

"And," said Sandy, "it would throw a wrench into the gaming business. And into the stock trading business. And futures trading, and currencies trading, and…"

"The news media would go wild. There would be speculation beyond all reality!" the prof said.

"There would be a panic on Wall Street!" I added.

"Governments would be forced into doing something, which will inevitably be the wrong thing!" Sandy said.

"And how many financial interests would force their way in, spying on FutureView…" Hal said.

We all grew silent again. Even the dryers stopped turning.

"…and threatening us." Sandy said.

"You think the people after us know the value of FutureView, and they want us because we built the time machine?" I asked.

"For the time being, we had better keep track of Kevin and monitor any FutureView messages," Hal said. "I'm not even sure Kevin is running the machine."

"What harm can Kevin do with the machine?" I asked.

"Not only does it allow you to have a limited view of the future, it also allows the operator to foresee the future, and therefore to change it," Sandy said. "Changing the future certainly provides the opportunity to gain financially, but it might also be the perfect tool for politicians, for military or police operations, for countermilitary or counterpolice operations, for criminals, for murderers, for terrorists, for dictators.

"It allows you to never make a mistake; to never get caught; to never be defeated; to never be overthrown. It allows you to try many approaches and to select the best outcome. These capabilities are far more important and far more dangerous in the hands of the wrong people."

"I see where this minor capability could lead to a disaster," the professor said. "I wish now that I had not built that infernal machine! Am I the Robert Oppenheimer of the time machine?"

"Oppenheimer," Hal said, "might have regretted where his technology ended up—competing countries with the instant ability to easily, or accidentally, destroy their enemies and then to be destroyed themselves. Oppenheimer was neither the cause for that condition, nor the only discoverer of the technology. Things might have been far worse if he had abandoned the Manhattan Project—no one has drawn out *that* timeline into the future. First, there would have been a guaranteed million more deaths of Allies, and five million deaths of Japanese, over the invasion of their homeland. The Russians were also looking at atomic weapons—what if Russia was the only country to build an atomic bomb?

"The FutureView machine has *not* destroyed civilization. In the right hands, it can be a virtuous machine. It can cause criminals to be captured, dictators to be overthrown, terrorists to be found out.

"The future is not yet written. We need to regain control of the FV machine, ensure that it does not fall into the wrong hands, and keep others from ever building another machine! We are the keepers of this technology and are the only ones who can assure that it is used for good.

"It can perfectly predict manmade or even natural disasters and allow for their preemption. Imagine how many lives would be saved if we knew in advance about major earthquakes, explosions, dam breaks, the path of firestorms, landfall location of hurricanes, volcano eruptions, tsunamis, train crashes, plane crashes, chemical spills, the name of a contagious carrier before he spreads a disease. Who knows, there could be a worldwide pandemic about to happen, and we could be the only ones able to stop it!"

The professor, always one to look at the facts, said, "For the current FutureView to be of value in avoiding a catastrophe, the event would have to be instantaneous, and with no reasonable warning. Not like a hurricane making landfall, where you already have days of warning, but more like a severe earthquake, where you could at least turn off the gas lines and take cover if you had even some short notice."

Sandy added, "The problem is probably not predicting the future, but may be more in the delivery of such a message and ensuring that people take action. Even today, tsunami warnings and volcano warnings go unheeded, and, even if believed, there are few clear directions or resources to disseminate a warning message, to prevent a disaster. After all, did the Japanese not realize that a tsunami, common to their island, would flood the Fukushima nuclear power plant, located right at the ocean's edge? Did the government of New Orleans not have ten years and the funding to ensure that Lake Charles would not overflow in an inevitable Cat 5 hurricane?

"FutureView would never solve the problem of the lack of long-term preparation for inevitable disasters. But early warning could save the lives of the attentive, the prepared, the wise, and the lucky ones," she went on. "Maybe if the machine can be improved in time range and message size, it could serve like a watchtower in the forest, a time's eyeglass to send out early warnings."

"With the current FutureView machine," the professor said, "we could, at best, give a two-hour warning—provided the event occurred between 12:00 noon and 2:00 p.m. and we were instantly aware of the event when it happened."

Hal said, "If an asteroid was about to hit Cleveland, we could warn everyone to leave town, but only if it struck between 12:00 and 2:00!"

There wasn't much more to say about that. So, like all those other planners, we considered the odds of an acceptable event so unlikely that it wasn't worth further consideration.

CHAPTER 27

Patriots' Game

November 25, 2019,
10:00 a.m., Thanksgiving Day

I T WAS MOST DEPRESSING FOR a Thanksgiving morning. No thanks were given, and the only family we were with today was the FutureView team. We gathered in the hotel lobby, waiting for Hal. Sandy was reading a romance novel. The professor was on the internet, reading something deeply technical. I was also on the internet, but I was playing *PUBG* with an army of other players.

At about 10:30, we walked over to the Dunkin' Donuts for some breakfast, such as it was.

I asked no one in particular, "Are we ever going to use the password to send our own FutureView message?"

"We need to keep that in reserve. It is our only 'Get out of Jail Free' card," Sandy said.

"What do you mean by that?" I asked.

"If we ever get in trouble, we can reset time and get an instant replay," Sandy replied. "If Kevin ever realizes we somehow got the password and can send a FutureView message, he will immediately change the password. We have to be very circumspect about our use of the FV."

I don't know what "circumspect" means, but I got the message.

We entered the ordering line and slowly put together the order for our group. The people behind grew impatient.

As we returned to our table, the professor said, "Unless we have a really pressing need, I don't think we want to risk our secret of the password."

As we ate our sandwiches and donuts, Hal said, "Today is the day we give thanks—for football! The Patriots are playing a home game against the Texans."

"What time is the kickoff?" the prof asked.

"The kickoff is at 12:30, but the pregame starts at 12:00. You are all welcome to come to our room for the game." Hal wanted to go down to Foxborough to see the game, but getting tickets was impossible. He had stocked up on snacks and beer, so it sounded like a good place to have lunch and watch the game.

Hal insisted on watching the pregame BS, but the rest of us were not that interested, so we drifted in after 12:00, not ready to give the game our full attention until the kickoff. The game was supposed to start at 12:30 but was delayed because of some jerk buzzing a drone around the stadium.

I took the opportunity of the delay to use the restroom and get another beer.

The food we had included blocks of cheese cut with a wire cheese cutter. The cheese Hal had included soft French Brie, hard Cheddar, Gorgonzola, Gouda, Swiss Gruyere, Danish Havarti, and French Roquefort.

The Patriots won the coin toss, so the Texans kicked off. The kickoff happened at 12:55. The Texans followed the airborne football downfield.

Then, suddenly, a tremendous *bang* sounded. It was so loud you could hear the echo from every television down the hotel hallway!

Since the camera was following the ball, we saw the explosion in the ground-level stands, throwing bodies and seats in the air. The explosion must have killed dozens, and a lot more were maimed! It would shock the country. No doubt the timing of the explosion was intentional, to show it live on TV to a large audience.

Hal finally spoke. "You know what just happened? An asteroid just hit Cleveland. This is the disaster that FutureView may actually help us prevent!"

I looked at the time on my laptop. I quit my computer game and opened the FutureView app.

Sandy put her hand over my keyboard and said, "We have time. Let's get as much information as we can pack into thirteen characters."

I wished, then, that I had created a disaster codebook for thirteen-character messages—something you only think of when it's too late.

Hal grabbed the hotel notepad and began writing trial messages. By his violent strokes, he must have been doing some quick edits.

I entered the password: *TIMESCAPE*. It worked!

The TV cameras scanned the scene, but most of the shots were unintelligible. We couldn't tell where the camera was pointing or what was happening under the smoke.

"Well, we should at least wait to see if there are secondary explosions, or if the announcers give any useful information," Sandy said.

The cameras showed people running, carrying bodies, screaming for help, and a large hole in the bleachers.

"The best I can make out is that it's on the north side, at the Texans' forty-yard line, in the front stands," I said.

I looked at the clock—it was 1:09. I set the message arrival time to 11:10 a.m.

"It's getting late, Hal! There's no more information coming. Tom! Send the message!" Sandy screamed.

Hal held up the pad of paper for all to see. There were cross-outs, but Hal had clearly circled one message:

BOMPATS125540

I counted the characters—thirteen exactly.

"I'm not sure how clear that message is!" cried the prof.

Hal said, "*I* will know what it means—send it, Tom!" He tossed the paper pad to me.

I entered our last words in my journal and saved the file to the FutureView tail memory. Then I entered the message.

Will we be any more prepared when we receive this message than we were when we sent it?

I hit "return," for certain this time.

CHAPTER 28

Patriots' Game 2

November 25, 2019,
11:10 a.m., Thanksgiving Day

W E SAT SILENTLY EATING OUR "breakfast" at the Dunkin' Donuts when we all heard that terrifying *ding* from my laptop. I opened the message immediately.

BOMPATS125540

"What does that mean?" I asked myself. It's too bad the tail message doesn't get transmitted with the message, but only appears after it's too late!

Hal answered, "An asteroid just hit Cleveland! The FutureView message we all feared!"

The prof said, "A bomb? At 12:55 today? But where?"

Hal shouted, "Isn't it obvious? There's a bomb that's going to go off at the Patriots game at 12:55 today in Foxborough!"

"Are you sure?" Sandy asked.

"Yes! I probably *wrote* this message!" he said.

"What does 'forty' mean?"

"It's probably a clue where the bomb is—we'll figure it out later. We need to leave—*now!*"

"I'll call 9-1-1," the prof said.

"*Wait!*" Sandy interrupted. "What are you going to say?"

The professor thought about it, mumbled something, and said nothing.

Sandy continued, "You're going to have to explain how you know about the bomb. They will already have your phone number and our location. They will ask you for your name."

Hal interrupted, "Let's figure it out on the road. If we leave now, we might make it in time!"

As we ran back to the hotel, he shouted, "Grab what you need! I'll drive."

I had my coat, cell phone, and laptop. What else could I need? I headed down to the parking lot while the others returned to their rooms. I set my laptop and half a cup of coffee on the roof of the Barracuda and powered up my computer.

At that point, we knew as much as you, the reader, do now.

What would you do, knowing only what you have read so far? In hindsight, today, it is pretty obvious what we should have done after receiving that message. But it wasn't the first thing we did, by a long shot.

The prof, Sandy, and I stood around the Barracuda waiting for Hal. I couldn't imagine what he needed to get since it looked like half of Hal's stuff was in the back seat. Sandy took out a credit card and scraped the frost off the driver's side of the windshield while we waited. The hatchback rear window would have to wait until we could get some heat on it.

Hal came out of his room and raced down to the parking lot. The Barracuda was from a time before remote car keys, so we had to stand in the cold until Hal could work his key into the iced-over door lock.

We all had our cellphones, of course. We were shocked when Hal produced a Glock G29 subcompact handgun and slipped it into the lower pocket of his cargo pants, along with a box of bullets. There was no time to ask where, when, or how he'd gotten it. It would be tough enough to get to Gillette Stadium, down in Foxborough, in time. We had to get on the road.

We were probably half an hour from the stadium on a normal day without thousands of others trying to get to the stadium. Hal was up to it, and took off smartly from the parking lot, leaving rubber where the tires hit dry asphalt and spinning wildly where the tires hit pavement wet from melting snow.

It was 11:16 when we finally departed from the hotel. While there are speed limits, there are no acceleration limits, so Hal took every advantage of his high-torque gearing. The fact that there were speed limits was also irrelevant, and Hal flaunted those limits, too. At least he kept an eye out for state troopers as he maintained a very respectable speed on the highway.

"Hal, didn't you say the game was to start at 12:30? Is that when they start the speeches or the actual kickoff?" Sandy asked.

"No, that's the kickoff time."

"But the bomb goes off at 12:55. If I were the bomber, I would want it to go off right at kickoff, when everyone is intently watching the game."

"Maybe the game was—or will be—delayed for something."

"Ah, I see what you're getting at, Sandy," the professor added. "If the bomb was going to be set off with a timer, and the start of the game was delayed, then probably half the fans, and the camera operators too, might be out getting hot dogs. The bomb *must* be command-detonated!

"If I were a terrorist and were going to do something this dramatic, I would sure want to be there to control the event and to set off the bomb at the precise time when the fans are all there and the TV cameras are looking directly at the stands where the bomb is hidden," Sandy added.

"And, incidentally, to watch for anyone tampering with his baby," Hal added.

"Yes," said Sandy. "If you were to call 9-1-1 about a bomb threat, they would probably evacuate the crowd. Before anyone could leave, the bomber would detonate the bomb."

It didn't take long for the highway patrol to scan the Barracuda and take flight after us. Hal kept a good lead, but another patrol car soon joined the race. We were still a long way from Foxborough, and this wasn't California.

"Hal, do you want me to call 9-1-1?" the professor asked.

"Go ahead!" he shouted.

Hal was swerving violently around traffic, so the professor entered the number on his cell, put it on speaker, and held the phone out for Hal to speak into it.

There was one ring, then: "What is your emergency?"

"I have an emergency and need to speak to the commander of the Massachusetts State Police out of the Framingham office. Could you connect me?"

"Yes, one moment, please. What is your name, sir?"

"This is Agent Blunt, out of the Boston FBI office," Hal said.

A moment later: "This is Commander Stevenson. What can I do for you, Agent Blunt?"

Hal went into his act and said, "I am currently attempting to reach Gillette Stadium, where a bomb has been emplaced. I believe a state trooper is pursuing me. Could you communicate with the officer and have him call me at this number? I am driving a red Plymouth Barracuda."

"Let me see what I can do. I'll have the officer call you."

A minute later, a call came in.

"Mass state pol-eese. This is Officer Harding. Is this Blunt?"

Hal replied, "This is Agent Blunt. Sorry, Officer, but I must get to the stadium. It's a matter of life and death. I have three civilians with me, and we need to get to Foxborough to prevent a terrorist bombing. I could sure use your help in getting an escort to the gate. The civilians I have with me are the only ones who can identify the terrorist. The terrorist is undoubtedly prepared to detonate the bomb or bombs if there is any attempt to evacuate the stadium or conduct a search. I need you to arrange for the stadium security, police, SWAT, and bomb squad personnel to meet me at the security office. Pass me and I will follow you to the gate. And, Officer—no sirens."

Harding started to say something when Hal ended the call.

"When you get the answer you want, stop talking," Hal always said.

Hal didn't even slow down. Eventually, Harding passed us and continued on. With his red and blue lights and an occasional chirp from his loudspeaker, we made it to the gate.

We pulled in front of an unlabeled side door of the stadium. The door was being held open by a guy that could have been an ex-Patriot. Officer Harding stopped his patrol car and got out, as did we. It was 12:11 p.m.

We entered a dimly lit tunnel hallway, then went up some stairs to a small office area. The guy who appeared to be in charge was an older, overweight, mean-looking dude.

"Special Agent Blunt, I presume? Could I see a little identification?"

Hal actually reached for his wallet but kept up the bluff. "We have a *bomb* in the stadium, and a *bomber* with a *dead-man* switch. It will go off at the start of the game. Let's not stop to chat just now."

While we were all looking toward the head guy, the cops approached us from behind. Hal turned quickly to see the approaching officers and backed away. Only Sandy figured out that our quest was about to end.

Head Guy became more aggressive, and said, "We checked with the FBI, and they have no record of you. If you don't have some identification, we're going to have to wait for a confirmation from Washington before we go anywhere."

"But what if I'm telling the truth?" Hal quickly responded, "Are you going to risk a bomb?!"

The professor, Sandy, and I were behind Hal. One cop then moved past me with his gun drawn, and a pair of handcuffs ready in the other hand.

Sandy whispered to me, "Hal's bluff is going to end—badly." She then started yelling, "Watch it! He has a gun in his left pocket!"

Everyone drew guns. Hal put up his hands immediately. They pulled him to the ground, then turned him over and cuffed him. The security chief led the rest of us to his office, while the police searched Hal, removed his Glock, and forced him to follow.

Sandy put on a show almost as good as Hal's. She started sobbing, messed up her hair, and started ranting like she was the victim of a carjacking.

"I was the victim of a carjacking!" she said. "My husband and I were taking my father to the hospital when we stopped at a light. This crazy guy then drew his gun and hijacked us. He drove us at dangerous speeds until the cops caught up. Then he used that phony story about being an FBI agent to get us here. Now, he told us that his 'comrades' planted a bomb in the stadium, and he had to get here in a hurry, to be part of the plot! You've got to find that bomb before it's too late!"

The security chief said, "I don't think we have anything to worry about, ma'am. We always run a full inspection for explosives before opening the stadium. We have dogs sniffing for any explosives. No one could even get a firecracker through the gate."

As they pulled Hal away, he looked at me and said, "Tom, I hope you're keeping a good journal on all this."

I understood. They hauled him off. I checked my watch. It was 12:30.

"Or maybe the bomb isn't put there until later," the prof whispered to me. "Or maybe it's well-hidden. But we already know, from the FutureView message, that *all* the current security measures *will be ineffective* in stopping this bomb. The *only* way this bombing can be prevented *has* to come from *us!* Any previous security measures are destined to be defeated!"

The Head Guy reassured Sandy, "Don't worry, ma'am. We're professionals at this. We know what we're doing."

What I had to do was clear. I entered the password to send a FutureView message. It was now 12:32 p.m., with enough time separation from the 1:10 p.m. transmission to prevent overheating of the FutureView machine. I would send the message to arrive at 10:30, pushing the limits of the FutureView time range. That was as far back as I could trust receiving the message.

At 10:30, we were in the hotel lobby and would likely hear the *ding*. There was no time to create a better message.

Before I did this, I closed the journal.

CHAPTER 29

Patriots' Game 3

November 25, 2019,
10:30 a.m., Thanksgiving Day

I T WAS MOST DEPRESSING FOR a Thanksgiving morning. No thanks were given, and the only family we were together with today was the FutureView team. We gathered in the hotel lobby, waiting for Hal. Sandy was reading a romance novel. The professor was on the internet, reading something deeply technical. I was also on the internet, but I was playing *PUBG* with an army of other players.

At about 10:30, we were ready to walk over to the Dunkin' Donuts when I heard the terrifying *ding* from my laptop.

The message was unexpected, as, of course, are all the messages from FutureView. I motioned to the others, and they quickly gathered around.

BOMPATS125540

"What does that mean?" I asked.

Hal answered, "An asteroid just hit Cleveland! The FutureView message we all feared!"

The prof said, "A bomb? At 12:55 today? But where?"

Hal shouted, "Isn't it obvious? There's a bomb that's going to go off at 12:55 today at the Patriots game in Foxborough!"

"Are you sure?" Sandy asked.

"Yes! I probably *wrote* this message!" he said.

"What does 'forty' mean?"

"It's probably a clue where the bomb is—we'll figure it out later. We need to leave—*now!*"

"I'll call 9-1-1," the prof said.

"*Wait!*" Sandy interrupted. "What are you going to say?"

The professor thought about it, mumbled something, and said nothing.

Sandy continued, "You're going to have to explain how you know about the bomb. They will already have your phone number and our location. They will ask you for your name."

Hal interrupted, "Let's figure it out on the road. If we leave now, we might make it in time!"

As we ran back to the hotel, he shouted, "Grab what you need! I'll drive."

I had my coat, cell phone, and laptop. What else could I need? I headed down to the parking lot while the others returned to their rooms. I set my laptop and half a cup of coffee on the roof of the Barracuda and powered up the computer.

The prof, Sandy, and I stood around the Barracuda waiting for Hal. I couldn't imagine what he needed to get since it looked like half of Hal's stuff was in the back seat. Sandy took out a credit card and scraped the frost off the driver's side of the windshield while we waited. The hatchback rear window would have to wait until we could get some heat on it.

Hal came out of his room and raced down to the parking lot. The Barracuda was from a time before remote car keys, so we had to stand in the cold until Hal could work the key into the iced-over door lock.

We all had our cellphones, of course. We were shocked when Hal produced a Glock G29 subcompact handgun and slipped it into the lower pocket of his cargo pants. There was no time to ask where, when, or how he'd gotten it. It would be tough enough to get to Gillette Stadium, down in Foxborough, in time. We had to get on the road.

"You know, there is something strange about this message," the professor said, looking at my laptop. "This message was sent at 12:32. The bombing will happen at 12:55, and the game is supposed to start at 12:30."

Hal had arrived with a gym bag; he threw it in the back seat. He was wearing his Patriots jersey with the name "Izzo" on the back.

"Why the shirt?" Sandy asked.

"As long as we have a few minutes, I thought I might dress like a fan to be less obvious."

We got in the car and Hal accelerated rapidly. I noted the time: 10:40.

"The prof thinks the time of the message is screwy," I said. "The message was sent *before* the bomb was detonated. Maybe we just found out early."

Hal bolted for the entrance ramp to the interstate.

"It's not likely that we could have found out any earlier than the time the bomb went off. We probably saw it on TV," the prof said. "I surmised that this might not have been the first FV message sent— just the first one we received."

Hal accelerated, going through the manual gears, shifting at high rpm.

"So, you think, in order to give us more time, we just relayed the message back in time?" I asked.

"If that were the scenario, why didn't we just transmit a little after noon, as soon as it was feasible, to give us the greatest advance warning?" Sandy asked.

Hal was weaving between cars, accelerating to 80 mph.

"What more likely happened is that we attempted to do something and failed. That would explain the delayed transmission," the prof said.

Hal got into a stretch of open highway and sped up to 90.

Sandy added, "Well, judging by what we just did, I would have to assume that, upon receiving the first message, we also would have headed for the stadium. We must have failed, or been close to failing, and realized the best path forward would be to just relay the message back to an earlier time! Maybe we crashed or were arrested for speeding."

Hal let up on the accelerator and the engine braked our speed down to 75.

"So, should we just try to do the opposite of what we most likely would have done, sort of like George Costanza?" I asked.

"Well, no," Sandy said, "It's hard to define what the opposite is. We might think about trying a different approach from our first thoughts. We also have at least a half hour more time than the last time we did this."

True to these estimates, another *ding* from my laptop heralded the arrival of a message. The time was 11:10.

"Want to bet what that message is?" Sandy said.

I quickly downloaded it.

BOMPATS125540

"This confirms the prof's theory. The first message we received must have been relayed from this message," I said.

We continued on toward Foxborough, but the traffic was getting heavier. I checked the WAZE app on my cell phone and saw considerable congestion ahead. I warned Hal.

To top it off, there was now a patrol car behind us. Hal kept looking in the mirror, nervously.

The traffic was getting thicker until it totally stopped. Hal pulled to the shoulder and skidded to a stop, jumped out, and waved to the cop behind us. I rolled down my window to hear.

"Hi. My name is Harold Izzo. My friends call me Hal. You may have heard of my brother, Ryan, who played for the Pats? I'm playing in today's game, but I'm *really* late. Could you help me get to the stadium?" Hal said.

He looked enough like Ryan Izzo to pass as his brother.

Hal rushed back to the car as the patrol car put on its lights and siren. The cop passed us and drove down the shoulder of the road. Hal followed.

"Officer Harding is going to lead us in," Hal said.

Then, at 11:40 a.m., another *ding*. I downloaded the message.

TOMFINDDRONE

The message looked pretty straightforward, so there was no discussion. Hal simply said, "At least *you* know what to do when we get there."

We were now approaching the stadium. Hal drove into the parking lot, rolled down the window, and waved off the highway patrol. Officer Harding waved back, then turned away.

It was now 12:00 noon. Hal stopped the car, and we ran swiftly to the admin entrance. Hal pressed the doorbell, then spoke into the speaker. "This is Special Agent Blunt. I need to see the head of security—immediately!"

The intercom went silent. We waited. The door opened.

"I'm with Security. What can I do for you?"

Hal rushed in, and we followed. "I believe there is a bomber in the stadium," he said. "We don't know his intentions, or where or whether he has placed a bomb here yet.

"This is my communication assistant, Thomas Edison…yes, that's his name. This is Professor Johnson, and this is Ms. Sandy O'Brien. They are witnesses to this bomber and can identify him. I need you to get a bomb squad ready, but keep them inside the concourse, out of sight. *Now*! My team will walk through the most likely seats to look for the bomber."

Sandy pulled up a layout of the stadium on her cell phone. We followed suit.

The security agent stood in front of Hal and said, "You sure as hell don't look like an FBI agent. Show me some identification."

"I'm sorry," said Hal. "My identification and my wallet were lost when we found out about the bombing. We could all wait for the FBI to respond, in case I might be trying to get into the stadium just to see the game for free, but then I could be telling the truth, and dozens will die. What are you going to do?"

"Well, I guess we'll go along with you."

"I am wearing this outfit to fit in with the rest of the fans. We don't want to spook this guy. He may have already set up a bomb and could detonate it remotely if he even suspects we are aware of his plans! Therefore, keep any uniformed officers and your staff out of sight. No one is to follow us or be anywhere near us. Here is my cell phone number. Give me a phone number to reach you when we find out where the bomb is."

"Anything described sufficiently fast is indistinguishable from genius." Wasn't that what Hal used to say?

We all headed out of the concourse to view the field. It was 12:15.

The stadium was huge, and fans filled the whole stadium. We couldn't possibly find a needle in this giant haystack!

"Hal, where do we go to look for the bomb?" Sandy asked.

"Look," Hal said, "the cameras are all on the south side of the field to avoid looking into the sun. The bomb will have to be on the north side."

"Forty—must mean something about the location—forty-yard line?" I asked.

"But there are two forty-yard lines," Sandy said.

Hal answered, "Depending on the coin toss, one team will kick from the thirty-five-yard line on one end of the field, and the other team will receive the ball and run back. The bomb must be emplaced near one of the forty-yard lines, and the bomb will probably be detonated when the ball, and all the TV cameras, are at that forty-yard line."

"We still don't know which forty," the prof said.

They then held the coin toss. The quarterbacks from each team moved to the center of the field and the referee tossed the silver dollar. The ref announced the results. "The Texans have won the toss and choose to receive the kickoff." The Patriots lined up for the kickoff, and the Texans dispersed at the other end of the field.

Hal shouted, "The ball is going to be kicked by the Patriots from their thirty-five-yard line toward the Texans. The cameras will probably follow the ball through the air, or when it is returned to the Texan forty-yard line. That's where the bomb is!" He pointed to the lower seats at the forty-yard line. "Let's go!"

Suddenly, a small camera multirotor helicopter drone flew down to the field and headed straight for the ball. Whistles stopped the game.

"Tom, there's your drone! Find the pilot!" Hal yelled.

But I was already ahead of him. Since I had been expecting the drone, I was watching the stands where the drone had first appeared and headed there to find the pilot.

Hal called on my cell and said, "Let's keep this call open so we can let each other know what's going on." I put on my earbuds and put my phone back in my pocket.

Hal, the professor, and Sandy moved swiftly down the concourse to the section nearest to the Texan's forty-yard line. They passed a concession stand along the way.

Hal bought Patriots' jerseys on the run, throwing money at the concessionaire, and handed them to Sandy and the prof. "Put these on—you need to look like the rest of the fans."

He looked at his watch and said, "It's 12:15. Remember, we are safe until 12:55, unless, of course, the bomber spots us messing with his bomb."

Hal said into the phone, "Tom, you need to stay far away from us, but keep us in sight. If anything goes wrong, send another FutureView message. Now, go look for your drone, and let's keep this phone call open."

While looking for the drone operator, I thought about the thirty-minute cooldown requirement for the FutureView machine. The first bomb message we got today was sent at 12:32. The original bomb message was sent after the bomb went off at 1:10. This last message, the drone message—I checked on my laptop—was sent at 1:40 p.m. It was now 12:25 p.m. W*ith only a two-hour time range and a thirty-minute cool-off requirement, there is no time window left to send another message!*

I raced toward the seats where the drone had first appeared. The drone started making swooping dives toward the players and the referees. If the pilot of that thing thought he was just observing, close up, he probably didn't realize how distracting the four screaming electric motors could be. The referee tried shooing it away, looking more like Buster Keaton swatting at pigeons. Between the shouting, the high-pitched drone of the drone, and the roar of the crowd, it was far from a silent movie.

The pilot had to be somewhere nearby. I looked around, knowing better than the security guards what to look for. I found one dude in the last row, wearing goggles, looking down while everyone else was looking up. *Of course!* He was watching everything through his drone's camera with a head-mounted video display! He had his hands in a large plastic garbage bag—probably working the joysticks on his transmitter in the bag.

There was an announcement of the delay in starting the game over the PA system.

Since this guy was looking only through his drone's eye, he didn't see me approach him, nor did he see how ridiculous and unofficial I looked. I grabbed his wrist and whispered forcibly into his ear, "I'm from the FAA. You *are* in violation of at least three federal rules, and I'm confiscating this drone!"

I grabbed the plastic bag out of his hand and ran down the row. He ripped the goggles off his face, but not before I quickly sat down at the end of his row. I worked the transmitter with my hands under my seat, directly observing the drone to at least keep it upright and out of trouble.

He rushed out, looking for that FAA guy. I pulled in my feet to let him pass.

From where I sat, I could see Hal, Sandy, and the professor walk down the concourse and out to the lowest level bleachers. The three separated and walked down different aisles, casually looking down the rows for anything that might be a bomb. If I were the terrorist, I would never suspect this motley crew was looking for my bomb!

However, the three ended up at the bottom row, apparently unsuccessful in finding the bomb.

I flew the drone by direct sight, hovering it high above the box suites, then checked the time on my cellphone. It was 12:52. I called Hal. "I've got the drone. What should I do with it?"

Hal said, "Damned if I know! Something will come up!"

I had to concentrate on flying the drone, but I heard Sandy's voice on my cellphone, "Hot dog steamer, halfway up!"

I pulled the drone up a safe distance and glanced over at our team. About ten rows up from the field, I saw the shiny chrome box set on an empty seat. A vendor must have just dropped it off. That explained why the pre-search never found a bomb! The vendor was long gone, but I knew he had an accomplice somewhere on the other side of the field, now intently watching that box.

Hal ripped a banner off the front of the stands, and the prof and Sandy each grabbed an end and carried it up to the row with the bomb. I figured out what they were going to do—mask the view of the bomb! I checked my watch again and realized then that they would never make it. It was 12:54 and 30 seconds! The ref whistled to start the game.

Hal turned his head, pointed to his watch, and looked at me to reset the timeline. *It can't be done! We are out of time!* The image of him looking at me was burned into my brain!

But wait, I thought, *I still have the drone!* I flew the drone down to the field again, back into the kickoff line, this time straight at the Patriots' kicker, causing him to fumble the hike! The refs were fast on their whistles! I kept my eyes on the drone and never looked back at our team. The next time I could glance at my watch, it was 12:58 p.m.

While Sandy and the prof held the ends of the banner, Hal stooped behind the banner, then reappeared out the other side. When Sandy and the prof dropped the banner, the steamer box was still sitting on the seat! The three headed smartly up the aisle and disappeared into the concourse.

The referee blew his whistle to start the game over. The kick was caught by a Texan on the twenty-yard line. He ran it back, avoiding a tackle, to the thirty, to the forty-yard line, to the fifty, and then, free of any defender, he ran for a touchdown. The crowd roared! There was no explosion!

"*Tom!*" Hal said over the phone, "Fly over to the opposite side of the field and look for anyone on their phone, probably a middle-aged male, who doesn't look interested in the game."

I did what he said.

The drone pilot was still out looking for some dude from the FAA, so I scooted back to his seat and grabbed the camera goggles he left on his seat. I then started looking for the bomber from the drone's camera, zigzagging across the stands.

Hal shouted, "You're close!"

I had no idea how he knew that, but I went into an outward spiral search from that point until I found the obvious suspect on his cell phone, binoculars in the other hand.

The game had started, but this guy was not interested. I hovered overhead, hung up my call with Hal, then called the head of stadium security. "Do you want to catch the bomber? I am the pilot of the drone, and I'm now flying right over the guy—you can't miss him. He's wearing a Patriots jacket, sitting in the Texans' stand!"

The bomber tried to escape, but he became the first tackle of the game.

I handed the equipment back to the drone pilot, let him recover the drone, and, incidentally, take the rap while I ran to the concourse to find my way back to the team.

When I got to the forty-yard line section, the game had been halted and that section of the stands was being evacuated. A sea of people filled the corridors. I fought my way through the crowd, Hal guiding me in by cellphone, and rejoined the team huddling on the side of the concourse.

"Nice thinking, Tom," Hal shouted, "delaying the game! I wouldn't want to do that again, in another timeline!"

I didn't have the chance, the voice, or the nerve to correct him. But the prof knew. I could tell by the way he looked at me, shook my hand, and said in my ear, "Closer than he thinks."

The head of stadium security came along and there were congratulations all around.

Hal explained, "I opened the lid of the hot dog steamer and saw a pile of nails, stacks of dynamite sticks, and a cellphone tied to a battery and detonator. It was pretty open. I just yanked out the cellphone."

The prof said, "Since the bomb would only be exposed for less than a minute, the bomber wouldn't waste any effort protecting it from being disarmed."

Hal continued, "When we got back to the concourse, I dialed star-sixty-nine on the bomb's phone."

Even the professor was confused and said, "What does that do?"

"That calls back the last phone caller," Hal said. "Any reasonable bomber is going to check out his bomb setup by first testing it by calling from his own phone before arming the explosives. So the last call received by the bomb phone would be the call from the bomber. I kept him on the phone until Tom could spot him with the drone."

"How did you keep him talking?"

Hal looked at Sandy, who said, "Hal handed me the phone. I don't think there is any need to go into my conversation with the bomber."

"I heard Sandy's conversation," Hal said, smiling. The two looked at each other. "When I heard the whine of your drone flying by, I told you that the drone was near the bomber."

While we were talking, none of us noticed the guy in a vendor uniform watching us. Hal saw him and offered the team, "Anyone for hot dogs?"

The vendor then reached into his hot dog steamer and pulled out a revolver, pointing it directly at Hal.

Hal had his gun in the lower pocket of his cargo pants and was in no position to draw it now. The security head was also taken by surprise. He never carried a gun.

The crowd panicked at the sound of a gunshot and everyone nearby dropped to the floor, as did I. Someone screamed.

Hal folded over and hit the floor.

He did not immediately realize that he wasn't shot. The bomber, though, was shot and fell forward to the floor.

For a second, I saw the shooter before he disappeared into the crowd.

Sandy put her hands to her face and shouted, "*Kevin!*"

CHAPTER 30

Silence

January 16, 2020

T HE MONOTONOUS SOUND OF THE clothes dryer and the warm, moist air of the laundry were getting to all of us, so we went outside, despite the light snowfall. The snow made everything quiet. Not just because it cushioned the sound of tires on pavement, stopped construction, and sent people indoors, but it seemed the falling snow itself threw a blanket over any remaining sound. Rain was just the opposite—it caused automobiles to make more noise as they splashed through rivers of water on the road.

The beatings of rain on your car, on your roof, on the street, add up to a tremendous roar. And, of course, the sound of thunder is the ultimate noise. But snow is silent and peaceful.

Kevin disappeared into the escaping crowd at Foxborough, and we never saw him again that day. A month and a half had gone by since, without our receiving any further FutureView messages. As perhaps we should have expected, Kevin also cut off our access to the transmitter function.

"The password is no longer 'timescape,'" I told Hal.

"Can we still receive messages?"

"I could gain entry to the FutureView computer for a while after the Patriots game, even though we couldn't transmit messages, but now we can't even get to the FutureView computer. It is totally offline."

"After the Patriots game, Kevin no longer had to guess about us—he *knew* we were both transmitting and receiving FV messages. He had every incentive to cut us off entirely."

"Incentive, yes," said the prof, "but I would have thought, for practical reasons, he wouldn't totally shut down access to the FV machine over the internet."

"How's that?" Hal asked.

"Well, he could easily stop us from transmitting by changing the password. Anyone who knows how to use a PC could do that. He can stop us from reading his messages by using some simple cipher—a letter substitution code. That would be a pain, but it could also protect him from his own people who might get a little greedy," the professor said.

"Shutting down the machine, or removing it from the internet, would be as simple as pulling the plug, something Kevin could also do. But if Kevin shut down the machine, it would defeat his entire purpose! Even pulling the internet connection would disable the remote controller, only hurting his own capability. He could, of course, spend his time in the Green Building, directly operating the machine," said Hal.

There was a pause in the conversation.

"Maybe I'll just go by the Cambridge lab today and see if I can get any information from the guards there about what he's doing," Hal said.

"Don't let Kevin see you there!" Sandy said.

I went back to my hotel room, then heard a car door slam and the unmistakable sound of Hal's Barracuda driving off, though the snow muffled the sound of his tires.

That afternoon, Hal knocked on my door and shouted out that he was calling a meeting in his room. I shut down my computer and joined the others in Hal's suite.

"Kevin's not in the Green Building," he said.

"Kevin wasn't there?" I asked.

"No, I mean, the lab was empty. The entire machine was gone. Nothing left but dangling power lines. Even the water-cooling system and the high-voltage insulators were removed."

"No one who looked at the machine would bother to take the plumbing," the professor said. "If I were moving the machine, I would build a better cooling system. It would work better and take less time than dealing with that rat's nest!"

"So, clearly, *you* didn't steal the machine!" Hal answered.

"Well, that's somewhat good news," Sandy said.

"That I didn't steal the machine?" the prof asked.

"No. That means that Kevin and his technicians wanted to move the machine but didn't have a clue how anything worked. So, the best they could do is to reassemble it *exactly* like it was set up in Cambridge."

***

We spent the next month trying to find Kevin and the time machine. Nothing was apparent from checks on the internet and in the business news. We looked for any sign that he might have gone back to the Holland cottage, his house, his office, or the FutureView Waltham office. We looked at some of Kevin's local hangouts, but there was no sign of Kevin or the machine.

Of course, we all considered his "Quantum of Solace" or whatever it was called. But we concluded Quantum was an apartment, or an office, or a cabin in the woods. He might have been there, but none of the sites where Kevin could be holed up were sites that could house the power-hungry FutureView monster machine. A month went by. We thought we might never find out where Kevin was. Then Hal called a meeting of the team to figure out what to do.

"We only have a limited time to find Kevin. With the lottery money he has now, he can change the internet connectivity, add serious encryption, or make several changes that could keep the machine secret from us. It's only a matter of time." the professor said.

"And, given enough time and money, he can have the technology reverse-engineered, and there's no telling where that would lead," Sandy said. "Even if he couldn't improve on the machine, he could build duplicate machines."

"It wouldn't take sophisticated knowledge of physics to add massive electrical power capability and the cooling system to go with it. That could expand the time range and the message length," the professor added.

Hal said, "Sam, if you haven't already, why don't you keep an eye out for anyone looking to hire physicists to deal with time travel? They probably won't come right out about it in a recruiting ad, but you could probably make up a phony resume that has all the right experience, post it on the recruiting websites, and see who puts a fishline in the pond."

"Sandy, if you could monitor the stock market to look for any trends that show someone is too smart for lucky. I don't know if there are any statistical methods to find out if FutureView is being involved."

"I'll see what I can do," she said. "If an unforeseeable event causes a major change in price of a stock or contract, then the successful buyer, or seller, would have to either be psychic or be Kevin. I can also compare markets with statistical histories, but I'm afraid if it's affecting major markets, we are already too late."

"Well, Tom, what can you do?" Hal said.

"I am still monitoring the internet connection for FutureView messages. If Kevin ever restarts the FutureView computer with a connection online, the FutureView computer will send a system diagnostic message over the internet. Kevin or Kevin's people would not be aware of this happening, but we should get a notice. I will, of course, keep my laptop on and monitor for FutureView messages."

"Well, thanks, everyone. All we can do now is wait," Hal said.

I stared out his window at the falling snow.

CHAPTER 31

Timebound

February 2, 2020, Groundhog Day

I EXCITEDLY CALLED EVERYONE TOGETHER AND announced, "I just got the activation message from the FutureView computer!"

"Was there any FutureView message?" Hal asked.

"No," I said, "nothing else yet. But the machine is totally back online."

"How about the tail message area?" the prof asked. "Was there anything new there?"

"I checked the tail memory to see if we possibly had our timelines realigned—but nothing has changed. I updated the journal in case there will be a change. The time machine was just down for two months. If Kevin used the machine, there's no sign of it."

I continued to monitor, hoping for a *ding* from my laptop during the morning window as I did most days, but again, there was no FV message. I was now keeping my laptop on 24/7, plugged into its charger.

In the afternoon I was deep into editing this journal, perhaps too many times, when I heard a *ding*. It was 2:45 in the afternoon, an unusual time. There was no reason the machine couldn't transmit late in the afternoon. It is just not possible to receive a message in the afternoon, when the receiver faces away from future earth. I rushed into the corridor and announced the arrival like it was a newborn child.

"Let's see the message!" Hal said as the team gathered in his room. I pulled it up.

G7R3UQ12Z7BLQ

The message was disappointing, as there was nothing intelligible about it.

"Actually, this now confirms my theory—Kevin has moved the machine to the West Coast," Sandy said.

Hal said, "All right, Sherlock, how do you figure?"

"Kevin can't play lotteries anymore—first, it requires operation late in the evening in the US, which he can't do without a receiving antenna on the other side of the globe. Even if he realized it, he would have to get some real engineering done, lease an antenna, and he doesn't have access to our special receiver/filter. Sports betting is not that lucrative, when you can find a good opportunity midday, so he's not likely to go down that path again, not after the Cicero affair. The only alternative, and frankly, the most lucrative, is to engage in market transactions in stocks, options, futures, and currencies. At least he was introduced to what is possible using stock options during our options demo."

"So what? How does that tell you where he's moved the machine?" Hal asked.

Sandy went on, "The most predictable and volatile stock price changes, and therefore stock option price changes, occur right after the market closes, at 4:00 in New York. That's because major announcements by companies, including changes in executives, quarterly financial reports, and other events that affect stock price are delayed and announced only after the market closes. Even though the market is closed, there is still trading activity in the aftermarket. On the West Coast the stock market closes at 1:00 p.m., Pacific time, so he can easily send a FutureView prediction after major announcements and their effect on stock prices. Kevin can buy and sell stock options with perfect knowledge of what will be reported. He doesn't need to develop an external receiver for that—not if he moves the entire FutureView machine to the West Coast. He wouldn't have to do *any* engineering at all. Keeping the receiver with the machine would also eliminate the risk of others figuring out what he is doing."

"He also wouldn't have to deal with all the snow and cold," I added.

"This message must then be related to stock price movement, in some kind of code encryption," Hal said.

The prof added, "Since these are most likely stock movements, it should be easy to find out what stocks have moved in the after-hours trading and use that information over multiple messages to break the code. I suspect Kevin is using only a simple cipher and not a complex code."

"What's the difference?" I asked.

"A cipher is a simple substitution for each letter or number digit. There is a table of what to substitute for each character. A cryptologist can break that type of code fairly quickly. I already see two sevens and two Q's. We know this message probably predicts highly profitable stock moves at the close of today's market," the prof responded.

"It's just like Kevin," Hal said, "no original thinking—just keep making money the way we showed him in the options demo. He may also have moved to set up a more secret and protected operation. Could someone be closing in on him?"

"Yes," I said. "*We* are!"

"Professor, I can get you the most likely trades Kevin was betting on today after the market closes," Sandy said.

"We won't be able to break the cipher with this one message, but if he keeps using the same cipher, every message will help break more of the code."

***

In the following days, more FutureView messages arrived at exactly the same time—2:45 p.m. Since the messages arrived regularly in time, we established a daily routine. I printed out each of the thirteen-character messages in a poster-size type font, then taped each message high on the walls around Hal's suite. Sandy searched the market results to find the most profitable trades that occurred after the market closed, then prepared a list that she handed to the prof daily, around 5:00.

The professor would write trial guesses for the encoded characters below each message. I borrowed a portable whiteboard from the hotel to keep the cipher translation table.

Around 5:30, Hal would arrive with dinner. We would all sit in the middle of the room, eat takeout, and take a stab at comparing Sandy's list of potential trades with the message and what we already knew about the cipher to translate the messages and break more of the code.

When we had a pretty good handle on the cipher, we would start earlier, as the 2:45 message arrived, to attempt to decode it immediately. I suggested we might do well trading on the same stocks and options. Hal was all for it, but Sandy was firmly against the idea, so it died. I didn't suggest it again.

Then, one day, the cipher stopped working.

"Kevin must have changed the code," the professor concluded as he dropped his scratch papers on my room desk. We all stopped trying at that point.

Sandy said, "You know, even before this, we have seen pieces of the messages that were indecipherable, literally. Well, I found some trades in exchange-traded funds, shorts, stock futures, and currency exchange rates that might have been in those messages."

Hal said, "So, you think Kevin has some people making more sophisticated trades?"

"Yes," Sandy said. "Some of Kevin's get-rich option buys could land him in trouble."

"Like what?" Hal asked.

Sandy replied, "What if Kevin didn't investigate the cause for a large swing in stock price, and it was caused by something like the CEO being killed? That might raise a lot of questions."

"I can imagine," Hal said, "that most stock price swings are owing to causes known only by the company executives. Kevin could be accused of insider trading, and he would have no defense. At least, he would have no defense that he would want to reveal."

"The dollar volume of his buys was getting big enough to interest the Feds," Sandy said, "as well as a lot of other traders. He had to move on to other trades and, I'm sure, needed to bring in experts in other types of trading vehicles."

"Do you think there may be someone else involved, a partner, not just Kevin? We need to find Kevin and the FutureView machine, and we need to do it soon," Hal concluded.

A few days later, we met again in Hal's suite.

"I think I know where Kevin moved the FutureView machine," Hal started.

"The machine needs a *lot* of electrical power, on a short-term basis. To avoid problems, you would like to avoid creating brownouts or drawing power that the power company is reluctant to provide. At least you don't want to blow circuit breakers, so you'll need a custom power line installation, like we had in Cambridge."

"On the West Coast, the Pacific Northwest has cheap, readily available power, because of the availability of hydroelectric power. California is underpowered, because of high demand and the mandate for solar or wind power," the professor said.

"But," Hal replied, "what source of electrical power is *free* and produces a peak output at midday, just when FutureView needs it? Solar power, of course. At midday, the sun shines brightest, but consumer use doesn't peak until much later in the day and evening, when more A/C is needed, people get home from work, cook dinner, watch TV, and plug in their Teslas. There's no viable storage for electrical power, so there is usually a shortage of 'clean energy' in the evening, but an inevitable excess at midday."

"Wouldn't they just shut off the solar panels when power isn't needed?" I asked.

"The power companies don't own the bulk of the solar panels. They're on rooftops of houses, stores, and factories, and on independent solar farms. They're privately owned. In California lawmakers' great wisdom, the law there *requires* power companies to buy all the solar power generated by private owners and pay full retail price for the electricity, whenever it is generated, regardless of demand! To top it off, power companies can't just disconnect the power grid either, they have to get rid of that power, and they end up actually having to pay other power companies out of state to take that excess power in midday!

"So, California is the most likely place to locate the FutureView machine, close to large sources of solar power. Southern California gets cloudless sunny days almost all year. The further north you go, there are more cloudy days, rain, and shorter days. In Southern California, it only rains enough to wash down the solar panels once a year. It's a pretty good bet that Kevin's in Southern California."

"I think I can confirm this," the prof added. "First, I have been noticing that some of the FV messages were being received pretty late in the West-Coast morning—once even after 12:00!"

"How is that even possible—given your tennis-ball theory of radio blockage by the earth?" I asked.

"Well," he continued, "we treat the time zones as if the sun peaks at exactly the local noon. Actually, on the east side of each time zone, the sun peaks later than the local noon, not to mention seasonal variations. There are some very large solar farms in the deserts of California, and the deserts are on the eastern side of the state and the time zone. I'll bet that's where the FV machine is."

"That's a pretty big territory," Sandy said.

CHAPTER 32

First Responders

February 28, 2020

W HEN WE MET AGAIN IN Hal's suite, I took the floor first. "We have been hiding out since last October, and it has been getting tiresome. I have no life. We have been searching for the elusive Kevin Brayton for quite a while, while avoiding someone who's after us. This Chinese virus is shutting down all travel, and, frankly, is putting us at risk, too! I'm really having a tough time thinking we should travel to California to find him. Maybe this is where we should stop."

"Mr. Edison," Hal said, "We have a limited opportunity to find the machine and get it back. If we stop now, we lose everything."

Sandy added, "Some may question your motivation, Hal. Is it the potential money you could make if you still controlled the machine? Is that why we are spending our lives chasing after Kevin—for you?"

The professor stepped in. "I thought we just wanted to find out who was after us and why. I was afraid that Kevin was the one, but I don't believe that anymore. He has full legal control over FutureView. That is unfortunate, but it means there is very little we can do, even if we find him. If Kevin has moved to California, has plenty of money, and now has the FV machine working, what does he care about us?"

Hal answered, "You know, professor, there are many people who, if they found out what the FV can do, would *kill* for it. I don't think we are at risk from Kevin—but I think we are at risk from others—the time machine is a golden goose. They would prefer to find Kevin and the machine. They might keep tabs on us in order to find Kevin or to force us to build them a new machine. We need to meet with Kevin and convince him he is a target, and to find out who is coming after him and us."

"Then, again," Sandy interjected, "is it possible that the people coming after us are part of Kevin's effort and want to make sure that we don't disrupt him or build another machine?"

Sandy added, "This is much bigger than winning a few lotteries, or even creating great financial wealth. While the ability to see the future seems to not be such a significant advantage, given the current short time range, the greatest advantage of the FV machine is the ability to always be right, at least in the short term, for now. The operators of the machine can redo any activity with perfect vision. Imagine what would happen with a FutureView machine with greater time range. Thomas Edison could have invented the light bulb in one try. Colonel Sanders could have perfected his chicken recipe on his first public attempt!"

"We could have found patient number one of the Coronavirus and stopped the pandemic!" I said.

"We could be using quantum computers that haven't been invented yet!" said the professor.

"Or, knowing the outcome, Hitler could have focused the Nazi efforts on early development of the atomic bomb instead of invading Russia," Sandy said.

We were silent. The machine would not be selective in supporting good versus evil futures.

"Isn't that a good thing?" I asked. "That our leaders would never make a dumbass mistake? Hell, some of them are pretty bad estimators of the future effects of even their own actions."

Sandy replied, "What if this technology got into the hands of a dictator? He could never be overthrown, could never be caught off guard. He could change any future that had him defeated. Imagine if the Terminator robot could send himself messages about the future. He could never be defeated."

"We certainly stopped a terrorist bombing at the Patriots game!" I said.

"That was not a great example. We were pretty lucky to even survive," the professor said.

"We haven't been too successful at changing the future, ourselves," I said. "I was just wondering if we shouldn't just let the government take over now."

I could see the weariness on everyone's faces. After I made this suggestion, we all looked toward Hal, as his words would clearly define our future. He hesitated. We all waited.

"I just have one thing to say," he began, then paused. "We honor the professionals in our communities who take on threats and risks for our safety and survival. These are the firemen and women, the police, the bomb techs, the soldiers, the medical technicians who put their lives at risk and who offer to do this as their job, whenever called upon. They deserve that honor. We call them 'first responders.'

"But they are not the *first* responders. The first responder is the fellow surfer who jumps off his board to rescue the swimmer attacked by a shark. He is the airline passenger who stops another passenger from lighting a fuse in his shoe. She is the witness to an automobile accident who pulls an unconscious passenger from the car just as it bursts into flames. These are the *first* responders.

"They are not trained. They are not equipped. They are not conditioned. They may be too old or too young. They may not be familiar with the area, the technology, or the threat. They are too out of shape. They are never forewarned. They do not even know their own limitations. They are seldom aware of the risks they take and often pay the price.

"But they act. They act because there is no one else. That is their only qualification, and it is the reason it is also their only duty. People will die if someone doesn't stop the bleeding, give CPR, or thrust the blockage from his throat—long before the professionals could arrive. They must act when the shooter is reloading, before the fire can reach the storage tanks, while the child is still above the water's surface and within sight.

"We are the people on the scene. *We* are the first responders. We're the only people who know how FutureView works. We are onto Kevin. The government does not know about this danger and has no basis for taking action. They don't even know how to deal with Facebook, much less FutureView. It is up to us. If FutureView gets out of control, we are the only ones who will know that we could have stopped it.

"If the only way to protect the world from an evil use of time messaging is to keep FutureView a secret, then we must *not* bring in the government, announce the technology to the world, or even warn the world about this technology. We cannot trust someone else to contain this secret. We are the only ones who can do that.

"We are the first responders. We have to pursue Kevin and regain control of the future."

I saw the team had reached the conclusion that Kevin and the FutureView machine must be stopped at any cost. There was no turning back. To the FutureView team, this was now an imperative.

"At least California will be warmer than here," I said.

CHAPTER 33

Minnie Winnie
March 1, 2020

WE ALL HAD TO LOOK at reality. We knew we were going to be gone for a while, and we needed to get our things in order. Hal arranged for movers to clear out our apartments and put everything in storage. He was careful to make sure there were no ties from the movers or the storage warehouses to any of us.

We each packed a suitcase from the storage for our trip to California. Hal paid for a service to close out our utilities, leases, and mail. It was a little shocking to depart like this, at least for me. I had never been out of the Commonwealth.

A week later, we all flew out of the Providence airport. People were getting nervous about the virus. There were fewer travelers in the airport and the middle seats were empty. International flights were being canceled. Our flight was uneventful, but I did get time to update this book and run through another clean edit, mostly for grammar mistakes.

We gathered our luggage from the carousel. I had a time gathering my stuff, as my luggage was overweight, and I'd had to buy an extra suitcase to divide up my tools. Sandy had only a carry-on bag, so I guess she wasn't bringing any formal wear. We carted everything outside to catch the hotel van to the Luxor.

I had to catch my breath. "It's as cold as hell!"

"I thought hell was supposed to be hot?" Hal said.

"Yes, and so was California!"

"You know," Sandy said, "we're not in California."

I knew we were actually in Las Vegas, not in California, but we were close enough that I expected more California-like weather. We stayed at the Luxor, on the Strip, as it was only $39 per night, one of the very few cheap expenses left in Vegas. That was, of course, not including the resort fee.

Hal headed straight for the blackjack tables. I was curious and watched for a while. He won at first but soon lost all his winnings. "You know what they say," he said, " 'What you win in Vegas, stays in Vegas.' "

Sandy continued in her role as CFO and kept whispering in his ear, probably some version of "All glory is fleeting."

We grew weary from the long day and began looking for food, avoided the expensive restaurants with long lines, and grabbed burgers at Shake Shack. It was an uneventful evening and, still being on East Coast time, we retired early to the hotel. The Luxor is an impressive imitation of a black Egyptian pyramid. Befitting the shape of the building, the elevators actually move diagonally up the building, sort of like the turbo lift in the starship *Enterprise*.

The next morning, we had to look far and wide for breakfast. I figured in Vegas, no one got up for breakfast. Fortunately, we found a Denny's on the Strip, and after breakfast, we gathered in Hal's room to figure out our next move.

The professor started, "I think our best bet for finding the FutureView machine is to look for the gimbaled antenna that we had in Cambridge."

"That will not be easy. There must be similar dish antennas all over the state!" I said.

The professor responded, "There's something unique about the FutureView antenna. Most dish antennas are receiving satellite transmissions from geosynchronous orbiting satellites. Geo satellites appear stationary in the sky because their orbits take exactly 24 hours, synchronized with the rotation of the earth. The orbits are always at the equator and very high—24,000 miles high, so any dish antenna in the northern hemisphere is going to be pointed upward and somewhat to the south. We know, however, that the FutureView antennas have to be pointed almost on the horizon, facing due west before noon and due east after noon. That should make it pretty unique."

Hal added, "There are commercial companies that produce timely aerial photographs with sufficient resolution to find our antenna. Those satellites are usually orbiting in low-earth orbits, so their cameras can be closer to the earth. By flying in a polar orbit—through the north and south poles—they can complete an orbit as the earth rotates under them, allowing their cameras to eventually cover the entire planet in wide swaths, always photographing around the local noon hour. They should have enough resolution to see a large dish antenna lying horizontally."

"There's another 'tell' for the FutureView machine," the professor said. "Kevin's going to need electrical power—plenty of it. That will require dedicated custom lines from a nearby power plant. That would be three separated cables, and the machine should be reasonably close to the power source or a substation, as it's expensive to string new power lines."

"We're going to need wheels to check out what we find, aren't we?" I said.

"I already have that figured out. Our transportation has arrived and is here in the parking garage," Hal said. We immediately headed down to the garage.

When we got off the elevator on the fourth floor, we were expecting a van or SUV, but the garage was pretty empty early in the morning—only a broken-down motor home was visible on the floor.

"There she is!" Hal said.

"Someone must have lost at blackjack," Sandy said.

Hal unlocked the entry door to the "Minnie Winnie," as it said on the side. It was a faded mustard color, with streaks of rust where the paint had once been. The front bumper had served its purpose. The

RV must have been a source of many family memories, judging from the hundred decals on the rear window and the Mickey ears silhouette on the side.

We were invited inside. Hal probably didn't notice her body language, as Sandy did not seem impressed. The RV was big enough to sleep four, even if Sandy didn't sleep with Hal, which was likely. It had a small kitchenette, with a refrigerator and storage for food. The propane stove was not working, and there was no propane tank installed, but we would be cooking in the microwave, anyway. There was a tiny bathroom with a shower, but the back of the shower stall that abutted the kitchen cabinets had been removed, probably due to water damage, and it needed to be repaired.

There was a most unusual addition to the RV that Hal was eager to demonstrate. Mounted in the ceiling above the kitchenette was a cylinder about nine inches in diameter. Hal pulled the cylinder down as it appeared to be a telescoping tube on a rotating mount. There were two arms on opposite sides of the tube that folded down into a horizontal position.

"It's a submarine periscope!" he exclaimed.

Well, it was certainly not to scale, but what a toy that must have been to the ten-year-old who traveled in this vessel! Daddy must have built the rotating mount and video camera on the roof. This was a modern version of the periscope—instead of looking through goggles, the lower cylinder was cut away, revealing a liquid-crystal video display connected to the video camera mounted on the roof. The junior commander could use it to survey the outside world. I checked out the camera on the roof. This was no toy—it was an expensive camera with motorized zoom optics and shielding from the sun. It would come in handy for our spying mission, too!

We continued to stay at the Luxor while we worked on fixing up the RV. I tapped into the video output from the periscope camera and ported it to the large-screen LED TV we installed on the wall. Since the TV had picture-in-picture capability, we could watch a game while monitoring whatever. Of course, we outfitted the RV with a hard-wired LAN, a satellite modem, a rack of storage batteries, and an inverter to provide electrical power for all the electronics.

Hal got on the phone and found a new tech company that provided real-time satellite surveillance photographs and automated photo-analysis. They could find missile launchers in Cuba—for a price. It was expensive, but we could get photo snips of every likely installation in Southern California. Hal seemed to cover the costs of our expedition, though we all tried to keep expenses down.

We kept up our monitoring of the FutureView messages from my laptop, and Sandy tried to correlate messages with large movements in the financial markets, but with limited success.

The professor tried to search for power line voltage drops that correlated with the 1:45 p.m. transmission time, since that seemed to be the regular schedule. Of course, as soon as we changed to Daylight Savings Time, we assumed the messages would be transmitted at 2:45, since midday was an hour later in the summer.

The team usually showed up in my room in the early afternoon, more to kibitz than to make sense of the daily FV messages, now deeply encoded.

"My biggest fear is that Kevin cuts us off from access to the FV messages," Hal said.

"There's no reason to do that now that he is encrypting the messages," the prof said.

I looked at them and gave them the bad news. "There was no FV message today. That is unusual for a business day, so I checked for a tail message at about 3:00 p.m., long after the assumed transmission time, to see if a message was transmitted. The access was dead. We no longer have any internet access to the FutureView computer!"

CHAPTER 34

Radio Research

March 22, 2020

"I GUESS WE GO BLIND FROM here," I said.

"Wait," Hal responded. "We had our remote receiver in Jakarta—why not build another receiver processor and antenna in California and receive the FutureView messages directly? Unless Kevin, or Kevin's people, get very sophisticated and start changing the message signature, we should still be able to intercept their messages."

The professor said, "I think by pulling the internet connection, they've protected the time machine from anything we might do. They would have no reason to add further complications."

"As far as building another receiver," I added, "that should be easy. I'm sure we can get all the parts we need. Las Vegas has a lot more than casinos these days. I think I still have the filter software stored on my laptop."

"But isn't the transmitter antenna going to be aiming directly at the location of Kevin's receiver antenna, not our antenna?" I asked.

"That's OK, Tom," the prof said, "the beam disperses so much over the distance between past earth and future earth that there is no need for the receiver antenna to be pointed exactly at the transmitter antenna. If we find a good antenna that can receive in X-band, in California, that will be good enough."

Hal handed me his credit card. "Be frugal," he said.

"And one more thing," Hal continued, "I got the satellite photos in from the automated pattern search for horizontal dish antennas. They found some candidates and sent us the photos. We should take a close look at them."

"I sense a road trip coming!" I said.

The satellite survey found fifty potential antenna sites. Applying the requirement for there to be three-phase electrical power, and therefore three separated wires going into the facility on high-voltage glass insulators, we narrowed it down to eighteen potential sites, all across California. We didn't even want to think about whether we should also look in Nevada or Arizona. We could also miss the site just because the antenna was down for repairs or the power lines were underground.

I plotted a road trip that had us going to each of the eighteen sites using a Traveling Salesman algorithm I downloaded. We packed up our bags and checked out of the Luxor. Hal covered the bill, but not without first reviewing each of the charges. Perhaps he was getting more careful about planning for future expenses, or maybe he was just running short of cash—or both.

We moved into the Red Rock RV Park at the edge of town, like some snowbird tourists. There I assembled the receiver filter unit, built into a desktop computer. We also bought many electronic parts, automotive parts, and "living room" parts to fix up the RV, on Hal's credit card.

It took us three weeks to get everything working. We weren't totally ready, but Hal disconnected the utilities early one morning, and off we went. He said, "We need to get going. In project management, it's called 'time to shoot the engineer.'"

We departed Las Vegas heading toward California. We left so quickly, I hoped we might get breakfast on our way out of town. But the transition from twenty-story casinos to empty sage was so sudden that we didn't see any place to stop.

"There's another casino up ahead," Hal said. "It used to be the last chance to get gas and water before heading out into the real desert. Today, it is the last chance to gamble away your last dollar."

I saw the sign for Primm, Nevada, and Whiskey Pete's Casino at the California border. Since we were already driving in the slowest lane, we couldn't miss the exit. Hal pulled up to the casino entrance and let us off at the curb.

"I'll move over to the gas pumps. Just bring me back a sausage and egg sandwich and a cup of coffee, one cream," he said to no one in particular, avoiding the impression that he was asking Sandy to do a "woman's chore." But it was to no avail.

We had an uneventful breakfast amid the clatter of the slot machines. We ordered our breakfasts, and Sandy quietly added an egg white and spinach sandwich to go. I paid for the breakfast, and a big tip, using Hal's credit card. We walked from the casino to the gas pumps. The temperature was still tolerable, but even in the early morning, Ole Sol reminded us who dominates the desert. We stood in the sun while Hal paid for the gas.

"It sure is lovely. You can see the mountains in California from here, like they're much closer than they seem," the prof said.

"I'm sure that was the talk on the wagon train when they got here, too," Hal said.

"And they probably didn't see the interstate going over the mountains," I replied.

"I'll bet the settlers didn't have a view of that, either," Sandy said, pointing to large circular clusters of what looked like solar panels on the rising slopes in the distance.

We boarded, and Hal started the slow drive up that mountain, as Teslas with dark-tinted windows, fully loaded semis, and the desert temperature all climbed ahead of us.

The professor sat at the kitchenette table and perused an antique Auto Club road map. The creases were well worn.

"I've already plotted our itinerary on Google Maps and mounted my phone so Hal could see the turn-by-turn and hear Siri give directions," I said. It was a good thing that I wired the RV with USB ports directly to the upgraded car battery to continuously charge our devices.

"You know, we're headed toward Barstow," the prof said. "Just outside of Barstow is the NASA Goldstone Deep Space Network station. I've never been there, but it could be a great place to find an antenna."

"We're going to be on a long trip. I think we can make a stop at Goldstone if it's on the way," Sandy said.

We stopped in Barstow and had lunch at Tom's Restaurant, where we all had hamburgers. Mine came with pickles that didn't sit well with me. It was hotter than hell outside, and there is nothing further I can say about Barstow. From there, we headed north.

Goldstone was not on our way. It was nowhere near Barstow. Barstow was just the last town with people in it. Goldstone had some big antennas, for sure. We're talking about dish antennas thirty meters across and weighing a thousand tons!

"These antennas were the means to communicate with every spaceship since Project Mercury!" said the professor. "Today, they are talking to the Mars rovers. You could put our entire FutureView lab inside one of these dish antennas."

We took the full tour. As soon as the prof heard that the earlier antennas were being used for odd jobs or were being decommissioned, we had our choice of the best X-band antennas on earth.

By the end of the day, we had installed my receiver box and tested it on a massive dish antenna kneeling toward the western horizon. Hal had convinced NASA that we were tracking a lost space probe stuck in space at the L5 Lagrange Point. The NASA center was more interested in justifying their contribution to science than adhering to any budget.

The rest of the road trip was extremely uneventful. We drove thousands of miles around California, going from one site to another, looking for the FutureView antennas. At some spots we could just drive by, see the site, and realize that FutureView would not be there. Other times, we had to camp out and reconnoiter. When we did so, we had to be cautious about getting too close. If it were really the FutureView site, Kevin would have it well guarded, and we, especially, would not be welcome. We knew we were now dealing with an opponent with nearly unlimited funds, and that would make it extremely dangerous.

Fortunately, there was now some interesting activity in the X-band. Soon after we installed our receiver at Goldstone, we started again receiving FutureView messages, transmitted through the internet to my laptop. We didn't have access to the FutureView computer, as it was still offline. As Hal predicted, Kevin had relaxed their security after they removed the internet connection, and their messages were no longer encoded.

It seemed Kevin had figured there was no longer a need to go through the encoding, then decoding—or the other way around, in this case.

The messages comprised stock symbols and option choices, as before. Sandy estimated that the potential trades were now generating tens of millions of dollars.

"I've figured out how Kevin is handling his stock trades," she said. "A reasonable investor or trader, even one willing to bet heavily on risky bets, will not double the risk in order to make only 5 percent more. The risk versus reward would not make sense, even for a gambler. But if you have FutureView, you are really taking no risk at all, and Kevin's people were buying everything they could cram into thirteen characters and winning every time.

"I've noticed another alarming situation," she went on. "Kevin's operation has opened an investment fund that is available to 'qualified' private investors. Their success rate must be phenomenal, probably well over 100 percent return annually. They are attracting so much business that it's affecting the market itself. But there's something worse happening. They now have such a reputation for success that their investments have become self-fulfilling. They may soon realize that they can manipulate the market. We have seen this phenomenon in the past—recently in some market niches like cryptocurrencies. Once you attain the ability to create your own success, you can 'pump and dump' anything, creating false expectations and stealing investors' money."

"Isn't that illegal?" Hal asked.

"Yes," Sandy replied, "but the gears of government are slow to turn. These ventures usually fail on their own, even if the Feds doesn't intervene, because eventually they lose their reputation and lose money. Every hot investment scheme at some point will take too much risk and will fail. But Kevin may never reach that point, because of FutureView. He will always know the future and does not have to fail. He could continue to grow without limits! This is extremely dangerous!"

"We have to find Kevin and the FutureView machine," said the prof. "Time is not on our side."

CHAPTER 35

No Dill Pickles

May 2, 2020

O NE DAY WE SAW AN unusual, text-only FutureView message.

NODILLONINTRV

"No dill pickles on hamburgers in travels," I said. "That is wise advice."

"I don't know," said Sandy. "It must be important—they gave up a lot of potential profits to send this message."

We started seeing more of these nonfinancial messages between stock messages. A week later, another strange message arrived.

NOCOMMENTJEWS

"Now this message is a total waste!" the prof said. "FutureView can only send thirteen-character messages, and whoever sent this one didn't even bother with abbreviations! Even if Kevin wanted to send this message, he wouldn't have done it so crudely. Someone else must have higher priority over the FV machine and is using it to give advice."

"Hardly specific advice at that," Hal said. "Something my mother might have said. Come to think of it, though, it's probably a lawyer's thousand-dollar advice…"

"…or a political consultant's million-dollar advice!" Sandy added.

"It sounds like political advice," said the prof. "Maybe we can find something in the news that would correlate with these messages."

Sandy said, "There's a recall effort to remove the governor of California. A lot of candidates are already running as if it's an election campaign. Maybe one candidate is getting some extra support from Kevin. We should watch for any candidate who might have a press conference early this afternoon."

Hal said, "Since the message is directing what *not* to do, you might have a hard time finding out which candidate is using this message. It could be reasonable advice for anyone. It could even be an inside joke because no one could come up with a winning stock market tip today!"

"I'll get on the internet, anyway," Sandy said. "Let's keep the TV on the news today and see what we can find."

Sandy got on the internet and checked the schedules of the candidates. "Goldmine!" she exclaimed, "*All* the candidates are having a debate today at 12:30 in Fresno. If we leave now, we could make it just in time."

We kept the TV news on as we drove. I was glad that I had thought about installing the tracking antenna for the RV, which kept the antenna aimed at our broadcast satellite as we drove, allowing uninterrupted television.

Driving through the Central Valley past all the empty farmland that no longer grew crops was not very exciting, so when news broke with a flash headline, we all watched intently.

"There was a mass shooting just this hour at the Temple Beth Chabad Synagogue in San Jose," the announcer said. "Observers reported hearing several shots from automatic weapons. The police are on the scene now and are assessing the situation before going in. The police have stated that there is no indication of terrorist involvement."

"Well," I said, "there's your Jewish connection! They're declaring no indication of terrorism? Of course, there isn't any indication. They haven't even entered the building yet!"

"We'll have to see how this plays out at the debate today. I'm sure that's what the message was about," Sandy said.

***

It was a little after 12:30 when we pulled into the Fresno City College parking lot. The lot was pretty full, and the Minnie Winnie was hard to maneuver, but Hal navigated to where he could park the RV on the grass, or what used to be grass. We all rushed to the entry check-in. They were eager to fill up the seats to make the debate look important, so there was no problem being a little late. We all passed through the metal detector and took seats at the back of the auditorium. We, of course, were wearing masks and sat on every other seat.

"Where are all the students?" I asked.

"The school is shut down over Covid. The students are probably watching this debate on a Zoom call," Sandy said, "like we should."

There were eight podiums in somewhat of an arc across the stage, but no candidates. The moderator was an older woman who stood at her own podium, but with her back to the audience, like a maestro conductor. She did, however, turn a well-lit profile view whenever the cameras were on her. There were as many TV cameras as there were TV vans in the parking lot—a lot. The cameras all pivoted as if on the same linkage arm, to follow each candidate as he or she entered and took a podium. There was undue applause for each. In case anyone we needed to identify said something remarkable, there were large nameplates on each podium, which was useful, as each candidate was wearing a large mask.

The moderator asked each candidate a question but was generous enough to suggest the correct answer without pausing. Each of the candidates struggled to outdo the others in his enthusiastic agreement with the moderator's position or her wittiness in response. It was sickening. I nodded off.

I was awakened, perhaps by a nudge, when the moderator finally asked what we all were waiting for. "What should we do about the terrible shooting incident today at the Temple Beth Chabad Synagogue?"

I wasn't fast enough to write down how each candidate responded, but I had the foresight to make a list of the candidates from their podium signs. I annotated each name with an "X" if the candidate gave an opinion about the subject; a check mark, if the candidate literally said, "No comment," or words to that effect, or a dash mark, if the speaker was just overwhelmed by others or otherwise could not speak.

That was all we needed to hear. We then just stood up and left the debate. The debate ended soon after that, and everyone rushed for the exits. We wound our way back through the parking lot to the RV, but by the time we all returned, Hal was blocked in by the traffic. We sat there and discussed what had happened.

"We have two candidates who directly stated that they would not comment, Antonio Valendez and Alexander Lamont," I said. "There were two others who didn't get to say anything, Joshua Arbongaza and Larry Elder."

"That means any of these four could be the FutureView candidate for governor," Hal said.

"Not really," Sandy said. "Those who didn't get a chance to speak wouldn't have had a chance to speak in the previous timeline, either. If the FutureView candidate were one of those, then he wouldn't have made a mistake in speaking, and there would have been no reason to send the warning FutureView message."

"Or," Hal said, "it could have been a candidate who spoke up about the Jewish shooting and simply ignored the FutureView warning."

"Not likely," said the professor. "If they went to all the trouble to send this FutureView message, then his handlers weren't just being cautious advisors—their candidate even *knew* the exact consequences. The candidate *had* to comply, to specifically not comment on the incident."

"I have to agree, then," said Hal. "The only person who could be the candidate supported by FutureView could only be Valendez or Lamont."

When the traffic cleared, Hal started up the engine on the Minnie Winnie, with an eye on the oil pressure light. Looking up, his jaw dropped as he stared out the window. "Quick, Tom, get on the periscope. Look at that black car over there! Can you get the license number?"

I glanced out the front window to where Hal was pointing, then rushed to the periscope roof camera and booted it as I pivoted the camera toward the front of the RV. Everyone watched on the TV screen. The parking lot was jammed as all the cars were now leaving. The car behind the black car was too close to allow me to see the black car's license plate. As the traffic moved, we all saw the back of the black Mercedes S-650. It was a Massachusetts plate.

791ERB

Hal confirmed the number with his notepad app, pulled up on his cell phone. "That's him! That's the Mercedes that was stalking us in Massachusetts!" There was no hope of trying to follow him, as the car was out of the parking lot before we could even move.

"Was he following us?" I asked.

"No way," Hal answered, though not confidently. "He was parked long before we got here. There isn't any way he knew we were coming."

"But this adds more strength to the link between the governor's race and the time machine messages," Sandy said.

CHAPTER 36

The FutureView Candidate
May 10, 2020

THE NEXT DAY, SANDY WAS scanning the news coverage on the governor's race, especially any references to Valendez or Lamont, when she ran across some editorial columns in the *San Jose Mercury News.* The article was critical of both Valendez and Lamont. She checked the author's name—William Dillon.

"Tom," she asked me, "do you remember that 'dill pickle' FV message we got last week? What was the exact message?"

I looked it up in a file I kept on my laptop and showed her on my screen:

NODILLONINTRV

"Stop, Hal!" she shouted.

Hal pulled to the side of the road, put the parking brake on, and rotated around in his captain's chair.

"I think the 'FutureView candidate' apparently had—I mean was to have—an interview with a reporter, William Dillon, from the *San Jose Mercury News*," she said. "Apparently, the interview went poorly—something happened. Maybe the candidate blurted out something that he shouldn't have. Maybe Dillon had incriminating information that this candidate later realized he might have validated during the interview.

"Anyway, the interview must have happened before the time range limit. The candidate's handlers realized the problem and sent a warning message to themselves: 'No Dillon Interview.' Even if no one knew why, they used FutureView to cancel the interview, retroactively, and thus prevented the embarrassing statement or revelation, or whatever. We just need to find out who was scheduled to be interviewed, sometime between 12:30 and 2:30 on May 2. That candidate must be the FutureView candidate!"

I got online to get the phone number for the newspaper, entered it on my phone, and handed the phone to Sandy. Before the first ring, she handed it on to Hal. He accepted it graciously and put the phone on speaker.

"Hi, I'm calling with some important information I'd like to pass on to your columnist, Mr. William Dillon," Hal said to the receptionist.

She stuttered something, then said, "Let me connect you to Mr. Dillon's office."

A man answered, "Hello? Can I help you?"

Hal hesitated, then said, "Yes, I'm looking to speak to Mr. Dillon."

"Yes, this is William Dillon. How can I help you?"

Hal hesitated, then said, "Well, you certainly don't sound like Bill. Who is this?"

"I'm sorry. Mr. Dillon is not available right now. Who is calling?"

It took one to know one.

"This is his cousin, Richard Thaler," said Hal. "I haven't seen Bill in years and just wanted to let him know that my wife, Sandy, and I were in town and wanted to get together with him."

Hal looked at Sandy. She grimaced.

"I'm sorry to have run you along, Mr. Thaler. This is Lieutenant Conrad of the San Jose Police Department. I am sorry to inform you that Mr. Dillon is dead, and we believe he was murdered. I cannot give you any more information. You can con…"

"Thank you," Hal said and hung up.

"You know what the means, Hal," Sandy said.

"Yes," he replied, "We need to drive back up to San Jose again!"

"Whoever is running the FV machine now is using it to gain power," she said, "and they will stop at nothing to get that power, including committing murder."

Hal rotated his captain's chair back into position, started the engine, and pulled back onto the road. He turned onto the northbound entry ramp to the 99 freeway.

Along the way, we kept tuned to the news about the shooting.

Sandy said, "Something must have triggered the decision to send that FV message. It wasn't just coaching. You don't need FutureView to do political coaching. There has to be something that happens before 2:30 to make the warning message."

We kept the TV on. I also brought up a California radio news station on my laptop, as well as a news website, to catch local updates.

The TV news show caught the San Francisco police chief in an impromptu news conference near the synagogue shooting. A reporter asked, "Was there any relationship between the shooter and the synagogue?"

The police chief replied, "Not that we know at this time. The shooter was Jewish, and he was the ex-husband of the female victim, but we found no connection with the synagogue…"

We all burst out in a cheer. It was decidedly uncaring to be cheering about a mass murder, but clearly this was no terrorist attack! It must have been a domestic issue that drove the shooting. Those idiots who pontificated about terrorism at the Fresno debate were going to regret it. The video of their statements will probably be on the evening news. The FutureView candidate, at least, did not embarrass himself.

To us, this was uncanny evidence of the use of FutureView for political purposes. You had to cheer for the guy who kept his mouth shut. Too bad others couldn't use their own forbearance.

We pulled into the *San Jose Mercury News* parking lot near the end of the day, though newspapers clearly work on a later time schedule. Hal parked the RV outside the gates, then went back and put on something like a business-casual suit—a sports coat over a white shirt with no tie. He asked Sandy and the prof to stay as he and I penetrated the building. We, of course, wore our masks.

"I'm Jedediah Gribenofski, and this is Wilhelm Nguyen. We're from the Proventual Insurance Company," Hal said to the receptionist/guard, "and we need to meet with your city editor right away. If you don't mind, I know the way. We'll try to stay away from the incident area. Is that all right?"

"Well, let me call him first," the receptionist said, as we just kept walking past him and into the corridor.

I guess using the insurance line was less threatening than pretending to be an FBI agent. Having two people in a scam also seemed to make it more believable. We could vouch for each other!

We could see that the scene of the crime was blocked off with police tape, and a uniformed cop was standing there, watching us approach. I thought this dude might be tougher to get past.

Hal said, "Let's not press this guy. We don't need to see Dillon's office; we just need to find out who he was going to see."

I saw a person giving directions and assumed he was some kind of manager. I approached him and said, "We're from the in…"

Hal completed my sentence, "…vestigative staff. I'm Sergeant York, and this is my assistant, Mr. O'Henry. I wondered if we could get a look at Mr. Dillon's appointment calendar. Who would we see about that?"

"The department administrator handles all appointments for Mr. Dillon. He's the gentleman over there," the manager said.

The young administrator looked easier to intimidate, but I wasn't even sure of my latest identity, so I let Hal take the lead.

"Hi, I'm Joseph Mastriani, and this is Stuart Little. The editor sent us over to follow up on any open ends that Mr. Dillon had. Could we look at his appointment calendar?"

"Certainly, Mr. Mastriani." He turned to bring up the reporter's calendar on his computer screen.

I whispered to Hal, "If that's all you wanted, I could have probably gotten his calendar up while we were in Fresno without leaving the RV!"

The administrator rotated his screen around so we could see. Hal reached for the mouse and scrolled back to May 2. There was nothing on the calendar near midday.

"We were particularly interested in following up some loose ends," Hal said. "Back a week ago there might have been an interview set up with one candidate for governor that was later canceled. I see there was nothing on the calendar. Do you, perhaps, remember canceling out an interview for Mr. Dillon?"

"Well, yes, as a matter of fact. Mr. Dillon was quite upset about it when I told him that the candidate had canceled out. He was scheduled around lunchtime—said it was the best time to catch him, but an important contributor wanted to meet him for lunch."

"And who was the candidate?"

"It was Mr. Lamont. Alexander Lamont."

CHAPTER 37

License to Kill

June 2, 2020

HAL THOUGHT WE SHOULD CHECK out one last site in the Sacramento area, though we weren't too optimistic about it. One thing we certainly kept up on was FutureView messages. Now that we knew there were political directives to support Alexander Lamont for governor, we were especially looking for messages that were not stock and options trading hints. Kevin, or Kevin's people, must have felt they had totally isolated their messages from us, as they felt no need to continue to encrypt messages.

Since we only expected to receive FutureView messages during the morning window from 11:00 a.m. until 1:00 p.m. (due to Daylight Savings Time), I set up my laptop during that window to receive messages from our Goldstone antenna.

One day I heard the *ding* at the fairly early time of 11:30 a.m. Kevin seemed to fall into the habit of sending messages every day to be received at 12:45 p.m., so a message at 11:30 already alerted us that this one would be different. The message was:

DENY4SBACCUSE

"This sure looks like advice for Lamont," I said.

"He is supposed to deny some accusation. Is he with another reporter again?" said Hal, talking to us while he drove the RV, "I hope the reporter has good life insurance!"

"Let me check his speaking agenda," said Sandy as she went to his campaign website. "All the top candidates are in San Francisco today for an important televised debate, and the debate starts at 1:00 p.m. I see someone had a hand in that choice of time!"

The prof beat me to the TV. He searched around for a California station covering the debate on our satellite system. The debate, however, would not start for a while.

"What about the rest of the message?" asked Hal.

"I'll bet the number four is a code for someone—the moderator, or a reporter, or another candidate. I have no idea what 'SB' stands for. We haven't seen that abbreviation before." Sandy said.

"All we know is that Lamont did something unethical…" Hal said.

"…or illegal," Sandy added.

"…and during the debate, he should just deny it. Which means it must be true! Too bad we can't reject his denial!" Hal said.

"When was that message sent?" the prof asked.

"1:30."

"So, whatever it is, it comes early in the debate. There may be more to this, later in the debate," the prof concluded.

I didn't take long after we beat that one to death that another message arrived, at noon, sent at 2:00:

USEJJRTOREFUT

"Whoever's writing their messages is not paying by the letter!" said the prof.

"I had to agree—the same message could be a lot tighter," I said. "What's a 're-fut'?"

"*Refute!* He just ran out at the thirteen-character limit. Just a follow-on from the last message, advising Lamont to use someone, I think with the initials 'JJR,' to refute the accusation that we saw from the last message," Sandy said. "JJR must be some authority who is going to lie for Lamont!"

It was my turn to get on the Lamont website to search for someone with those initials, but with little luck.

"So," Hal shouted back to us, "denying didn't work! Something hit the fan during that debate. Mr. Number Four must have something on Lamont!"

We eagerly awaited the next message, which would undoubtedly come after the thirty-minute cooldown limit on the transmitter. With the two-hour time range limit, there would be another message at 12:30, transmitted at 2:30. It arrived on schedule.

K4+JJR8JYT342

This was now getting cryptic. No one jumped in with an interpretation. Hal asked twice for someone to read him the message, character by character, but he only muttered it to himself.

"I see the number four, again," the prof said, "and 'JJR,' but the rest is unintelligible."

"Those other numbers and letters look sort of familiar," Hal said, but with little to follow.

We continued down the freeway, puzzled over the meaning of the message, when Hal shouted, "Look at that Toyota!"

We all looked out the window, but there didn't seem to be anything unusual about the Toyota. It was just a Toyota Sienna that needed a car wash.

"Look at the license plate!" he said.

It was a California plate, 8GWM554.

"I don't understand—what about it?" asked the prof.

"The license numbers in California!" I said, "That's the same format as the rest of the FutureView message! The number eight, followed by three letters, then three digits."

It was getting close to noon and promotions for the upcoming debate were running on the TV. Suddenly, the local channel broke in with a "Breaking News" banner.

"Really?" I said. "The debate is not something everyone is eager to watch in the middle of the day?"

But the breaking news was, indeed, related to the debate. A reporter with a microphone, carrying his own camera, was doing an on-the-spot report from the street in front of the auditorium for the debate.

The reporter, panting, said, "We are outside the governor's election debate venue where a horrific drive-by shooting occurred, killing the limo driver and two passengers. One passenger was the front-runner candidate for governor, Mr. Larry Elder. The police are not sure whether Mr. Elder was targeted, because he was a passenger in an automobile that had no connection to the Elder campaign. No one planning to assassinate Mr. Elder would know that he would be in that car. The police are looking into the possibility that the other passenger was the target of the attack."

The camera scanned the black Chevy Tahoe with bullet holes in the passenger door. As the camera shot zoomed back, we all saw the license plate on the vehicle, a standard California plate:

8JYT342

With Elder out, the leading candidate for governor was now Alexander Lamont.

CHAPTER 38

Pyrocumulonimbus

July 13, 2020

H AL SAID, "IT'S ONE THING to take advantage of knowing the future for financial gain—it is quite another to use it to commit murder for political gain."

"Whoever is running FutureView now is freely taking advantage of future knowledge to commit crimes. Imagine what a criminal could do with an improved time machine," Sandy said.

"I'm sure they are already developing remote antennas to give them twelve hours per day operation," said the prof. "Kevin already knows we accomplished that when he won the lottery!"

"That alone would give them the opportunity far better than political polling—they could correct any gaffs; they could give their candidate apparent foresight into economics, warnings about crimes or disasters—the candidate could seem like a wise man, with well-thought-out insight into the future, at least within the limits of a two-hour time range," Hal said.

Sandy added, "Or whoever runs FutureView could avoid leaving evidence of a crime, could foresee any flaws in their criminal plan and could murder any witnesses, turncoats, or undercover agents. This is far more dangerous!"

"Remember also," said the prof, "that with millions of dollars generated by the machine, this machine could become much more powerful, even if the only effort is scaling it up. It could have increased time range, larger and more detailed messages, the ability to try multiple futures by eliminating the cooldown delay. With that, they could easily protect themselves from any effort to find the machine or shut it down!"

"Which is why we need to find Kevin and the machine now, while he is still vulnerable!" said Sandy.

Our search, however, was becoming depressing. The last potential site in northern California also came up as another dry well.

We were getting worn out. Covid-19 was gripping the country. That didn't so much affect us on our isolated journey, but we still had to take precautions. A lot of restaurants and stores were closing. It seemed there was a big run on recreational vehicles and at least twice we were offered cash for our decrepit Minnie Winnie. The offers were greater than what Hal had paid for our mobile abode, but he turned them all down. I figured he didn't want us to get any ideas about stopping the search. The troops were getting restless.

Hal parked the RV on the side of the road somewhere. He took charge of cooking a steak dinner on the small barbeque we carried with us. It took forever to cook the meat and baked potatoes. I wonder, in hindsight, whether Hal kept the briquette heat down low intentionally, so that we were forced to face each other and decide what we should do next. I don't know if any CEOs were using the technique— starving the staff until they committed to a common strategy—but it sort of worked.

Hal said, "There are many reasons we couldn't find the machine. The dish antenna may have been down for repairs. It may have been replaced with a different antenna. It may have been camouflaged..."

"Yes! We've heard all these excuses," Sandy said. "The only important question, though, is 'What should we do now?'"

"What about a power survey?" Hal said. "Could we look for large power spikes that correspond to the transmission times for FutureView messages?"

"That may not be very fruitful," said the prof. "The high voltage and high current drain would require dedicated power lines that would be isolated from the public grid. I'm sure FutureView would cause quite a disruption if it were on the grid."

"How about checking for a company with unusual material supply requirements?" Sandy asked.

"The machine is already built," said the prof. "There is no need for special resources to keep it running. Now, they probably want to hire some smart people who could understand the machine and build a bigger time machine. That might be a source."

"Of course, they wouldn't advertise for time-travel experts, per se. Would they?" Hal asked.

"Not directly. But I think I could search for certain skills, if they are advertising for physicists, both theoretical and experimental physicists."

"I doubt they would even try to advertise," Sandy said. "Maybe it would be better if you had them come to you. Could you prepare a false resume and put it out? You could probably put words and references in it that would catch a computer search algorithm."

"I could put out a good resume. See if I get any requests for an interview."

"In the meantime, we should probably head back to Las Vegas," said Hal. "I think that's the area where the time machine would most likely be located."

The next morning, we packed up and headed back to Vegas. It was another long drive through desert and parched farmland in a hot summer. It didn't help that the A/C in the Winnebago was only marginal.

The professor thought it might be more tolerable to drive east, toward Lake Tahoe, then south, through the mountains, rather than drive down through the Central Valley again. We were amid a major summer heat wave, and there were a hundred wildfires burning in California alone. Though the route through the mountains would be more pleasant, it would be longer, and perhaps blocked by fires. In the end, we agreed to keep focused on our mission.

I was still monitoring for FV messages every day, especially now that they had taken on more importance. The 2:45 p.m. to 12:45 p.m. messages seemed to be the standard, probably making it easier for a larger organization to receive and transmit regularly.

We were also monitoring social websites and the general political media for news about the California governor's race. Lamont apparently had a shady background. It is amazing how easily they could erase an embarrassing history with enough money—money for lawyers, money for media advertising, money for attacking his opponents, accusing them of the very faults and sleazy activities that were his history. If history is only recorded on the internet, with enough money, you can change history.

That day, we did not receive a FutureView message. That was quite unusual based on the past months, but it was the third day that no message had been received. Sandy calculated that the lost profits, based on her market watch after the close, were over $1 million.

Finally, at the end of a long day, we came down that long downhill into Primm, Nevada, and thirty minutes later, we were back in the Red Rock RV Park. We were all beat. Hal offered but we all declined to catch an Uber into town. We thought it might be nice to put some folding chairs out and watch the sunset instead.

The sky grew dark, with heavy clouds that often led to intense downpours in the desert. A sudden cooling, a brisk breeze, then a dead calm was a warning not to stand tall in the open desert, or you'd risk becoming an electrical conductor. But, as is often the case in desert thunderstorms, we expected rain and were disappointed. The clouds thinned and the sun returned just before sunset to heat the air again. The only evidence of a storm that remained was a sound of thunder.

"Pyrocumulonimbus," the prof said. "Smoke particles from the fires cool when they rise in altitude, collect moisture, and form clouds, causing thunderstorms."

Just then, Hal called the professor and asked, "What would happen if a thunderstorm happened over a solar power plant at 2:45 PM?"

"That's interesting, Hal. Maybe Tom can compare Doppler radar maps for 2:45 p.m. on the days that there were no FutureView messages."

I overheard and started collecting the weather maps immediately.

Hal returned to the RV in the early evening. When he walked in, I asked, "Lose all your money?"

"Sort of. Sandy has me on a gambling budget."

"Anyway, I was interested in whether you have found anything based on the smoke theory."

By then, I already had the map overlays ready. I showed everyone on my laptop by routing the display to the wall TV in the RV.

"Here are the areas in California where there were clouds or smoke at 2:45 on the days we did *not* get an FV message, marked in blue on this map of California."

I could see the disappointment in the team, obviously because so much of the state was covered in blue, owing to all the smoke from the fires.

"This doesn't look like it will help us," I added. "A lot of the state was covered in smoke at the critical time, when they would have wanted to send a FutureView message."

"Do you have maps of the cloud cover for the other days, the days when we *did* receive a FutureView message?" Hal asked.

"Sure," I said. "I have a map of the Doppler radar for every day at 2:45 p.m."

"Pick a day when we received a message, but when there were a lot of clouds and smoke. Increase the transparency of the colors on the map, and overlay it with this map," Hal said.

I did what he asked and figured out why. I put the image of the western states with the two cloud overlays on the screen. "Here it is," I said.

"The FutureView machine is most likely in the areas that show only light blue," Hal said. "That's where it was cloudy when FutureView did *not* send a message and was clear when a FutureView message *was sent*."

I added, "Here is an overlay of the map showing dots where there are large solar farms."

"There is only one site that met all the criteria!" the prof exclaimed. "It's a place we passed by twice, without even looking. The Ivanpah Solar Power Plant in California, behind Whiskey Pete's Casino."

CHAPTER 39

Zzyzxx

July 15, 2020

E ARLY THE NEXT DAY, WE packed up again and drove out of Las Vegas, heading west, now with more interest. As we approached the California border, we could see three brightly lit towers on the desert upslope in front of us. Each of the towers sat in the middle of a large, light blue, circular disk that must have been a half-mile in diameter. As we approached, I could see that the disks were really circular arrays of hundreds of thousands of solar panels.

"Every solar farm I've seen," I said, "has the solar panels in a rectangular array, with every panel synchronized to follow the sun. But why are these panels arranged in concentric circles?"

"They are not solar panels," said the professor, "they are large mirrors, mounted on separate gimbals."

The mirrors were reflecting the sun's light onto the tower in the center of the array. Then I realized the towers were not lit up with spotlights but were actually white-hot from the convergence of so many beams of sunlight.

We took the now-familiar exit at Whiskey Pete's Casino and parked in the back, where we could see the power plant. We all got out of the RV to get a good view.

"This is the Ivanpah solar energy plant," said the prof. "It simply uses old-fashioned steam boilers and steam turbines in those towers."

"They are still captive to the same economics as solar-panel plants," Sandy said. "No one needs the electrical power when they generate the most, and they can offer a good deal to FutureView to power the machine when the machine needs it most. We need to look for a building near the power plant, with power lines leading up to it, and a big dish on the roof!"

The sight was amazing. "They must have spent billions of dollars to make this!"

"Have you seen Hal?" Sandy asked.

I swung the periscope around toward the casino to look for him. "He is back at the casino gas station, talking to someone with a cowboy hat."

"What does the hat have to do with it?" Sandy asked.

"Nothing, really," I replied.

I followed Hal with the periscope as he returned to the RV, and warned the others, "You won't believe what Hal has now. And it includes the hat."

We could all hear him as he got near, riding a four-wheel all-terrain vehicle, a "quad."

Hal shut off the engine and said, "With this, we can look the part of a vacationing family, and have the perfect excuse for tooling around the mountains!"

"You go ahead, Tom," Sandy said. "I'm still trying to decipher some of the earlier FutureView messages. By the way, my list of the messages seems to miss a few. Have you been keeping a list?"

I grabbed my hat and sunglasses, eager to join Hal, idling on the quad. As a professional hacker, I had always been reluctant to share my passwords, even among friends. Just a practice I had instilled in myself.

"You know, I've seen Hal keeping his own spreadsheet of the messages," I said. "Why don't you look on his laptop?"

"What's his password?" she asked.

"Hal's password is 'don't ask me for the password,' one word," I said.

Sandy gave a nod, so she must have understood. Hal gunned the quad, drowning out any further conversation.

Hal and I spent the day surveilling the mountains surrounding the solar plant on the quad. We found some heavy truck tracks on the dirt road and followed them up a newly carved access road on the side of a steep canyon. It led to a metal building at the top of a small hill. We didn't get far up the trail toward the building when we were intercepted by a uniformed security guard on an even louder quad.

He must have seen us coming to have intercepted us so soon. He waved us off. Hal turned around immediately. I could see that they had a gate on the road up ahead, with a small guard shack. They had total control over access to the building.

"There is no need for us to get closer and have them ID us," Hal said. "This must be the FutureView building."

We returned to the RV and reported what we had found. "It's the perfect location," Hal said. "No one could even get close, and there's no one out here to complain about noise, flashing lights, or power drops. I could see that they were wired for plenty of three-phase high-voltage power."

"They have a good view to the east, but the site is blocked by the mountains to the west. How can FutureView even work?"

"The east-facing transmitter antenna looks like our old dish, right on top of their building—that has to be tied directly to the time circuits," the prof said. "Being up on the slope, with a clear view over the desert in Nevada, they would have good clearance to the east. The receiving antenna, as you know now, can be any antenna that operates in the X-band frequency. They probably mounted that on the west side of the mountains, where it would have an unrestricted view to the west. Actually, this is a pretty good setup."

"Tomorrow, we need to move the RV to a ridge out there," said Hal, pointing out the adjacent ridge, "where we can monitor the building, yet still be far enough away that no one will bother us. But first things first. Professor, you thought you might get hired by them. Let's work on that, too. We will need to get inside that building."

We had dinner at Whiskey Pete's. I thought we should celebrate. After all these months of searching for the machine, we had finally found it! Hal opened his wallet for the best food and extra wine, despite the casino namesake. Sandy didn't say too much.

After dinner, we returned to the RV. It had what you might call a master bedroom, a double bed separated only by a privacy curtain from the rest of the vehicle. Hal and Sandy were having a conversation in there, but it was hardly a private one.

The professor was working at the kitchen table, and I was sitting on the bunk over the cab. It had its own little window and a USB charging port, and I could use my laptop there late into the night without disturbing the others. But neither of us could ignore their conversation, nor have one of our own.

"I was looking for your spreadsheet of the FV messages. Tom said you might have been keeping a list on your laptop," Sandy distinctly said. "I found it, and found that you had neatly tracked every message, its date, time, content, and my interpretation of the stock option action. But I also noticed that you added another column to the spreadsheet. The column was labeled 'profit' and several FutureView messages showed thousands of dollars in that column. Before you make up some bullshit explanation that I'm sure you've already conjured up, I will tell you that, as long as I was on your laptop, I checked your brokerage account and found some matching numbers in the activity history there. You have been betting along with Kevin—making money off of the FutureView messages!"

"Yes, I was," came Hal's rebuttal. "How do you think I've been paying for everything on this trip? Why not take advantage of it? Every financial advisor does basically the same thing—predicting the future. FutureView happens to just do it better."

"But it makes me wonder why we spent months chasing Kevin all over. Maybe you didn't really have the incentive to end it sooner? Did you ever consider what damage Kevin may already have done in the meantime?"

"Honestly, Sandy, I did not keep us from stopping Kevin. Now that we're here, I think we can take back control of the FutureView machine…"

"Take back control! You think that's what we need to do? We need to destroy that machine. We need to destroy it now, at any cost!"

I assumed from the conversation that Hal might sleep in the front of the RV tonight.

The professor had been checking his email and made an announcement that at least changed the subject for a while. "I just received an inquiry from a strange new company called the Zzyzxx Corporation. This company could be FutureView."

"How do you spell it?" I asked.

The prof spelled it out.

"They don't have a website. There is another company with a similar name, but with only one 'X'," I said. "I've looked up the name on Wikipedia. 'Zzyzx' is the last word in the dictionary. It was used to name the last desert town in California near the Nevada border, but the town went away. The only thing left is Zzyzx Road, an exit off the interstate."

"Sounds close enough," said Hal. "This is probably FutureView. Can you get an interview?" He stepped out from behind the bedroom curtain.

"They've asked for a Zoom call—maybe because of the virus, maybe because they don't want to reveal their location. But that should make it easier for me to be in disguise. I will set it up."

"They probably won't reveal what you'll be working on," said Hal, "but if it is FutureView, you would certainly have an advantage over any other candidate—you're the only candidate who knows what they want."

We moved the RV to the overlooking ridge, though not without some serious trepidation by those of us who were not driving it. I led with the quad and spotted the bad ruts in the road. In position, we had a good view of anyone coming or going to the FutureView building, and we could ID them using the periscope. If anyone came knocking, we could claim to be a vacationing family, and had the quad, barbeque, and folding chairs to fit the script.

We spent some time watching the comings and goings at the FutureView building and continued monitoring their FV messages. When they transmitted, the sound of escaping steam from the water-cooling system echoed across the ridges, and you could see the steam escaping from the large heat exchanger next to the building.

The professor observed that the building itself seemed much too large for what was needed to house the FV machine, so we wondered what Kevin had in mind. We saw private cars and a passenger van arrive at shift changes for the guards, technicians, and scientists—we could tell from their clothes—as they entered the building.

One other interesting thing I observed was the sign on the building entry. It read:

Zzyzxx Corp

CHAPTER 40

Dr. Montrose

August 3, 2020

"**D**O YOU THINK I CAN get by wearing a mask on the Zoom call?" the professor asked.

"Kevin knows you. I think we need to give you a disguise, not just for the interview, but also to get you onto the site," said Hal.

"Given the ruthlessness we have seen, the professor would also be at much greater risk than just getting a rejection letter," Sandy said.

"We have to disguise you well enough that you could shake hands with Kevin at a luncheon for new hires," Hal said. "No one is going to object to you wearing a face mask when you're inside."

"I used to be a pretty good Shakespearean actor in amateur theater and did my own makeup," the professor said. "I can do some conservative hair coloring and facial prosthetics such that my daughter would not recognize me."

"Well, make yourself look like a physicist, not the king of Scotland."

The professor seemed eager to be cast in this "play." He even produced a makeup kit that he must have carried since we left Cambridge.

Hal continued, "That's all we need for now. What about a resume? Can you create something that will get you hired, yet can't be tripped up by a verification effort?"

"That's already taken care of, the prof said. "I have a friend, Dr. Anthony Montrose, who has an excellent CV for this purpose. I embellished it some to make the FutureView—I mean Zzyzxx—recruiter jump to recommend him—I mean me. They can verify any of his degrees, jobs, and publications because they are all real."

"Be careful about saying anything about FutureView—that will give you away for sure," Sandy said.

Hal asked, "Won't this Dr. Montrose have a problem with you using his name?"

"I don't think he would mind. He passed away last month."

I helped the professor in the social media field, setting him up with a new email account, a revised LinkedIn profile, a few new photos to be photoshopped into Dr. Montrose's real Facebook page, and a few touches to make Professor Johnson pass for Dr. Montrose, even if it wouldn't pass a full FBI investigation.

Hal said, "You should be familiar with Montrose's history and publications, and the names of recent professional supervisors and family members."

He could, of course, claim a short-term loss of memory, an out that I could not use.

The prof did his Zoom interview, using my laptop computer. He sat at our kitchenette in the RV, with a four-by-eight sheet of white melamine behind him. I captured a JPEG of the library of a distinguished scholar off the internet and electronically inserted it as the background for his Zoom call.

The professor was in full makeup, and indeed looked like the king of Scotland, without the crown. But he did well. There were more gaps in their questioning than in his answering—always a good sign. What really helped was the prof's statement that he could start any time, and that he was currently living in Pahrump. I figured that had to be something Hal made up, but Pahrump, Nevada, is real. The town was close enough for the prof not to need relocation, yet far enough away to avoid anyone checking him out.

Getting a Social Security card would be essential for any employment. It had to be Dr. Montrose's original Social Security card, not a new number. This took some skill and dealings with the dark web, and I had to open a bitcoin wallet to pay for the effort, but I won't dwell on that business. I did hand him a brand-new Social Security card with Montrose's real number for him to sign.

"The long pole in the tent is getting you some identification," Hal said. "We need to get you a driver's license—that's essential."

The next day we drove the RV into Vegas to the Department of Motor Vehicles and applied for a Nevada driver's license under the prof's real name, using his Massachusetts driver's license.

Hal somehow got behind the DMV counter, pretending to be an "office manager's assistant," and escorted the professor's application along. That included surreptitiously dropping the application to me while I stood at the counter, so I could change the applicant's name to *Anthony Montrose*, with hardly a disruption in the office efficiency. The prof was in full makeup when they took his driver's license photo, and we were set.

As soon as we got the professor's temporary Nevada driver's license, the next step was a small used-car lot far off the Strip, where he bought and registered a car in Montrose's name. It was a beat-up old Honda Civic, so it didn't set off alarms when the prof paid for it in cash. Hal, of course, provided the cash.

The vehicle was sorely needed to keep us from having to drive the big RV up and down that treacherous canyon road, and it gave the professor a car he could drive to work if he got the job.

*****

A week later, he received an email that he got the job. They must have been eager to have him, as he was asked to start the next day. We were all disappointed, however, when the address they provided was for an office in Las Vegas.

"I'm sure they don't want to just send every new hire out to their secret site," the professor lamented. "I can build their confidence in me enough for them to invite me out there soon. After all, I know more about their machine than they do!"

We shopped in Las Vegas to buy the prof a new suit and tie. He looked like a compromise between a Harvard law school professor and Liberace—given the location, he didn't seem too out of place.

The professor got up early the next day for his first day at work. I think it reminded him of his amateur acting career, and he loved it. He applied his makeup and dress with extreme care, like Patton dressing to go into battle with Rommel.

The professor insisted he go in alone. If he was found out, there was nothing we could do anyway. He had his cell phone and would call if he needed to. But we were in a rickety RV, parked in the desert mountains.

We heard nothing from the professor during the day, not even when he would have been on a lunch break. The prof's progress was on my mind. I knew it bothered Hal as well, but our hands were tied.

CHAPTER 41

Sandy's Run
August 21, 2020

Throughout our tour of California, Sandy would rise early and go for a run before the sun could do its damage. She often would wear a small backpack that included a bottle of water or two. She said she preferred that over a runner's water belt, as those bounced with each stride and disturbed her rhythm. She would often return with the water bottles still mostly filled. I suspected she was carrying more water than needed and using the backpack to add to her workout. I admired her self-discipline but wondered why she felt she had to hide it.

Now that we were essentially camped in the desert, she was up every day to run down the unimproved roads and coyote trails in the early dawn light.

I was awakened by her movement behind the privacy curtain one morning, and the sound of the backpack being zippered. I got up and prepared the coffee, though the others were sound sleepers and would not be up for a while. More out of courtesy than common sense, I offered her a cup.

"No thanks," she said. "I'm going for a run." She hesitated at the door, then added, "Tom, if I have not said it before, I want to make sure your efforts and dedication were appreciated on this extensive venture we have been on. You have been a tremendous help."

"Thank you," is all I could think to say. I had not had my coffee yet.

"Could you give this thumb drive to Hal when he gets up?" she asked, handing me a bright red USB thumb drive.

As she went out the door, she said, "I wish you the best of the future." Her backpack seemed pretty heavy—maybe she was bringing extra water for a long run in the dry desert.

That strange statement puzzled me. Why not just "See you later"? I sat down and drank my coffee, feeling a sense of uneasiness as I grabbed her thumb drive in my right hand.

I had to see what was on that drive. I loaded it onto my laptop. The drive contained only one file, "ForHal.docx." I opened it.

Hal: The FV is a weapon of tyranny. It creates the wealth and power that prevents it from being stopped. Our only hope is to end it now. If I fail, you are the only one with the ability to take the action needed! -S.

It was just as I feared. I knew now that Sandy would not be back for breakfast.

"Writing an email to your girl back in Boston?" Hal asked from behind me.

I tilted the lid down on my laptop. "No, just some notes for the journal," I lied.

"Did Sandy leave already?" Hal asked.

"Yes, she left on her run." I copied the file to my desktop, then powered down, but Hal saw the unmistakably red thumb drive.

"Is that Sandy's?" he asked, pointing to the drive. He knew it was. I had to give it to him.

"She left this for you." I handed it over.

Hal opened his own computer and attempted to put the thumb drive in its USB port. It didn't appear to fit, so he flipped it over and tried again, but that didn't seem to work either. He flipped it back and finally had it connect. Enough time then passed for him to have read the message, but he said nothing.

I went outside and lit the grill. While it heated up, I then broke some eggs into a bowl and scrambled them. The professor was up and stepped out of the RV with a cup of coffee.

The sun was rising. Hal came out and scanned the hills with binoculars.

"Hal, she left with a full backpack of her things," I said. "I see now that her laptop must have been in it, too. I don't think she's coming back."

CHAPTER 42

Plan A

September 2, 2020

U SING THE PERISCOPE AND SHORT ventures out with the quad, we surveyed the Zzyzxx site from all sides. It was a veritable fortress. The approach to the site from below was up an unclimbable slope covered in loose gravel and rocks. The only reasonable way in was by the access road, blocked by a swinging fence gate guarded 24/7. We surveyed the exact coordinates of the building by establishing lines of sight using the periscope and a camera with the GPS compass app on my iPhone. From that, we could locate the building exactly on a satellite terrain map.

What Hal called his "Plan A" was to load up the Honda Civic with explosives and run it through the guard gate and into the building. Hal would drive it, then escape by jumping off the steep rock-covered slope. I would pick him up in the canyon on the quad. This would happen before anyone could get a shot at us in the desert, where there was no vegetation or cover.

Not much of a plan.

It sounded too much like *Road Warrior*, except that our opponents would not be shooting arrows. When Hal described it, he spoke in generalities. Sandy wasn't there to ask any critically detailed questions about the plan.

I avoided criticizing Hal's plan, but I might have been a little impolitic when I asked, "What is Plan B?"

Hal did not answer.

The professor rolled in around 6:00 p.m. I could see him approaching by following the dust cloud in the periscope. When he finally arrived, we were cooking dinner outside and offered him a brat. He seemed in good spirits.

"I spent the morning doing the usual corporate in-processing stuff," he said. "The human resources agency they hired provided no information about the company or the job. They are going to check all references. At best, we have two weeks before they find out that Montrose is dead."

"Did they admit to operating a time machine?" I asked.

"Not hardly. There were some more senior people there. We engaged in some discussion to determine the purpose of a time-dilation circuit they brought into the room. I think I impressed them. But they don't have a clue."

"I recognized the circuit board. It had too much solder on the connections—clearly one that I built, not one of yours, Tom! But the son-of-a-bitch argued with me about how it worked! Clearly, he had little experience in circuit design. They had to rush the circuit board back right away. I would guess it was needed for the 2:45 transmission."

"Did you see Kevin?"

"I caught a glimpse of him consulting with my new boss," the professor replied, "but he seemed more preoccupied with the current operations than the development of a new machine. He raised his voice and seemed like he was under a lot of pressure. He didn't stay in Las Vegas very long. Did you see him come out to the site?"

"Yes," I said, "we saw him arrive today at 12:30 to receive the message. He stayed until after the transmission event, at 2:45. He doesn't have to—am I right?"

The prof continued, "Actually, he has to be there for *every* transmission event at 2:45. I found out that he is still the only one with the transmission password and has to be there for any message to be transmitted. Of course, in the final timelines, where a message is received, he doesn't have to stay."

"But he stayed today," I said. "I mean, he stayed until the power-up at 2:45 in the last timeline today."

"There was a manager-type person in Vegas, and he said I should be cleared for the program and would invite me out to 'the site.'"

"Don't hold your breath on that," Hal said. "It sounds like Kevin's already built a bureaucracy."

"Clearly, they are working on reverse-engineering the FV machine, and eventually they are going to succeed. They have the money to do it, and they have a lot of smart people. I have to be careful. If I tell them the wrong thing, they may think I'm a hack and keep me away from the machine. If I tell them too many of the right answers, I will help them build another machine. Have you come up with a plan yet?"

I said, "Ask Hal about Plan A."

The professor went into the RV to discuss Plan A with Hal, and I had another bratwurst. I couldn't hear what they were saying, but Hal did a lot of arm-waving and exaggerated movements, while the prof stood with his arms folded, asking a lot of questions.

The professor returned outside and grabbed a bun, to which I added the last brat. He said, "I heard some talk about the Ivanpah power plant today. They offer a tour on the weekend. Maybe we should take the tour. It could be interesting, and maybe we can ask more questions about the arrangement they have with Zzyzxx."

"Sounds like a good idea," Hal said.

Perhaps Hal agreed to appear to be open to other ideas after we showed the extent of our enthusiasm for Plan A.

CHAPTER 43

More About the Zs
September 15, 2020

AFTER THE PROFESSOR DRESSED, DID his makeup, and headed off to "work," Hal spent a good deal of time on the phone muddling through the bureaucracy to buy explosives, to get a permit to buy explosives, and then to get a mining permit to get an explosives permit to buy explosives. It was not going well. I could see that "Plan A" was going to take months.

Hal also seemed to search for other sources for explosives, some nontraditional and some nonlegal. "It seems so much easier in the movies," he said.

It was making me nervous. I made it a point to the professor that we might think about alternatives to Plan A.

During the day, I kept my eye on the periscope camera image projected onto the wall TV. We kept the camera aimed, focused, and zoomed at the Zzyzxx building. Kevin arrived every day at 12:30, like clockwork.

Maybe he was worried that his golden goose might give up the ghost in its violent spasms during the transmitting. Certainly, the desert heat and the hot summer didn't help. It was a regular practice for the technical people to vacate the building at 2:30 to be sure that everything was secure and people were safe before all that energy was released. It was probably damned hot in that metal building too—not a pleasant place after the machine ate all that electrical energy.

Apart from the security people, who stayed comfortably in their air-conditioned guard shack, everyone left in the van and private cars as soon as they exited the building. Today, I noticed one car there that I recognized—a beat-up green Honda Civic.

"It looks like the prof got invited to the site today," I told Hal.

"Good," he said. "Maybe he found some other vulnerability we can explore."

I also watched the security people. Clearly, they could see anyone approaching long before anyone could get close. Early in the morning, there were some coyotes testing the security perimeter and losing. The guards were well-armed and took any opportunity to practice their marksmanship on the coyotes. They must have also had thermal imaging capability, as we could hear gunshots before dawn. I sure wouldn't want to be sneaking up there in the middle of the night. I told Hal about that.

Hal tried calling Sandy's cell phone and attempted to leave a message, but the automated answering robot said that the voice mailbox was full. I could hear that recording from his phone across the room.

That evening I used the periscope to watch for the professor driving back up our road. It was easy to just set up the periscope, then watch on the flat-screen TV on the wall.

When he walked in, I asked, "How was your day at 'work'?"

"It was easy getting recognized as the top student in the class when you secretly have all the answers to the test," he said. "I impressed them so much with my 'theories' that they invited me out to the site. I have some good news and some bad news."

"Go ahead. What's the good news?" Hal said, reluctantly playing the straight man.

"The bad news is that they are building a new, massive version of the FV machine next to our machine. That's why they built such a large building. They have hired some of the best talent in the world. Money is no object when you own the golden goose."

"Yes, we saw the entourage leaving at transmit time today," I said.

"There were a lot of nontechnical people there, too," the prof said. "I think they were financial people, and some pols, for sure."

"You mean political types? How could you tell?" Hal asked.

"Just by bits of their conversations and what they were interested in. They were clueless about the science. I saw Kevin arrive and kept my distance. There was another suit who also kept staring at me, though. I didn't recognize him, but he may have met Professor Johnson at some point. I'm also going to avoid him. If he sees through my makeup, I may also be cooked."

It seemed strange for the professor to refer to himself in the third person. I could also swear that he had developed a midwestern accent, for some reason.

"I hope that was all the bad news," Hal said.

"The good news is that I actually got inside the machine. Everything is laid out like it was in Cambridge. I looked behind the rack that included the FutureView computer and saw that the Ethernet cable was still there, just not plugged-in. Someone had duct-taped over the connector and attached a warning note, not to plug it in. Maybe Kevin kept the cable there so he could use the remote controller on the internet, if he needed to."

"You know," I said, "maybe we could attack them by literally pulling the power plug at the power plant. There's a regular tour of the Ivanpah solar plant every Sunday. We ought to take the tour tomorrow."

"I agree. It starts at 10 a.m. Let's be there. Dress like a tourist," Hal replied.

While we were eating dinner, we caught the news on our satellite TV. The California news showed a lot of smoke and fire videos but told us very little about where they were. From the videos, they could have been using stock footage from last year.

The announcer introduced another story: "The governor's race is heating up, as people pick winners. Since the death of Larry Elder, the current leader in the polls is the relatively unknown candidate, Alexander Lamont. He has developed quite a lead on the other candidates, now only four weeks from the election! Governor Newsom is out on the road campaigning for votes against the recall motion as well."

"Do you think they would consider murdering Newsom too?" I asked.

"Not if we succeed in our plan," Hal said.

The story showed Lamont touring the Ivanpah power plant. "That guy was at the Zzyzxx site today!" the prof said. "I guess unlimited money can buy you anything."

The TV reporter said, "Lamont seems to be the only cool-headed candidate and has shown uncanny insight into the problems in California. That is one reason he seems to have taken the lead after the death of Larry Elder. He has been quite open and has arranged a daily press conference and free lunch at noon for the reporters following his campaign."

"That's a convenient time for getting the right answer to any question," Hal said. "Listen for the comments from the reporters, then revise your answers to the questions. How could you go wrong?"

CHAPTER 44

Plan B

September 29, 2020

T HE WALKING TOUR OF THE Ivanpah solar power plant started in the forest of mirrors. One hundred thousand of anything is impressive, but 100,000 mirrors reflecting the sun produce an extremely bright light beam, brighter than even the marquee at Caesar's Palace. Upon close examination, there were two mirrors the size of Ping-Pong tables mounted on each pivoting pedestal. The pair of mirrors pivot fore and aft, and side to side, to maintain a specified and constantly changing angle to the sun.

The tour guide said, "While it is old hat to pivot solar panels somewhat to maximize their exposed cells to the sun, the precision needed to keep these mirrors exactly reflecting the sunlight onto the boiler tower in the center of the array has to be a hundred times more precise!"

I climbed under one of the mirror-sets to examine the gimbal and slipped on the carcass of a dead bird. It reminded me of the Jerry Seinfeld line, "If the bird doesn't realize it's a mirror, why would he fly directly into that other bird?" But this bird didn't fly into a mirror—this bird was barbequed! I could still smell the charred meat.

"Yeah, a lot of birds fly into the wrong place at the wrong time," the guide said. "We have a cleanup crew picking up the birds at night."

"Not politically convenient to the environmental crowd when you're trying to sell clean energy," Hal whispered.

Our tour took us through the control room, so I asked the tech, "With such precision required in pointing the mirrors, has there ever had a problem when the pointing was off?"

"We don't talk about it much, but there was an incident when the station first came online. The mirrors were pointed too low on one tower. The sunbeams melted the steel structure of the tower in an instant! There's no way to turn off the beams, so it can be pretty dangerous. There is now strict control of the mirror pointing system to prevent such problems. We aren't even allowed access to the 'pointing' computer. The development company engineers are the only ones allowed access," he said with a sarcastic tone, pointing to an engineer who sat reading an X-Man comic book in the back of the room. The engineer was wearing a teal-green golf shirt with a lightning bolt logo of the development company on his back, quite different from his own white and blue shirt.

From the tone of his voice, I could detect that there was little shared respect between the operational people and the developers.

"There was probably a considerable gap in salary range, too," I said to the prof.

Eager to show his stuff, that engineer came over and logged onto the computer. I took a video of him on my cellphone, and he really thought I was impressed. He ate it up. When he entered his password, you could see that this guy was no great software expert. He entered the password with his two index fingers. Any competent software developer would never be so lame and would touch-type with all ten.

The computer showed a page on the screen:

Data Set for Solar Array Number One

The engineer pointed to the screen and said, "This is the data set for solar array number one."

Hal rolled his eyes.

"These are the three coordinates for the tower boiler: longitude, latitude, and altitude. Each of the reflecting mirrors uses these coordinates and its own surveyed location to determine its vector from the mirror to the tower. Combine that with the vector to the sun, which is the same for all mirrors, but varies with time of day and day of the year, and you know what angles to tilt each mirror."

"What happens if there is an emergency during the day?" I asked. "Say, a boiler springs a leak. You can't turn off the sun. What do you do then?"

He showed me the emergency routine software. I could read the simple code and comments on the computer screen even before he could explain.

"You can't shut off the mirrors," he said, "but you can have them all point their beams straight up. We do that by just changing the altitude of the target location to 99999. That effectively puts the focus of the beam where it can't do any harm."

"So, the beams only converge at 100,000 feet and surely won't fry an airplane flying at 30,000 feet. Won't all that light blind a pilot who might fly overhead?" I asked.

"Since the beam is not focused and is always directly above the site, the FAA has our site marked as a no-fly zone on pilots' sectional maps. Pilots flying into McCarran Airport in Vegas are more worried about laser pointers from partying drunks than getting a flash of sunlight from us."

"The development engineers make adjustments and run tests only at night—it's safer that way. The operational crew goes home when the sun goes down, so there's less of a conflict."

The tour concluded with the mandatory drop-off at the gift and souvenir shop, where they sold desktop vanity mirrors, shot glasses with the lightning-bolt logo, and other useless crap. Hal bought two of the teal-green golf shirts with the lightning bolt on the back.

The sun felt extremely hot on my back as we walked out to the Honda. I realized that it probably was hotter than usual in midafternoon in the California desert in the hottest month of the year, but I was also thinking, as we all were, about how damned hot the combined beams of 100,000 mirrored suns would be.

We all looked up and saw the Zzyzxx building on the hillside behind the Ivanpah.

"What do you think, Sam? Would it work?" Hal asked.

"I think so," said the prof.

"We need to work out Plan B before the engineering shift comes on at seven tonight," Hal said.

"But it's Sunday," the prof said. "They said that the engineers rarely come in on the evening shift on Sundays, unless there's an emergency."

"I think there will be one tonight."

"All we need now is to determine what time, tomorrow, the emergency should occur," Hal said.

"It should be timed to take advantage of Kevin's usual transmission time at 2:45," the prof said. "That way, everyone will be safely out of the building, and the combined energy from Ivanpah and the time machine will ensure its destruction. We should plan on diverting the mirrors at 2:55 p.m."

The professor's voice fell off at the end of his statement and his face dropped. I could see that it might now have occurred to him he was now planning the death of his only child.

The thought made me realize as well that Hal was no longer talking about "taking back" the time machine. He seemed to accept the idea of destroying the machine, too.

I probably said the wrong thing next. "I guess we're all on board with Sandy's goal. It's too bad she's not here to see us do it."

No one spoke.

"Tuesday's her birthday, too," Hal said. "If all goes well tomorrow, we should be out of here as soon as the beams hit."

***

That evening, we went back to the Ivanpah power plant. I felt uncomfortable in the teal golf shirt and khaki pants. Hal created a script for me, and I practiced a bit in the car on the way over. We drove to the control room for solar array number three, the one closest to the Zzyzxx building. We waited on the access road until dark. The day shift operational crew had all left. There were very few cars left in the parking lot—probably only a skeleton security staff. Certainly, anyone who might have seen us as tourists during the day was gone.

I walked into the control room and announced, "Hi, I'm here to make some minor changes to the control software this evening."

The senior person in the room looked up from the newspaper he was reading, looked at me, and said, "Well, you know the rules. Even a minor change cannot be installed without the approval of Quality Assurance, so you will not be making changes tonight."

"Hi, I'm Hal, from Quality Assurance. Am I late?" said Hal as he entered the room, also dressed in the teal golf shirt and khaki pants.

I walked over to the control computer and entered the password, while Hal said, "Is there any way I can get a cup of coffee around this place?"

I had trouble getting to the log-on screen but figured it out before anyone saw me struggling. The password was easy to extract from the video I had taken of the two-finger typist during our tour. It worked on my first try.

I didn't have to change any of their existing software—that would involve more complexity than is apparent in the movies. Programs are written in a high-level source code that is not usually available on the operational computer. The changed software would then have to be re-compiled, linked, and loaded with special software tools. That would not be a simple hack. Fortunately, we only needed to change a few data constants, without changing any of the software, thanks to the information provided by the day crew. These values could be edited directly on the operational computer.

The first data to change were the "safe" target coordinates for all the mirrors when an emergency occurred. I simply looked for the altitude value of "99999" and replaced the coordinates with the GPS coordinates of the Zzyzxx building.

At the effective end of the power-generating day, when the sun is too low on the horizon to generate any useful heat, the mirrors are also directed to the safe target coordinates, to assure that no worker would be injured or blinded by concentrated sunlight that might still be collected before sundown.

It was then a simple matter for me to change the constant representing the time of the end of the power-generating day from 6:30 p.m. to 2:55 p.m.

These changes would not be noticed until the destruction of the time machine the next day.

We thanked them all, thanked them for the coffee, and made it back to the RV.

***

"There are certain things that we have to assure get destroyed," the professor said.

"What things?" Hal asked.

"The most important thing is The Old Man of the Mountain."

"Your master design notebook!" I said.

"Yes. It has the explanation of the physics of time messaging and the detailed design of the machine."

"I thought you said you didn't have any such material?" Hal asked.

"I said I never took it out of the lab. It is well-hidden, in a fireproof, locked safe built into the side of the console. That was the first thing I looked for when I got into the building. They never found it! If it isn't destroyed in the fire, they might find that notebook and rebuild. The only way to assure that it is destroyed is for me to get in there."

"So, you think you can just waltz in there, open the safe, and pour gasoline on the notebook? Won't somebody say something like, 'Hey, don't do that!'?" I asked.

"The power applied during the transmission is tremendous. They know that, and everyone vacates the building no later than 2:30. Their messages are transmitted at 2:45 p.m. on the dot, and the solar heat won't appear until ten minutes after that. That gives me plenty of time by myself to empty the safe. I'm sure they won't let me walk out with anything, but I can assure that it will be destroyed."

"What if they don't make a transmission tomorrow?" I asked.

"You should monitor the FV messages. You will know by 12:45. I will stop at Whiskey Pete's and wait for your phone call before going to the site. Even if Kevin doesn't send a message tomorrow, the staff will still evacuate at 2:30, so I can access the Old Man. I will just make sure it burns up with the time machine."

Hal said, "You know this will be our last chance to stop Kevin."

"We don't know," the prof replied. "Maybe we're already too late—we can't see the future."

"But this *will be* our last opportunity," Hal said. "If these guys ever find out what we are about to do, what we will have done, or even what we will have attempted, they are more than willing to kill us, and they have tremendous resources to find us.

"And let's not forget the laws we are going to be breaking. We could be investigated, arrested, and convicted. The only thing that would keep us from serving long sentences is that we might be dead."

With that and a last toast of the remaining wine, no one having come up with a better plan, we all went to bed.

CHAPTER 45

Judgment Day

September 30, 2020

A GUST OF DESERT WIND ROCKED the RV, and I awoke. The predawn desert was usually dead calm, so I wondered what that unusual gust of wind meant. It was warmer in the Minnie Winnie than outside, mostly because of its shelter from the wind. A hot cup of coffee gladly provided some more warmth. Hal and the professor must have also felt the wind and were up soon after.

The desert can be bitterly cold at night, despite the heat of the day, so I relished the coffee. The only breakfast we had left in the RV was a granola bar, one each. No one spoke much, even though today was going to be our last day, our victory day. It didn't feel like a victory. Maybe we just had to execute the plan today, then we might feel more positive.

"I guess I'd better get dressed and into Vegas," the prof said, as he stood and finished dressing for work. "I think they trust me enough now that they will let me travel to the site on a regular basis. They have to call ahead to the guard shack, but I should be able to get in before midday."

"We've got to do this, and we've got to do this today," Hal added, for no apparent reason. "Yes, this is what we must do. It doesn't matter what it costs us. This is the right thing to do, not just for what the machine might be used for today, but for what it could become. Our mission is extremely critical now, for the future."

This didn't sound like the guy who used to bet the company payroll at Texas Hold'em.

I could see that the red USB memory drive that Sandy had left for Hal was still sticking out of his laptop. Perhaps he had read it again last night. "If Sandy were coming back, we will not be here much longer," I said.

"Tomorrow is Sandy's birthday," Hal said, "but come success or failure, we are going to have to move out today, as soon as it's done."

"The Ivanpah will shine on the Zzyzxx at exactly 2:55 p.m. today," the professor reminded everyone. "There is no stopping it, no delaying it. It is now inevitable."

"So be sure to be out of there when we stage our coup," Hal said to the prof.

"Don't you mean our '*coup de grâce*'?" the professor asked.

***

The morning dragged on. After the professor left, Hal and I prepared the RV to leave, packing up what we could. We planned on towing the quad with us and selling everything in Barstow on our way to LAX. We already had ads on Craigslist.

Hal said little. He had his laptop open. While his screen was facing away from me, I could see that he was intensely looking at the screen, not typing. Hal shut down the computer, pulled out the red thumb drive, and slammed his palm down on the cap to snap it on. He slipped the thumb drive into his pocket.

"We will destroy an extremely valuable asset if we go ahead with our plan," he said suddenly. "Is there any way, Tom, that we could save the critical time circuits so we might rebuild the machine later?"

"You mean, after we destroy the time machine, you want to build it back?" I asked. He nodded. "Well," I said, "the circuits we would have to save would be massive, physically massive. There's no way the prof is going to get out sneaking them under his shirt. Have you asked the prof about building a new machine?"

"No, I haven't asked Sam yet. It just seems like such a waste to destroy everything we worked for."

* * *

I monitored the site with the periscope camera, viewing on the TV, just to make sure that Kevin didn't somehow disrupt our plan. I was also careful to monitor the time. The professor needed to avoid Kevin and get in and out.

Key to the entire plan was the assumption that Kevin would conduct business as usual, transmitting a message at 2:45 p.m. that is received at 12:45 p.m.

"I'm at Whiskey Pete's right now, as we planned. Have you received any FutureView messages?" the professor asked.

"None yet."

"I'll wait until 12:50, just in case. Even if anyone wanted to send a later message, it would be difficult to receive anything that close to midday—one o'clock—because of the low antenna angle required to receive the message."

We waited.

At 12:50, I called the prof back.

"We still haven't seen a message today," I said. We hadn't planned on this contingency. We needed the machine's massive electrical power, added to the solar heating from Ivanpah, to assure the destruction of the machine. I was concerned.

"We go ahead as planned," the prof said.

"Wait a minute. If there is no message, then the machine won't be starting up at 2:45. They won't vacate the building. Weren't you counting on everyone leaving?"

"Yes," he replied, "but last week when I was there, everyone vacated the building like clockwork, at 2:30, every day, even when there was no message that day. They even have an alarm bell set for that time, telling people to vacate. They don't actually need for someone to tell them a message was received, because the message may not have been received, but it still could be transmitted. If I were running such an operation, I would also make it a regular clock-driven event to evacuate the building, for safety. You don't know for sure whether someone is going to transmit, even someone in another timeline!"

"OK, good luck!" I said, though I still wasn't totally assured. "Yes, the plan required their staff to vacate the lab, and that's taken care of. But aren't we also counting on the energy content from the FutureView transmission operation?"

"Aren't you forgetting something, Tom? We could be in the first timeline, where no message is received. It is essential that a message be transmitted in this timeline. That's my only job—make sure a message is sent!"

"But if you're still there at 2:55, won't you be toast, so to speak?"

"If this is the first timeline," the professor said, "there will never be a 2:55 in this world. I'll call you in the next timeline!"

He was right, of course.

To be honest with the reader, I had no access to the FutureView computer, so I couldn't save a journal describing what happened during this timeline. This is only my construction of what I believe would have happened.

CHAPTER 46

Judgment Day 2
September 30, 2020, 12:30 p.m.

"I'M AT WHISKEY PETE'S RIGHT now, as we planned. Have you received any FutureView messages?" the professor asked.

"None yet."

"I'll wait until 12:50, just in case. Even if anyone wanted to send a later message, it would be difficult to receive anything that close to noon, because of the low antenna angle required to receive the message."

We waited.

"I just received a FutureView message!" I said, after a few minutes. "It came in at 12:49 p.m., with a transmission time of 2:49 p.m."

"Kevin must have been a little late in sending the message. Everything should still be OK. I will head up to the site now," the prof said.

"Leave your phone on," Hal said to the prof. "Leave it on speaker and carry it in your shirt pocket so we can hear what's going on. Tom will keep his phone on mute, so we don't give you away. If we have to tell you anything, he will turn off the mute and tap on the phone with his fingernail three times. Then let us know when we can talk."

"Got it," I said. I put my phone on speaker and mute and set it on the shelf next to the periscope.

I followed the professor with the periscope, tracking his dust cloud as he drove the Honda up to the Zzyzxx site. The professor stopped at the guard gate.

"I'm Dr. Montrose," the professor said. "I believe they sent a note ahead that I would come to the site? Here is my ID."

"All right, Doctor," a voice said. "Go ahead. Remember the rule: for safety reasons, everyone has to be out of the building when the alarm sounds at 2:30 p.m."

"Yes, sir."

"I'm at the site now, Tom," the prof said, "and I'll be going in shortly."

I heard the car door open and close. As I watched the prof enter the building, I heard the corresponding sound of the building door opening and loudly slamming shut in the desert wind.

"Dr. Montrose!" a voice shouted. I jumped. "We need your help to understand this circuit. We can't figure out why it's laid out so inefficiently. What do you think?"

There was a pause.

"Well," said the professor, "you must have taken this from one of the later stages. We are dealing here with higher frequencies. The circuit has to act more like a wave guide than a conductor at these frequencies. The developers probably had to learn the hard way, judging from how this circuit was modified from the original. See how the original circuit was cut? That's probably why the layout is so strange. If you are redesigning this, I suggest you eliminate all of this part of the circuit and redesign it for a clean layout. Does that help?"

"Oh, thank you, professor, for your tremendous insight and knowledge!" Hal said, mocking the professor. My phone was still on mute. We both grew anxious about him wasting time. I reached for my cell phone, but Hal grabbed my hand.

"We still have plenty of time," he said to me. "Let's not interrupt him when he's with others."

The professor said, "We're getting close to transmission time. Be sure to get this back into the machine."

We waited.

"Dr. Montrose!" said a voice, suddenly, on the phone. "It's almost time. Don't stay long."

"Yes, of course," said the prof.

A few minutes later, the warning alarm went off. I heard the pulsing alarm sound, both on the phone, and with a slight phase delay, directly across the desert, right on time at 2:30.

Then the sound of people shuffling out of the building, the door slamming shut in the desert wind. Then silence.

"My God!" the prof said.

"What…?" I said.

Hal looked up from his laptop.

"I'm into Kevin's desk here," said the prof. "I've found a printout of an email that Kevin received from Ronald Fox, the other investor in FutureView. It speaks to a major program for mass-producing the time machine, based on the reverse-engineering of the prototype, to be completed after the shutdown in October! We may just have caught this in time—otherwise we might be searching for a hundred new machines!"

"There's a lot of flammable stuff here, including some drums of transformer oil and petroleum solvents. I'm going to spread some of it around. It won't take much heating to set this stuff off and create a pretty massive fire."

Meanwhile, Hal was separately watching the access road through binoculars. "There's somebody coming up the access road!" he said.

I took my phone off mute and said to the prof, "There's someone coming up the access road!"

The prof responded, "That's strange. I wouldn't have expected Kevin to come in this late on this timeline since the message had already been sent in the previous timeline, and received this morning. Then again, maybe that's why the message was transmitted late."

He continued, "I now have the Ethernet cable that connects the FutureView computer to their local network and the internet. I am plugging it in now."

My laptop was on and connected to the internet. I hit my number-one bookmark and immediately saw the familiar access web page from the FutureView machine. Now I could at least check the Ephemeris program for the extent of the transmission timing window available to transmit a message. I was relieved when the automatic download of my journal entries was executed, storing the latest entries in the FutureView tail memory. It would be more reassuring if we could also transmit a FutureView message in case of an emergency, but I didn't have the password.

The prof continued, "I pulled out my Old Man notebook from the hidden safe in the control room. After all this time, they never found it. Thank goodness! Half of my life is in this notebook."

Hal moved to the phone from across the room and said, "Is there any way you could carry that out with you?"

"No, there isn't. You know this will have to be destroyed, along with the machine. I will leave it here on the counter. It will definitely burn."

I put my phone back on mute then swung the periscope over, locking onto the dust cloud from the car racing up the road.

Hal watched on the TV and pointed to the monitor. "Is that a Mercedes?"

It was.

The road curved so that we now saw the car front-on, as it continued up the road. I zoomed down to the license plate. Hal read off the plate:

Massachusetts

791ERB

"That's the Mercedes from Cambridge!" I shouted.

The Mercedes slowed as it reached a more treacherous part of the road. Suddenly, the rear passenger door swung open. A person fell out and rolled down the rocky road! The car stopped. A man jumped out.

He quickly recaptured the prisoner. It was a woman! He dragged her back to the car.

Since they were now stopped, I could zoom in a little more. As the dust cloud blew away, we could now see more clearly.

"That's Kevin Brayton!" I said.

I moved the camera a bit. The prisoner looked right at us!

"That's Sandy!" Hal shouted, rushing to the back bedroom.

"Professor!" I shouted. "Kevin is driving up the road, and he's captured Sandy with him!"

I heard no response.

The Mercedes didn't even slow down at the gate. The guard just waved him through.

I realized my mistake, took the phone off mute, and clicked the phone three times.

"Go ahead, Tom," the prof said in a loud whisper.

"Kevin is coming in. He has captured Sandy!"

Hal tossed me his cell phone and said, "Call the police!" He stuck his gun under his belt, and pulled his shirt over it, then bolted out the door. I heard him start the quad, gun the engine loudly, and drive off quickly.

"Put your phone on mute, Tom!" said the prof on the phone.

I hit the mute button.

As I watched, I thought, Sandy was gagged and her hands tied when she rolled out of the car. She must have known that she had no chance of escaping down that steep embankment. She was apparently injured and had difficulty standing, but she was looking directly at us! That was why she did it! So we would see her!

I grabbed Hal's phone and dialed 9-1-1.

"What is your emergency?" the operator said.

I hesitated, realizing that I might accidentally reveal too much about the time machine, I said, "I'm calling about an emergency at the Zzyzxx corporate site, near the Ivanpah power plant."

"Yes," the operator replied. "Is this about the man and woman who were electrocuted today? We have already dispatched police and an ambulance, and they should be there in about thirty minutes."

Thoughts ran through my head. Who called this in? Regardless, the cops would obviously not get there in time to prevent anything.

"Yes," I said. "I just wanted to warn them to please stop at the guard shack and wait for the all-clear. It would be very dangerous to go directly into the building!" *I had to tell them that, at least!*

Kevin had already set this up, I then realized, so he could get away with murdering Sandy…and someone else…the professor, of course! They must have known about him and planned to make it look like an industrial accident. The machine would be the perfect cover for a murder or two!

I scanned the road with the periscope. When the Mercedes arrived at the building, no one left the car. It remained parked near the entrance. The windows of the car were heavily tinted, so even someone walking past would not notice Sandy inside.

The door to the building sprung open and a line of people rushed out. They got into cars and a small passenger van, queuing up to leave the small parking area.

When the employees had all departed, the driver of the Mercedes got out of his car and walked toward the building. I had seen that guy before—Ronald Fox, one of the original investors!

Kevin emerged from the back door of the Mercedes, stood up, then hesitated. He pulled Sandy from the back seat and the two walked slowly toward the building. Sandy was limping.

Suddenly, she turned and darted back to the Mercedes. Kevin stood and blocked Fox, who drew his gun and fired at her! I heard the shot on the cell phone and directly, as if an echo, from across the canyon. She fell to the ground.

"What was that?!" the prof said. "I'm going to hide in the resonant chamber!"

But Kevin had disrupted Fox's aim, and the shot missed.

All was for naught. Fox, now aiming directly at Kevin, forced the two into the building.

I took my phone off mute and said directly into the phone, "Fox has a gun and is bringing Kevin and Sandy into the building. I believe now that he intends to kill her *and* you by being electrocuted in the time machine and have it look like an accident. Kevin tried to save Sandy, so he might be next!"

The building door slammed shut in the desert wind.

The prof whispered, "I hear them now."

I said, "Hal took the quad and should be there shortly. He has a gun!" I put my phone on mute again.

"Hal is our only hope," the prof said.

My phone beeped. I looked at it. *Battery Low*. I hit "ignore."

He then whispered, "It sounds like they're opening the hatch!"

I heard what I recognized as the echoing sound of the chamber hatch being unsealed and opened.

An unfamiliar voice said, "…now put her in there."

The next voice sounded like Kevin. "Fox, you can't do that. When the machine powers up, it will kill her!"

"Do you really think we've gotten this far without spilling a little blood?" Fox said.

"I will not do it! You've gone too far now!" Kevin protested.

"Or not far enough!" Fox said. "I have news for you—I have the password now. I can finally operate without your sniveling. You have lost your usefulness, Brayton! Get in there or I will shoot you first, then stuff both of you in!"

I heard struggling, and the sound of the hatch being slammed shut.

The prof then whispered, "I see through the porthole that Fox just discovered the Old Man, and he's taking it with him! Tell Hal! He has to stop him!"

"Hal should be there by now!" I said. "I'll call him."

I reached for the other phone before realizing my stupid mistake. All I could do now was to turn back to my cell phone and tell the prof, "Hal needs to get you out of there before the sun shines."

"Dr. Johnson?" Kevin asked from inside the chamber.

"You knew?" the prof replied.

"Yeah. We knew from the day you were hired. We hired the real Dr. Montrose back in Cambridge. He worked for us until his heart attack. Maybe it wasn't a heart attack, now that I think about it."

"Then why did you let me in?"

"You've been a great help. You've answered a lot of our questions about the technology. Any question we needed answering, we just had somebody ask you about it."

"What a fool I've been."

I heard a moan from Sandy.

"Sandy, are you OK?" the prof said.

"I think she lost a lot of blood," Kevin said. "She's injured pretty badly."

"Hang on, Sandy! Hal is on the way!" I shouted into the phone.

She must not have been able to speak.

Kevin continued, "As fools go, I have you beat by a mile. At first, Fox and I were just business partners, in a very lucrative business of future prediction. He was never satisfied, though. He wanted the power FutureView gave him, as well as the wealth. He realized he could manipulate the future. The man was unstoppable. The only reason he couldn't turn on me was because I knew the password. He can't get away with this! He's going to need a talented lawyer to explain our dead bodies!"

"I'm afraid he already has a cover story," said the prof. "If they check for fingerprints on the control panel, they will find only yours, Kevin. He's probably already down the road and passed plenty of witnesses for his alibi. Our only hope is Hal. He should be here soon."

"There's going to be a power-up at 2:49," Kevin said. "Is there any way we can short out the machine? Can we do anything from inside here?"

"Not with these voltages!" the professor said. "And that's not our only deadline. We need to get out of here!"

"Professor? Sandy?" It sounded like Hal shouting from outside the chamber.

"We're here, in the chamber! Sandy, Kevin, and me!" the prof shouted back.

"The chamber door has been wedged shut! There's no way I can get you out in time!" Hal said.

I could hear the time machine powering up. The time was 2:49.

I knew what Hal would want to do. "You'll have to override the thermal lockout to send another FutureView message so soon. It can work, but the machine won't survive. Just hit 'ALT 5' before transmitting!" I shouted.

The prof shouted, "The machine should survive long enough to send a message!"

I checked the Ephemeris program to see if the window was still open to send a warning message. I had to tell them. "The transmission window has expired! It's too late! The window is closed! Get out of there, now!"

"Look at the Ephemeris program again, Tom," the professor requested. "Do you see some unusual windows?"

"That's strange," I replied. "There's something strange about the program. Other windows are popping up! There is a strange window for receiving a message at 11:30 tomorrow morning, October first—in the future! I don't understand!"

"I'll run the machine directly from here, Tom!" Hal shouted. "I know what has to be done, and I know now how to do it! It's getting hotter than hell in here! Brace yourself! I'm going to send another FutureView message!"

"Kevin!" Hal shouted. "What's the password?"

The machine began its latent power surge for the morning message. I heard the cooling pumps and fans come on. I could hear the strain in Kevin's voice as he shouted to Hal.

"Copacetic!" Kevin shouted. "*C, O, P, A, C, E, T, I, C!*"

My phone battery died.

The only thing I could do now was close my journal entry and hit "return."

There were no further entries in the journal for this timeline. It was closed on 9/30/20.

CHAPTER 47

One Year Earlier

October 1, 2019, 11:30 a.m.,
Sandy's Birthday

THIS STORY WOULD NOT BE complete as it stands, so I will continue. To understand what happened, I will now relate from my memory and the current journal, what took place a year earlier, on October 1, 2019.

The professor and I spent the morning making good progress on cleaning up minor issues and software changes to prepare for the demonstration for Mr. Brayton that evening. One change I thought important to implement was a full display of the transmission time and reception time on messages.

Both Hal and Sandy were with us in the lab as they were also a little nervous about making sure we performed well in this evening's demonstration and wanted the test to be unambiguous proof of the validity of FutureView.

We were all gathered in the office area when the professor said, "While we will use the Jakarta antenna to receive the twelve-character message that Kevin will transmit this evening, we still can run one last test of the system using our local antenna, here in Cambridge. For this test, I am planning on receiving a message this morning that will be transmitted this afternoon."

The Ephemeris program determined the transmitting antenna pointing angles and the time windows for transmitting and receiving times that meet our power limitations, so the program needs to keep a database of where the receiver antenna is located. This evening's run would require the use of the Jakarta, Indonesia, receive antenna, but for the local test, I was switching the antenna location back to Cambridge.

"Now, all we have to do is select a receive-time, and remember to transmit to that time this afternoon," I said. It was then 11:45 a.m.

Hal said, "11:52 should be as good as any. Go ahead and transmit your test message."

I mentally noted the message time, and seeing that I had a few minutes, I poured myself another cup of coffee.

The FutureView computer *dinged* and caught me by surprise. I put down my coffee and noted the time: 11:46. "Oh, something is off here," I said. I knew that this was too large an error in receive time to just be a clock synchronization effect.

I was apprehensive as I opened the message but completely shocked to see the length of the message. It filled the display screen. The message displayed was:

Hal: The FV is a weapon of tyranny. It creates the wealth and power that prevents it from being stopped. Our only hope is to end it now. If I fail, you are the only one with the ability to take the action needed! -S. STOP LOT, RANCHERO

We all stared at the screen.

The professor looked at the message parameters and calmly said, "In case you are wondering how such a long message got transmitted, you might look at the transmission date-time."

"It was sent at 5:49 p.m., but from yesterday, September 30th? Sent from the past?" I said, "And look at the length of the message! How can that…?"

"No, Tom," the prof replied, "While it was sent on September 30th, at 5:49 p.m., look at the date. It was sent from the year 2020, a year in the future! My God! What a fool I've been! We've been limiting ourselves to a two-hour time range, limited by our transmission range: how far the earth moves in a few hours. I never considered that, after a full orbit, the earth is extremely close to its past location. Close enough to enable us to send a much longer message, a much shorter distance!"

We all then stared at the screen and read the message.

The professor continued, "To send this desperate message to us, now, we must have seen that we needed to take action today, this year!"

Hal then said, "It looks like the time machine may turn into a terrible development. We do not know what will go wrong, what prompted this message, or what might happen."

"No, Hal," the professor said. "This is not what might happen, this is what *will* happen."

"The only chance we have to change the timeline," Sandy said, "is to take action directly because of this message. We know that everything else, every effort, every action, every random event, everything that will happen, will create this future! Isn't that right, professor?"

"Absolutely," the professor said. "This is not an estimate of the future, this *is* the future. The only thing that is different from this future is this message! The only changes to events that can happen are those resulting from receiving this message!"

"It sounds pretty definite to me," I said.

Hal continued, "Let's keep calm. This is a warning of what will happen if we lose control of the machine. We just have to make sure that it never happens. This is a warning message sent from a timeline that is now replaced with our current timeline, a timeline where we now know what has to be done. We have to protect the FutureView from being used for evil purposes!"

"But can you be sure that won't happen?" Sandy said.

"Aren't we in total control of this technology now? With the proper precautions, some increased physical security, and proper diligence about keeping it a secret, we should be able to prevent this desperate timeline from occurring!"

Sandy said, "Hal, see that letter, 'S'? I'm the one who wrote this message. I know myself—I know how I write and how I think. This is no dire warning—this is a desperate attempt to change the timeline because something happened, something that we could not stop, despite efforts over the next year! I think we need to pay heed, or we are headed for an unrecoverable catastrophe. Consider the timing. This may just be our only opportunity to take action. Clearly, we need to act...today!"

"Did you notice, Hal," the professor said, "the line, 'you are the only one with the ability to take the action needed!' Why is that?"

"I think we all know why I said that!" Sandy said, turning to Hal. "Only *you* have the ability to pivot. Yes, to pivot! To change direction 180 degrees, while traveling at full speed, in response to something as simple as a message, a message from the future!"

Hal said, "What you say may be true. We will have to see. Here's what I will do: At the first sign that we might lose control of FutureView, I will pull the plug, I swear!"

The two stared at each other with determination.

Another message then dinged and appeared on the screen.

HELLO WORLD!

I said, "Our test message worked fine."

CHAPTER 48

Sandy's Birthday 2
October 1, 2019, 9:00 p.m.

"WHERE THE HELL ARE YOU guys?" Hal said on the phone. "It's getting close to the message time, and you need to be here and set up."

"We're heading out right now," the prof responded.

Hal was not one to complain about timeliness. After months of additional engineering and testing, tonight was going to be the final, shining demonstration for the venture capitalists. We had even made a final test run that morning using our Cambridge antenna and everything checked out.

I was put at ease by the lengthy message from the future we had received. While it was an ominous message about the future, it also provided a demonstration that the system would work well. The message also shined a light on a greater potential for the machine—the ability to provide a view of the future a whole year in advance!

I thought Hal would want to promote that potential to our investors that night. However, given the ominous content of the message, we had agreed not to speak of it. Hal felt it could easily end our investors' interest in the project.

The prof and I rushed down to the parking garage with the remote controller and a box of party favors in hand. To make sure that we beat Sandy there with enough time, I called all the elevators and sent them to the lobby with the prof and me, leaving her standing outside the lab.

She was none the wiser about our prank. As the prof and I hurried out of the parking garage, she was just walking in. I saw her in my rearview mirror and almost ran into a pair of black Chevy Tahoes with tinted windows coming up the ramp.

"Is the president having a drink on campus tonight?" I quipped to the prof on my cellphone as we headed to the Waltham office.

After working so many long days and nights, we had finished and were ready for the evening test. We arrived early at the office with the remote controller to set it up in the conference room, and also to prepare the room for a small party—both to celebrate the completion of the FutureView machine and this final test, and to celebrate Sandy's twenty-ninth birthday.

Sinatra sang "My Way" on the conference room speakers. She had been kept unaware until she entered the room with Hal (and keeping Sandy unaware of anything is difficult). We sang an off-key rendering of "Happy Birthday to You" on top of Sinatra. It made for an interesting tune.

In place of a traditional birthday cake, I had arranged a collection of cupcakes in a circle on the conference room table next to the remote controller. The cupcakes were frosted half black and half white, representing the earth in positions in orbit around the sun. The layout reminded me of this morning's message and the ability to transmit messages a whole orbit into the past. There were candles on each cupcake, but the candles were, of course, not combustible, containing multicolored LEDs, a lithium battery, and a Bluetooth receiver. There was plenty of food and drinks, and a good time was had by all.

In all the singing, no one noticed the banging at the front door until Hal rushed to the lobby to escort Kevin and his party into our soiree, quickly offering Kevin a Sam Adams.

Kevin introduced his associates and their titles, a strange mix of people I had not seen before. His associates looked like they never refused cake, and they didn't. None of the usual suspects showed up since the venture capital company had sold out their interest to Kevin

Brayton. Mr. Fox was the only other person I recognized; I presumed he was still an investor.

This morning's cryptic message from the future had me on edge. Did the timing of that message have anything to do with the demonstration tonight? Were we being forewarned of the immediate danger? These strange people arriving tonight didn't help my fears. I glimpsed Hal when he wasn't looking at Sandy. He seemed worried, too. This worried me even more.

"I would again like to thank this team for their hard work and excellent achievements at FutureView," Kevin began. "I would like to congratulate Sandy on her birthday and everyone on the success of the FutureView machine. Also, after the party and the machine demonstration tonight, I have an important announcement. Sandy, why don't you tell us what we're going to see today?"

"Since this is a demonstration of the time messaging machine," Sandy said, diplomatically handing the meeting back to Hal. "Mr. Harold Hawkins, the president of the FutureView Corporation, will describe what we will see tonight. Hal?"

Hal looked miffed by Kevin, but immediately took command of the meeting. "Thank you, Sandy. What we will see this evening has been a challenge. First, we have had to extend the message size to twelve characters. I believe the team achieved the ability to actually send messages of thirteen characters. Well done! We are also extending our nominal time range to two hours—so we should receive a message at 9:30 p.m. that will not be sent until 11:30 this evening. And executing this message at this time of day might not seem to be significant, but it has been a major difficulty. Since it is almost 9:30 now, we had better get ready to receive the message."

I thought about the morning's message. That was a hell of a lot more text than thirteen characters. Would we be able to achieve that great an expansion in capability in one year? Thirteen characters and a two-hour time range are embarrassing and of little practical use, but sending large messages a year into the past? That was something worth working on!

The receiving computer in the FV remote controller booted up smoothly, passing quickly through the startup screens for Windows 10. After booting up, it displayed the time: 9:28 p.m. We watched until the display read 9:30. I keep feeling that there is something special about the FV messages always being on time, but computers can read clocks better than humans, and it is only humans who miss deadlines.

Almost immediately, the receiver *dinged*, and we saw the message appear, just as Kevin had requested—twelve digits.

224195180468

Kevin wrote the numbers down carefully in a small notebook that he returned to the inside pocket of his suit coat. The professor then shut down the remote controller and pressed the button on a small electronic box on the table, lighting up the LED candles on the cupcakes.

Sandy blew out the birthday candles as if they were real. They flickered under her breath then died, except for one that remained lit a few seconds longer before joining its mates. I had to take credit for that simulation, executed in an Arduino processor.

The professor commented something about compressing a message to fit more into the thirteen-character limitation. But we had already seen a full-page message, received this morning. All of it was in ASCII character format, as well. Why bother with better compression? My thoughts went on to other things. Hal and Sandy were also not interested and drifted away.

I asked Hal, "What information is Kevin sending in these twelve numbers? What is this for?"

"I have no idea," Hal said.

This morning's message made me paranoid about the events of this evening, even the meaning of this numerical message.

"Maybe he'll let us know when he creates the message later tonight," Sandy suggested.

"Well, that may not happen," the professor said. "Remember, there is no need for Kevin to send a message at all. This message has already been received. That means it was already destined to be sent from a timeline that no longer exists."

This logic always disturbed me. I added, "I always wondered how anyone could assure that a message would be sent, when it comes from an alien world with a different sequence of events, different priorities, and maybe even different people."

The professor replied, "You assure everything is in place so that, even in the timeline where no message is received, the equipment, the FutureView machine back in Cambridge, and the operator are ready, and that the operator has the *intent* to send the message. If all that is in place, then the message will be received. So, everything must…I mean *will operate* just fine since we *received* Kevin's message already. I have insisted in the past that Tom go through the motions and send the message even after it is received, anyway, as there is no harm done, and it assures that you would have sent the message in the previous timeline as well. All that is unnecessary, but it provided me confidence in the results."

Hal, Sandy, and I stood around and chatted, while Kevin drew the professor away in a separate conversation.

"Do you have the time, Tom?" Hal asked.

"Yes, it's 10:01," I said.

"Are you sure you're looking at the time and not the date?"

I felt embarrassed and looked again, but he got me.

"The end of this morning's message—what did it say?"

"It said 'Stop lot.' "

"Could *lot* mean *lottery*?" Hal asked in a whisper.

"Do you think Kevin's message is a winning lottery number?" I asked.

A minute later, I got back to Hal. "Twelve digits is what you need for a lottery number—five sets of two-digit numbers and one more set for the grand prize."

"Still," Hal replied, "This would be the perfect application for FutureView, and the timing is consistent with tonight's drawing of the winners of the Mass Millions Lottery."

Kevin rapped with his fork on his beer bottle, silencing the crowd to make his announcement.

I shut the lid on my laptop.

"Since we have already received the digital message, I must congratulate the team on the proof of the success of FutureView. To commemorate this achievement, I have had engraved plaques and photographs of each of you made that will be mounted in this conference room, as we move into Phase II."

Phase II? I thought. I'd never heard of any phases on this project.

I looked at Hal to see if he had taken part in this plan. His mouth hung open. He looked as perplexed as I was; actually, more so. *That's not good!*

Kevin continued, "And I want to announce a more practical award to each of you in recognition of your outstanding achievement."

His associate then passed out envelopes to each. They were windowed business envelopes with the name exposed in the window—the colored pattern of a check was visible. I ripped open mine, revealing a check and a tri-folded paper. The others followed suit.

Hal nervously read the paper before looking at the check. "What is going on here?"

He read the letter before I could, and immediately interrupted Kevin, saying, "You're taking over the company? You're taking over the company!"

The room became very silent. The music from my iPhone ironically disconnected from the conference room speakers.

"Yes, since I have now acquired a majority share of the company stock by purchase and execution of my warrants, I now have controlling interest in the company, and as the self-appointed CEO, I am terminating all current employees, immediately, as allowed by our at-will employment agreement, under state law."

As if to defend his statement, Kevin handed a single-page printout to Sandy. Sandy scanned it over and gave Hal a shallow, vertical nod. That was not what I wanted to see.

"Those papers included with your severance check are a copy of your own employment agreement that you signed, and the penalties for violating protection of the company's trade secrets and intellectual property."

"You mean we're all fired?" I asked no one in particular.

"No, you are just laid off," Kevin responded. "Now that the FutureView machine is operational, we are moving into Phase II, and you will no longer be needed. We can certainly provide you with a good reference for your fine work at FutureView."

It finally hit Hal in the face. "You son-of-a-bitch! You've just been waiting until we perfected the machine. Then you take over and make yourself rich!"

Kevin didn't respond, and he didn't have to. His "associates" had well-developed upper body strength and physically escorted each of us to the door. I grabbed my laptop and the last cupcake.

Outside the door, Hal leaned against the wall and said, "Oh, shit!"

CHAPTER 49

Stop Lot

October 1, 2019, 10:30 p.m.

W E ALL STOOD THERE THINKING about the message—the message we called "The Future View Message" and the future of humanity. None of us had expected this critical turn of events to happen so soon and so suddenly. Clearly this was the event that would determine whether we lost control of FutureView.

Hal turned to Sandy and said, "So you think I'm good at pivoting? Watch me!"

To the rest of us, he said, "The bottom of this morning's message read: 'stop lot.' Kevin's going to use this FutureView message to win the Mass Millions Lottery. That's being run tonight! I'm going to Dorchester to stop the lottery drawing! Everybody get over to the professor's apartment. I will call you."

He raced out of the parking lot in the Barracuda; I could smell the tire smoke as he took off. We got in our cars and headed for the prof's apartment.

We passed the Quickie Mart along the way and saw the unusually long checkout line winding through the store. The prof suddenly hit his brakes and pulled to the side of the road. Sandy and I stopped too. We all got out onto the sidewalk.

"Why don't we just buy our own lottery ticket?" the professor said.

I handed him my laptop and said, "Here, take this. The lottery number message should still be showing."

He grabbed my computer. As we stood there, a BMW pulled up to the store entry and double-parked. Kevin rushed in.

I chuckled. "Hal was right."

The professor entered the store and got in the back of the line. Kevin never noticed us. Sandy and I returned to our cars and proceeded to the professor's apartment.

When we got to the apartment parking lot, I noticed a red Ford Ranchero parked in the back of the parking lot. Two guys sat in the car, in the dark.

"Didn't that message from the future end with the word 'Ranchero'?" I asked.

"Yes," Sandy said, " 'Stop lot Ranchero.' "

"Well, look over there," I said, then called 9-1-1. "Yes, I'd like to report there are some tough guys here, with guns, about to go into the Revere House Apartments in Waltham. They are in a red Ranchero pickup in the parking lot…"

We parked on the other side of the parking lot and waited for the cops to arrive. I joined Sandy in her car as Hal called on my cell.

"The professor had the idea to stop at the Quickie Mart and buy our own lottery ticket," Sandy said to Hal.

"That sounds like a good plan," Hal replied. "But the warning message was clear—Stop the lottery. I am going to have to push it to get there before the balls drop." I could hear the roar of his engine over the phone. "Have you seen a Ranchero, by the way?"

"It's right here at the professor's apartment. The cops are on the way."

"Make up a story if you have to. Get the cops to search the car."

The professor arrived, and the three of us headed up to his apartment on the second floor. From the top of the stairs, I could see that the cops had the "rancheros" sitting on the curb, in handcuffs.

On the way up, the professor said, "The twelve digit message was not the winning lottery number. It looks like Kevin encoded the number somehow."

Sandy added, "I guess Kevin doesn't even trust his own crew with the real number."

"I tried a fix for the problem, but we really need Hal to stop the lottery," the professor said.

As we entered the professor's apartment, Hal called. Sandy put it on speaker. You could hear the roar of his engine and the squeal of his tires as he raced to the Lottery Commission.

"I've been thinking about this," Hal said. "Not only do we have to stop Kevin from winning the lottery, we also have to take back control of FutureView and make sure no one else is interested in it."

"Too bad we have spent all this time trying to convince everyone that FutureView works," I said, "and that it's not just a scam to get their money!"

Hal answered, "You never know who's holding and who's bluffing until the end of the game. And, if you're holding good cards, the task is to make everyone *think* you're bluffing."

"I think I can do that for the card demo," the prof offered.

"And I can tear apart the options demo," said Sandy.

Hal said, "That leaves me. I have to take care of the lottery!"

Hal left his phone on, but he couldn't hear him over the roar of his engine noise as he drove madly through Dorchester.

The prof then said, softly, to us, "Kevin's lottery number message was received *after* we received the future warning message, so anything that Hal does as a result of that message has already been accounted for. Kevin has already won the lottery, and there's nothing Hal can do to change it. The deed is done!"

The professor turned on his TV and switched to a channel that was showing the Massachusetts Millions Lottery draw. This was a more dramatic lottery than usual, and the Commission clearly was trying to draw it out for more excitement. A cute young lady came on stage to the rotating cage full of numbered Ping-Pong balls. Her job was to push the button that released each numbered ball from the cage and then announce the number as each ball came to a stop.

She released the first ball. "41!" she said.

We then heard an extremely loud crash! The sound coming not from the TV but from the cellphone.

She flinched, but the young lady kept smiling and went on, unflustered, to release the rest of the six numbered balls on cue, continuing the lottery drawing as scheduled.

Hal's phone connection went dead.

There was nothing further we could say or do.

***

At 11:30, the late evening news came on. The Boston newscast led with a story on the Massachusetts Millions Lottery.

A news story about the car that smashed into the lottery commission building followed. The Barracuda was no match for the brick building. They showed Hal being carted off on a gurney. "He had severe but not life-threatening injuries," the reporter said, "despite the lack of airbags in the 'muscle car.' "

Sandy's cellphone rang. Hal's name showed as the caller, so she quickly answered and put it on speaker.

"This is Officer Muldowney of the Boston Police Department. I'm sorry to inform you that the pah-tee with whom you were conversing has been in an accident in Door-chest-ah."

Sandy spoke out, "Is he all right?"

"The young man received medical attention at the scene of the accident and is currently in transit to Mass General Hospital. You will have to call the hospital to ascertain as to the state of the pah-tee's condition."

"Thank you, Officer." She ended the phone call and stood staring at the wall.

We sat in silence until Sandy broke it, saying, "We need to go back to the FutureView office tonight! I'll drive."

The three of us went down the outside staircase to the parking lot. The two rancheros were being assisted into the rear seat of a squad car. "Watch your head," the officer said.

We all got into Sandy's Mini Cooper and took off. I discovered that the back seat of a Mini Cooper was never intended to carry an adult passenger.

When we got back to the office, the professor handed Sandy a deck of Bicycle playing cards held by a rubber band. "Put this deck somewhere where it'll be found, with the face side up."

She looked at the deck and nodded recognition, then put the cards in the outer pocket of her purse, where I saw she also had that ubiquitous red notebook.

She drove quickly to the FutureView Waltham office. The professor and I watched as she went to the office door and knocked on the glass. An older male guard who came in with Kevin's entourage came to the door, unlocked it, and talked with Sandy. I couldn't hear the conversation, but the body language was unmistakable. *"Oh, please, I just left my monogrammed handkerchief in the conference room! Could I please go in there and get it? I'll only be a second! Pretty please?"*

Sure enough, she was in. A moment later, the lights came on in the conference room and the professor and I watched the play unfold. The guard entered the room and stayed with Sandy. She bent over to look under the conference table. We could see her through the glass walls, but the guard stood over her and could not see what had transpired under the table. We saw her pull her red notebook out of her purse before standing with it in hand.

The guard demanded that she hand it over. He opened and examined it. While he was distracted, she slipped the professor's deck of cards, face side up of course, onto the wall shelf next to the conference table.

The guard apparently read enough to confiscate her notebook, and immediately escorted her out of the room and out of the building. She got back into the car.

As we drove away, Sandy said, "The deed is done."

She drove to the exit of the parking lot, only to meet up, front bumper to front bumper, with a BMW rushing to enter. Kevin got out of his car.

"You're too late!" Sandy shouted.

Too late for what? I thought. I looked at my watch—it was midnight.

Kevin looked at his watch, and slowly returned to his car. We drove off.

I turned on the radio in the car in time to hear that there had been a single winner of the Massachusetts Millions Lottery that night, and that the winner had bought the winning ticket at the Quickie Mart in Waltham. My hopes sank.

CHAPTER 50

The Showdown

October 15, 2019

I TRIED LOOKING FOR WORK IN the Cambridge area over the last few weeks, but with no success. I still had my FutureView app running on my laptop, but Kevin did not need to run the FutureView machine, as far as I could detect. He probably didn't need FutureView right now, not with all that lottery money.

Since it was only a little out of my way to stop at the MIT campus, I went over to the Green Building, where we had spent so many late nights building the machine. I could easily take the elevator all the way to the eighteenth floor without a problem, and there apparently were no guards around. The lights were out, and the lab was still locked up. It looked abandoned. I was confused.

Hal sent me a text saying that we should meet at the FutureView office in Waltham. I thought Kevin might have a problem with us back at his office, but I showed up early, with curiosity.

I saw Sandy's Mini Cooper in the parking lot and a beautiful 1969 Jaguar XKE convertible, well-polished, and in mint condition, probably Kevin's. There were, strangely, no other cars in the parking lot.

Sandy welcomed me at the door, and let me into the conference room, where Hal and the professor were having bagels and coffee. Kevin was nowhere to be seen. It seemed like the old days at FutureView again.

I could see immediately why Hal didn't have a car in the parking lot. He was wearing a monstrous arm cast. He limped over to the cream cheese. A pair of crutches was leaning in the corner. Sandy must have been doing all the driving. Since Hal's left hand was the one in a cast, and as he was left-handed, Sandy also had to do all the signing. Probably for the better, as she would take far more care in reading what she signed.

I helped myself to a sesame bagel and looked out the window at the parking lot. Since Kevin was obviously not there, I wondered, *Who owns the Jaguar?*

"Admiring my XKE?" the professor said, standing behind me.

That was not the only shock I would get.

Hal started, "I called this meeting to get the team back together for a couple of reasons. First, we should probably update everyone on what happened on Sandy's birthday, and then discuss our new mission."

"Let's start with Sandy," Hal said. "Tell everyone what happened when you came back here the night of the lottery."

"The professor gave me a deck of cards, held together with a rubber band," she began. "I took the cards and my red notebook back into the office. With Kevin gone, I could easily get the guard to let me back in on the excuse that I left my 'personal' notebook in the conference room."

I chuckled, remembering the scene.

"When I got in there, I reached down under the table and pulled my notebook out of my purse, as if I had found it there. I also dropped the deck of cards onto the shelf next to the conference table, faceup, as the prof asked. When I asked to leave, I knew they would want to check out the notebook. As soon as they saw the tabs on some pages, they knew it was about FutureView and the guard immediately confiscated it for Kevin. Kevin has been dying to see that notebook even when I worked for the venture capitalists. That was my plan."

"What was in the notebook?" I asked before the others could.

"The notebook had all my notes about how the FutureView demonstrations could have been faked, especially the options demo. You remember, Tom, that you didn't actually prove the viability of making money in stock options using FutureView because the answer could have been preinserted in the FutureView message buffer. The machine would not even have to send a message in time to get that answer. I'm sure Kevin would question whether that test was valid or just a bluff."

"What was the deal with the playing cards, professor?" Hal asked, pouring another cup of coffee.

"Well," he replied, "At the time of the card demo, we really didn't have the machine working yet, but I desperately needed you and the VCs to keep funding the project! So, I played this little card trick. I generated the FutureView message that would match the card that Kevin would pick from the card deck the night before the test."

"How can that be? Kevin pulled a random card from the deck—the six of spades. How could you know that in advance? He didn't even pick the card until after the message was received!" I said.

"When I put that deck of cards on the shelf, the six of spades was showing on the top of the deck," Sandy said.

"Yes," the professor said, "I was sure *that* card would immediately catch Kevin's attention, given how important it was in convincing him to fund the project. I assumed he would want to take that card off the deck and probably frame it! However, as soon as he took the card off the top of the deck, he would immediately see that the next card, and then every card in the deck, was also the six of spades."

"OK, so Kevin then thought that the demos might have been faked," Sandy asked. "What about the lottery? That would seem to remove all doubt about FutureView. Kevin transmitted that FutureView message himself. Didn't he win the lottery?" Sandy asked.

"No," Hal started, "Kevin didn't win the lottery."

"But you weren't able to stop the lottery. Kevin's plan *must* have worked! Didn't he have the winning lottery number?" I asked.

Hal said, "While I was rushing to Dorchester to have the lottery stopped, I realized I would be too late. The only thing I could do was hope to cause a disturbance."

"That you did!" Sandy said. "But you weren't able to stop the lottery or change anything! We saw it all on the TV broadcast. The cute young lady barely flinched and kept on drawing the numbers, like nothing happened."

"I think I understand what happened," said the professor. "The winning lottery number is determined by releasing numbered balls kept in constant motion in a rotating drum. Hal may not have stopped the lottery, but that cute operator definitely heard the crash. Even if she hesitated only a split second, that would have been enough for the balls to be in an entirely different position in the cage, and a different lottery number would be drawn."

"How could that be?" I asked. "By your theory of time travel, Hal couldn't influence the winning lottery number, as Kevin's lottery message was received *after* we received the message from our future, so Kevin's lottery number message had to be determined by the latest timeline, including any influence Hal might have made on the lottery!"

"Yes," the professor said, "but Hal acted based on *both* the lottery number message, telling him that Kevin was betting on the Mass Millions Lottery, *and* on the message from our future, motivating Hal to take desperate action that he wouldn't have otherwise taken. The message also gave Hal an early clue that the FutureView message was a lottery number. Hal's actions were the *only* thing that could change the winning lottery number!"

Then Sandy said, "Kevin saw the card demo was faked, the options demo was faked, and his own lottery message, a message that he personally transmitted, was a loser. He must have feared by then that he'd been snookered. Kevin knew Hal's pattern of bluffing from their poker games and that Hal sought vengeance after Kevin took him for everything in their last Texas Hold'em game."

Hal added, "Kevin also pulled in other investors to buy the controlling interest in FutureView. One investor was a Mr. Ronald Fox, who wouldn't take lightly to being swindled. Fox was probably behind all the thugs that were after us. Fox is not a betting man—when he invests heavily, he makes sure that his investments pay off. It would have been an interesting meeting to be there when Kevin had to explain it all to Fox. They both became highly motivated, we might say 'desperate' sellers of the company."

The professor continued, "Fortunately for them, the Macduff Group expressed interest in buying the company for its 5G capability. Brayton and Fox sold out at two cents on the dollar. The deal closed last week."

"So that's why the FV machine hasn't been running. Kevin sold the company," I said. "Who is this Macduff Group, and how do you know so much about it? It seems like that would be pretty confidential information."

"Actually, *we* are the Macduff Group," said the professor. "When I went into the Quickie Mart and discovered that Kevin had encrypted the winning lottery number, I did the logical thing. While waiting in the lottery ticket line, I simply noted the time, then mentally committed to transmitting the actual lottery number after the lottery drawing. Immediately, I heard the *ding* on your laptop and a new FutureView message appeared with the real winning lottery number. I thought I was just getting the same lottery number Kevin had."

He continued, "I bought a lottery ticket and submitted it. Back in my apartment, I still had your laptop after the winning number was displayed on TV. That's when I would have sent the message. When we found Kevin lost the lottery, I figured my ticket was a loser too. But my lottery number message was the last message received and reflected the true winning lottery number."

"Wait a minute! When the lottery drawing took place, and Kevin found he didn't have the right number, wouldn't he just go back to the

Waltham office and use the remote controller to transmit the actual winning lottery number?" Hal asked.

The professor answered, "I had a conversation with Kevin during the party, earlier that evening, when he so innocently asked me for the transmitter password. When he questioned whether I was giving him the correct password, I reminded him that since his numerical message was already received, that was the proof that the password was guaranteed to work. I also pointed out that there was no need to even stay late to send the message, in the current timeline, as once the message was received, 'the deed is done.' He apparently went home or to a bar or somewhere to watch the lottery ball drop."

Sandy added, "I think Kevin might have panicked and tried to rush back to the FutureView office. He almost hit us when we left the parking lot. He must have been desperately trying to get back into the office before midnight to send another FutureView message with the right lottery number! After midnight, the earth blockage would prevent sending another FutureView message."

The professor continued, "I was shocked when I found I was the sole winner of the Mass Millions Lottery! After taking the discounted immediate-payout option, paying state and federal income taxes, funding my retirement plan, and buying my XKE, I bought the company from Kevin and the other investors, through a lawyer, for the Macduff Group."

"Who is Macduff?" I finally asked.

The prof answered, "Macduff was the king of Scotland who was killed by Macbeth."

"So, what is the new FutureView Corporation going to do? Make 5G transmitters?" I asked.

"We are going to finish the 5G transmitter development, but that will be a cover for our actual mission."

"To destroy the machine?"

"I'm afraid we can't," Hal said.

"That's right," The professor added. "Remember the conservation of energy requirement? The FutureView machine has to be turned on and powered up with full electrical power at the time that any message is transmitted, even if the message was sent in another timeline. If it's not, then that message is never received, and everything reverts to the previous timeline."

"So, all of this will be erased if we don't keep the FV machine working for another year?" I asked.

"Yes, we have to keep it working, but out of the hands of people who might abuse the technology. If we don't, then the timeline will revert to the previous timeline, and we know that timeline does not end well," Sandy added.

The professor continued, "That's why I'm hiring Hal, Sandy, and you, to protect the machine."

"There's another reason to keep the machine running," I said.

"Why is that?" Hal asked.

"All my notes on what happened in that other timeline are in the tail memory, and that journal won't appear until October 1, 2020! We'll have to wait until then to find out what happened!"

I grabbed the last bagel and generously applied garlic cream cheese.

"You know," I said, "there is still something that bothers me about the lottery."

"What's that?" said the prof.

"When Kevin returned to the office to send a new FutureView message and failed to get there before midnight, I didn't say anything, but I think everyone forgot about something."

"What was that?"

"Everyone forgot we were on Daylight Savings Time. Kevin could still have sent a FutureView message until 1:00 a.m."

THE END

FOR MORE INFORMATION

If you like this novel you will find more information, other books in the FutureView series, and notifications of the release of future books in the series at:

www.MichaelLimeski.com

(If you didn't notice the secret
hidden in this book, find out more about it on the website!)

I am depending on you, the reader, to provide feedback on your experience with this book, and would appreciate a brief review, good or bad! Please send your comments to:

MichaelLimeski@gmail.com

Or comment directly, and rate this book, at the distributor where you purchased it.

Michael

FOLLOW THE FUTUREVIEW ADVENTURE...

FutureView – Saving the Future

The FutureView team knew they only had one simple mission…to save the future by *not* using the time machine. But that was not an option when they had to use the time machine to save themselves. And what can they do when someone else is changing the timeline? Which teammate will have to die to Save the Future?

To be Released Fall, 2022

Receive notification of this and future book releases in the FutureView series by signing up at my website:

www.MichaelLimeski.com

AUTHOR
MICHAEL LIMESKI

I am an engineer. I designed aircraft, flight controls, a record-setting high-altitude drone for NASA, a self-driving off-road vehicle for DARPA, and a human-powered vehicle to attempt the world speed record. I have started a manufacturing business. I was an army electronic intelligence officer. I flew hang gliders off mountains. I teamed with others in publishing *Model Rocketry Magazine*. Now, I write science fiction novels based on this wealth of experience in Southern California.